These M

of Faith

Book II: Heaven's Avenging Angels

Andrew Richardson is an author, teacher and father. This is his second novel.

Heaven's Avenging Angels is the second book in the series *These Matters of Faith.* The first book, *This Matter of Faith,* is out now on Kindle and in paperback

For more information on the author and forthcoming titles in the series, see
www.thismatteroffaith.net

For Amelia Jean and her mum

Heaven's Avenging Angels

Heaven's Avenging Angels

32: Death of a Titan

It is ten days since the death of Surrey. At Whitehall Palace, there is a curious mixture of industry and inaction. The weather is cold, bitterly so, and the river threatens to freeze over. Few of the usual footmen and domestics are about their business outdoors, giving the palace a feel of desertion, but the windows are lit by fires within. The fermentation has spread by rumour, and many of the nation's great men have convened on London, including our old acquaintance, the Earl of Shrewsbury. He is quartered some way distant from the palace, but that does not prevent his continued presence each day. He is attended by a retinue of liveried footmen. Among them is one whom the reader will immediately recognise as Guy Fletcher, attaching himself to the nobleman for the duration of his visit, instead of his usual duties with Longshawe. He is grown considerably in both stature and confidence since our first meeting with him in Doncaster.

Such is the state of the palace. Absent are the three royal children, dismissed by the powers that have been running the machinery of state for some months. Edward himself has been sent to Hertford to live with the Seymours, but the brothers have both come to the palace and installed themselves in rooms close to the king's. Wriothesley occupies the next suite, and is in constant communication with Edward Seymour. A procession of doctors pass in and out of the rooms, each arriving looking grim and leaving looking yet more so.

Inside the king's chamber, Henry lies on his bed. His body is covered with black patches, the ulcerated wound on his leg oozes yellow, and his breath rattles. He calls to the guard. Longshawe, for it is he, comes over and leans in to hear the king's whisper. "Save me from these blackguard ignorants who call themselves doctors. I want nothing now other than that my passing might be eased a little. Send your friend."

Longshawe disappears for a minute, and returns slightly breathless but wearing a smile. He approaches the king's bed once again, and bows deeply. "It is arranged," he says.

Five minutes later, Strelley, who has stayed at the Palace in the entourage of the Earl of Shrewsbury, is leaving it in the direction of St Paul's. He walks through the streets which are quiet, but not unusually so. The chatter as he passes is of the king, and his imminent death. Such conversation may be officially forbidden, but this has not stopped it happening, nor has the lack of a concrete statement from the Palace prevented speculation throughout the city.

A few minutes later, he walks up to the door of Gilbert's warehouse. It is, as usual, open, but there is a no sign of activity outside. He goes through, swallowed by the gloom inside. Gilbert sits at his desk, reading through a ledger list.

"Good morning," he says to Strelley, without his usual bluster. "I hear our great King Henry is not long for this world."

"Do you? I understand that it is treason to foretell the death of the king."

"Are you here for anything, or just providing me with legal advice?" Gilbert looks up from his list.

"The king wants something for the pain."

"Tell him to go see the apothecary."

"It's the truth. For Henry himself."

Gilbert pushes the paper sideways, leaving the desk in front of him clear. "I want something in return."

"What can I give you?"

"An undertaking."

"You want me to promise you something? I am not in a position to offer a great deal."

"Ah, you misunderstand me. I don't want money, nor do I want you to steal the Crown for me."

"Good." Strelley sits down in the empty chair in front of Gilbert's desk. "What, then?"

"Pay attention." Gilbert pulls the paper back across the desk. "This here is the shipping manifest for a vessel that I chartered. There are four items missing from it, both from the manifest and from the delivery. I know those items were aboard, and yet I do not have them. Can you see my problem?"

"You are sharing your profits with one of your employees. How do I come in?"

"My employees know that there is nothing to be gained in defrauding me. This is a legitimate delivery, Master Strelley, entirely above board. This manifest is not the original. The authorities that govern this port have taken liberties with my stock, and I do not like it."

"I still do not see where I can be of assistance," Strelley replies, reading the paper.

"That is because you lack imagination. You have access, I believe, to the Lord Chancellor."

"I have met him."

"I have no doubt that it is he who is profiting by this larceny. I would like you to discover the items that he has taken."

"I am no thief, Sir."

"I do not need you to remove the items."

"Nor am I a spy."

"Then you shall become one."

"All this for something to dull the king's pain?"

Gilbert appraises Strelley with a long, searching look. "No. I'll sell you the king's medicine either way. But *you* want to know that a man of my connections is on your side, Master Strelley. For your own benefit, perhaps."

"I shall do what I can. Short of criminality, of course."

"My thanks." Gilbert rises, and picks up a clay pot, two inches high, from a shelf across the room. It is sealed with wax. He hands it to Strelley. "That, my friend, is the best you'll get. His Majesty will appreciate it, I don't doubt."

Gilbert picks up a pen and a piece of parchment, on which he scribbles four words. He hands it to Strelley, saying, "Find any one of those in Wriothesley's possession, and you let me know." Strelley reads, folds the paper and holds it over a candle, letting it take flame. He casts it on to the stone floor of the office.

Gilbert smiles. "Dramatic, Edward. I like it. Now go." He waves Strelley out of his presence.

An hour afterwards, Strelley passes the pot to the king's groom. Henry dismisses his doctors, haranguing them with curses out of his bedchamber. Strelley too bows and leaves, past Longshawe who is still at his post. Longshawe doesn't watch as the groom breaks the seal on the wax pot and applies some of the oily substance within to the king's ulcerated leg. Henry gasps with pain at the first touch, but soon appears more comfortable. His eyes take on a sort of glaze, and he stares at the fire without moving. The groom withdraws to the edge of the room. Longshawe's eyes drop to the king's corpulent form. He says nothing, but his face speaks concern at Henry's illness. After a moment, Longshawe raises his chin again and settles into his stance, looking at nothing in particular, but focused nonetheless.

Across the palace, Strelley walks into a withdrawing room, where the Earl of Shrewsbury and his son are seated. The earl is reading from a pamphlet. George Talbot rises as he sees Strelley come in, offering him the smallest of bows.

"Master Strelley," the young Talbot says. "What news of the king?"

"The king will not last another two days," Strelley replies. "His doctors are certain that his malady will take him, and soon."

"So you did not go to find him a cure, but merely to ease his pain?" George Talbot sits back down as he asks his question.

Strelley nods in reply. "My Lord?" He solicits Shrewsbury's attention. Shrewsbury makes a face that suggests that Strelley can ask his question. "Have the executors of the king's will been assembled?"

"Master Strelley," Francis Talbot replies, "what interest have you in such politicking? How does it matter for you whether the king's executors are told or not of his condition?" Talbot focuses on Strelley, looking at him for some moments. "What concerns you?"

Strelley casts his eyes about the room, uncomfortable. Eventually, he decides to speak, palms up to show that he is in earnest. "When the king names Edward as his successor... There are those who might contest that succession, are there not? If nothing else, the Pope-"

Talbot raises his hand, silencing Strelley. He thinks before making his statement. "You fear a war, perhaps, with the French, the Scots? You fear that the Catholics will rise up and put Mary on the throne?" Strelley is motionless, but Talbot has it right, and it shows in his eyes. "Well you might have such fears. But the removal of the Earl of Surrey and his father has somewhat lessened the focus of any Catholic party... As has the defection of Wriothesley." At this, Strelley's eyebrows rise. "To those who had faith in him, Wriothesley is nothing better than a traitor." Talbot invites Strelley to sit as he finishes speaking.

Strelley sits forward on his chair. "Were you...?"

"A supporter of Surrey? I suppose I was, in my way. I have no great desire to see this nation dragged through a civil war for the sake of doctrine, but neither should those who hold power use it to silence those who stand against them."

"The earl brought about his own downfall, though," Strelley says, rather too quickly.

"What do you mean?" Shrewsbury asks.

"His persistence with Lady Mary... His suggestions about his sister becoming the king's mistress... His display of the Sainted Confessor's arms... All of these things that forced Hertford to make his move against him. Surrey, more than anyone, and without intending to, has done much to promote Edward Seymour's cause."

"You must understand that the earl thought all of these things appropriate to someone of his station. The marriage with royalty, diluted though her dignity was by her demotion, even that he thought would bring some of his family's honour to the Tudors, not the other way. I think he did think he ought to be king, but not at the expense of Henry."

Strelley waits, unsure whether Shrewsbury has finished. The earl looks at him, still trying to fathom Strelley's intentions. "There is no desire among the nobility to depose Edward in favour of Mary. That is what you wish to know? Even those of us who adhere to the ancient ways... There are many things that the king has done that we regret, but that does not entitle us to presume that we know the will of God."

"So the Pope will not call for a crusade against England?" Strelley's eyes narrow as he asks his question.

"His Holiness is concerned that England should return to the flock, but he does not require loyal Catholics to bear arms in that cause."

Strelley draws breath deeply. "You have been in contact with the Pope...?" It is unclear whether he asks a question or makes a statement.

"Master Strelley, I do not follow. You have no interest as a servant of the Lady Elizabeth, nor as my client, in my dealings with the king and the Pope."

"I am trying to choose my camp carefully, My Lord."

"I still do not understand."

"I only wish to avoid the penalties that come with making the wrong choices."

"You have no conviction? No strong pull in any direction?" The earl leans back, folding his arms across his chest.

"I hope God will guide me away from the stake. Those who make the wrong choices now..." Strelley trails off. "Am I safe in the Lady Elizabeth's household?"

"Cleave tight to the prince and his family. My offices cannot protect you. You, and Longshawe, are beyond my influence."

Strelley stands and bows to the earl, before turning to his son and bowing again. He turns to leave.

"Master Strelley," George Talbot calls after him, "Good luck!"

It is later that evening when the palace sees a brief flurry of activity. Amongst others, Lord Chancellor Wriothesley crosses the grounds, as does Edward Seymour. Several riders leave in the direction of Hertford a few minutes later, Seymour among them. One of their number bears the Royal Standard.

Inside the palace, Longshawe, no longer wearing his guard's uniform, passes down a corridor. As he does, he knocks on a door that leads to Lady Mary's suite of rooms. The lady herself is absent, but a familiar face appears. De Winter gives Longshawe an inquiring look.

"It is over," Longshawe says, quietly, "but not yet announced."

"And?" de Winter asks.

"Nothing yet. The Seymours have set off."

"The boy..." de Winter begins. "King..."

"In name, at least." Longshawe nods his head.

"We shall soon see whether Hertford manages to take hold of power."

Longshawe puts his hand on de Winter's shoulder. De Winter's face shows a mixture of sadness and fear.

"Do not be troubled, George," Longshawe offers, but he is not himself convinced. "I must go to Edward." De Winter takes Longshawe's hand, looking at it. A moment passes, then Longshawe withdraws the hand, turns, and is gone. De Winter curses quietly as he closes the door.

Longshawe makes his way to Strelley's attic room. He knocks on the door, opens it without waiting for an invitation, and finds Strelley sitting at his his tiny desk, reading by candlelight. Strelley turns to face him, face eerily uplit by the flickering candle. Longshawe lowers his head.

"Henry is dead, then," Strelley says. "Long live the king," he adds, a flicker of a smile at the edges of his mouth.

"What now?"

"You continue as you were. So do I. I spoke to Shrewsbury." Longshawe sits himself on the edge of Strelley's pallet as his friend continues to speak. "He seems to think that there's no threat from abroad, but I can't imagine that the Catholics won't see this as the ideal moment to strike. They simply declare Mary to be queen, ignore Edward as the bastard son they think he is..."

"Calm yourself, Edward," Longshawe soothes. "Edward is Henry's rightful heir, by anyone's reckoning. Remember, Queen Catherine died before Henry married Jane."

"Legitimacy is only one criterion."

"Yes, and the king's will names Edward, doesn't it?"

"So Wriothesley and Hertford say. But with a boy on the throne..."

"The king's named Council will protect him, and see him to his majority."

Strelley focuses on his friend's eyes, flashing in the low light. He holds his gaze for a long time, before replying finally, "We must look to each other's welfare. There are dark days ahead."

33: To the victor, the spoils

Strelley sits with Grindal in a room flooded with the low winter sun. Lady Elizabeth, tucked neatly into the embrasure of one of the windows, studies from a small book, occasionally adding a note in the margin. The two men are quiet, not productive, in contemplation rather than idleness. There is a knock at the door. Before it is answered, a page enters.

"I have the notice that Master Grindal requested." The page bows to the lady, but she ignores him. He shuffles over to Grindal and hands him a roll of paper. Grindal slips a coin into his hand, dismisses him, and falls to reading. Strelley rises and stands behind him so he too can read.

Grindal taps the paper with his finger. "It seems that the Council has been led to dissolve itself," he says. "Hertford – I should now say, rather, the Duke of Somerset – has been declared Lord Protector to His Majesty, King Edward. Look at this! Wriothesley an earl! It seems that Seymour has bought the king's men, too. Paget and Browne both spoke in favour of this appointment."

Strelley points to a different part of the document. "And his brother, it seems. Baron Sudeley! What a grand title for Master Seymour."

At this, the Lady Elizabeth's attention shifts from her book to the discussion between her tutor and his servant. "Thomas Seymour is to be elevated to a Baron?" she asks. Grindal looks at her with head tilted in condescension. "I shall take your scowl to be an indication of your affirmation," she says, raising her chin and narrowing her eyes. "My brother will need a strong nobility on his side if he is to rule this land." She returns to her book.

Strelley leans in to Grindal. "Seymour's brother is a preening, strutting fool," he whispers.

"Keep your judgments on your betters to yourself, Edward," Grindal hisses in reply. "You will do yourself no good if you persist in reckoning yourself qualified to comment on such matters."

Strelley reads the rest of the notice in silence. After a pause of a minute or so, Grindal's face breaks into the merest hint of a smile. "Though I should not," Grindal says, his tone much softer, "wish to have him for a master either."

"No. But we are both likely to be subject to him."

Grindal looks up at Strelley, puzzled. "What do you mean?"

"I mean that Baron Sudeley has made his move on Dowager Queen Catherine."

"His move?" Grindal asks, still not catching Strelley's point. Strelley raises his eyebrows, and Grindal understands. "Ah. So the Baron will be married to royalty. Of sorts, at least."

"Not just that. I understand that Sudeley's ambitions extend to the guardianship of the last remaining royal child up for grabs."

"Elizabeth? Surely not."

"It makes sense, does it not, for him? Mary is grown up, and though I wouldn't put it past Tom Seymour to have had designs on her, I suspect Hertford – Somerset – is clever enough not to let his brother marry into the succession. Edward Seymour will not allow himself to be leapfrogged. Not if he has any sense. So Tom Seymour and Catherine arrange the next best thing."

Grindal sits back in his chair, contemplative. He folds and unfolds his fingers, and more than once looks at Strelley as if to speak, but doesn't find the right thing to say. It is Elizabeth who breaks the silence.

"So my stepmother is going to marry the Baron Sudeley, is she?"

"You heard, Mistress," Grindal observes, drily, eyeing Strelley with an accusatory look. "Master Strelley says there is a rumour to that effect."

Strelley takes up the thread. "As you know, the queen – Catherine – and the baron once shared an affection-"

"Do not temporise with me, Master Strelley. My father was well aware of the position of Seymour in Her Majesty's heart, and he did what he thought best to make it easier for Catherine. Seymour must not have been in England for above a month in the last five years. Perhaps, rather than removing Seymour from court, he ought to have removed his head from his shoulders. It at least has the merit of permanence, if not subtlety." Elizabeth laughs at her own grisly suggestion. Grindal tuts.

Strelley catches Elizabeth's eye. "With your permission?" he asks. She nods. "Just like your brother does now, your father needed his nobles. Think what happens when over-mighty subjects find they no longer have any affection for or loyalty to their king." As he finishes, he chews his tongue. "Your grandfather-"

"Oh, don't try to mollify me, Master Strelley!" Elizabeth throws her head back in a haughty gesture. There is a moment of wide-eyed worry before Strelley can, just about, see her concealed smile. "My grandfather was no over-mighty subject, but the rightful king of England, and as God saw fit to seat him on the throne, who are we to question it?" Her mirth breaks through, and she laughs aloud. "I haven't seen you worried like that very often, Edward! Though I shall not hold it against you, might I suggest, for policy's sake, that you avoid further comment on the succession. Some are simply not born to do so." She holds her book up, giggling behind it. Strelley does not reply, but concentrates instead on re-reading the recently-delivered proclamation. Grindal looks at him for a moment. When Strelley's eyes rise from the paper, Grindal offers him a mocking smile. Strelley masters his urge to frown, instead remaining impassive.

Lady Mary walks across the palace, attended by her several retainers. Susan Clarencieux is there, as is our friend George de Winter. He wears the look of a man troubled by matters outside his control, following a few paces behind the lady, staring out but unaware of his surroundings. Mary herself leads the party to the royal presence chamber, and is admitted immediately by the two guards who stand watch. A herald announces her presence, carefully intoning her title of 'lady'.

Edward sits at the far end of the room, dwarfed by the same carved wood throne which his father lately occupied. His unremarkable frame is enhanced by layers of cloth and fur, his chains and jewels equally calculated to impose. The effect, doubled by the memory of his father, is pathetic, accentuating his smallness and his youth. His high voice welcomes his older sister.

"My Lady." He offers her the faintest of nods, presuming it to be dignified. "I have summoned you to speak with you on matters concerning your faith."

"My brother," Mary replies, and seeing the scowl that her words elicit on his face, changes tack. "Your Majesty, my religion is a private matter-"

With a gesture that mimics the action, but without the

conviction, of his father, Edward silences her. "Sister, you are mistaken." He tries desperately to sound authoritative. "Your faith, I say, is very much a public matter. Your continued failure to distance yourself from the Bishop of Rome is an embarrassment to our great House of Tudor. To the people of this realm it provides an example which they must not see fit to copy."

Mary fixes her look on her brother. He returns her gaze, his eyes shifting their focus, while hers remain absolutely still. Neither wants to concede this little contest, a sort of combat of nerve that holds great significance for both. Edward wants to show his authority over even the heir to his own throne, Mary by contrast wanting desperately no to have to bow to her young brother, a child of nine years.

It is Edward who speaks, conceding the game but choosing his words to change the battleground. "Sister, I will not allow you to continue to practise the old ways."

Mary draws a slow breath, composing herself for her reply. "Your Majesty must remember that my cousin, the Emperor, will not suffer me to be forbidden."

Edward's anger bursts, his voice rising to an uncomfortable shriek. "You will not browbeat me, sister! I am not afraid of your cousin, nor should I be. God will protect those who follow the true religion. Has he not seen to it that I have become King Edward to lead the people of England to the light of reform?"

Mary smiles wryly. Edward sees and slaps his hand down along the arm of his throne. The noise is small, unimpressive. He continues, "I am the Church, and I shall have my word obeyed!"

Mary bows to Edward, turns, and leaves. His heavy breathing is still audible as Mary's entourage exit the chamber. As she strides away to her own apartments, she fulminates.

"The ignorant child!" she spits. "Edward Seymour has put him up to this. I shall see to it that he answers for this persecution."

Susan Clarencieux holds Mary's hand. "You should not allow your anger to cloud your judgement, Madam. You would not wish to bring a charge of treason upon yourself."

"It is not treason to practise a faith," Mary replies bluntly.

De Winter coughs gently, signalling his wish to speak. Mary nods her assent, and he begins. "With the greatest respect, My Lady, the boy and the puppeteer have all the power. Should he wish it, he can

15

declare you a traitor because he, by your father's reforms, is the legal head of the Church in this land."

"I do not recognise that authority," Mary says, her bluntness coming partly from anger, partly from genuine conviction.

"Perhaps not, but that will not stop them trying and finding you guilty," de Winter returns. "Your safety, Madam, your life itself, is at issue. You might consider joining your cousin away from this court, beyond the reach of Seymour's arm."

"Don't be ridiculous, Master de Winter. I am not in danger from my brother."

Clarencieux takes Mary's shoulder now, grasping tightly. "My Lady, you must listen to us. George is right, you must not mistake your brother for a child. Whether or not he is just, he is king. And Seymour has his ear. You must not antagonise him. He is your father's son, and what fate befell so many at your father's hand?"

"My father had Protestants burned at the stake. Remember Askew?"

"I do, Madam." Clarencieux shudders. "Only too well. But such an act of faith will not serve! You are heir to the throne. Please do not throw away your life so recklessly!" She embraces Mary, her eyes shining with tears.

The party enters Mary's rooms. De Winter is dismissed, and Mary disappears into her chambers with Clarencieux. He leaves Mary's apartments, in search of his friends.

Fifteen minutes later, de Winter enters Strelley's garret room. Strelley is in there, reading from a manuscript which seems to be in Greek. Every now and and again he alters a word on another piece of parchment. He looks up to see de Winter.

"George! To what do I owe-"

De Winter does not allow him to finish the greeting. "That boy!" he growls. "The king. He has been indoctrinated."

"What do you mean?"

"He refuses to allow Lady Mary to practise her religion."

"He will not let her hear the Mass?"

"No. He is convinced that he is the true leader of the Church in England, and that he is chosen by God to convert the people to Lutheranism. Starting with his august sister, it seems."

"I cannot say I am surprised. How did she react?"

"Not well. She does not seem to have any fear of him, despite his power. I advised her to get out of England to somewhere safe."

Strelley shakes his head. "That plan has more than a hint of treason about it."

"If it's that or lose her life-"

"I thought you were in favour of martyrdom," Strelley interrupts.

"*I* do not matter. Lady Mary is next in line to the throne. She could restore England to the flock."

"Perhaps. She certainly will not do so if she is abroad."

"Though of course she could return from Spain to claim her throne. I doubt Our Lord would intervene to return her from the grave."

"Then you doubt His power...?" Strelley smiles. "No, you are right. We should speak to Longshawe. He may be able to help you."

And so, another five minutes later, Strelley and de Winter enter together the barrack room, where Longshawe is reposing himself, feet up on a barrel, picking away at a nearly-bare hock of mutton. He acknowledges the arrival of his friends with the slightest of nods, and swaps his bone for his mug of ale.

"Gentlemen," he says, through a mouthful of beer.

De Winter looks around the room. Only the three of them are present. Longshawe watches him as he approaches close and sits down.

"Well then," Longshawe smiles, "it seems this is a private matter."

"Indeed," de Winter replies. "A private matter that might see all three of us hanged if it found the wrong ears."

"My discretion, as ever, is assured." Longshawe allows himself a laugh. "I can't speak for Ned, though."

De Winter looks over his shoulder before speaking. "How difficult would it be to get the Lady Mary out of the Palace, out of the country?"

Longshawe's beer jets out of his mouth. He recovers himself with a cough. "To leave the country? Impossible."

De Winter's face falls. "Why?" he asks.

"Because Seymour has his eye on everything that goes on. At least half the Warders report directly to him or to Wriothesley, and the same is true of many of the retainers. They read the king's correspondence before the king does, and no doubt they know the contents of every scrap of paper that passes in or out of Mary's rooms likewise."

"They take such measures?" De Winter's tone betrays his surprise.

Longshawe smiles again, this time with an extra roll of his eyes. "Seymour is hardly secure in his power, is he? He guards it with jealousy, so that anyone who doubts him is suspect. From the little I have heard about it, though, he does have the support of the rest of the nobility."

"But it is *his* evangelism that is leading the king and country astray!" de Winter hisses.

"You shall not persuade me, George. I am loyal to my king. God has seen to it that he rules over me."

De Winter shakes his head and stands. "Thank you for your advice. I see that Seymour has already won." He offers Longshawe an exaggerated twirling bow, before stomping off. Strelley remains behind.

"How much of that is true?" Strelley asks.

"All of it. And more. Seymour and Wriothesley know most of what goes on among the great and the good. Seymour is the boy's uncle, though. He's not setting himself up as king."

"No, I think that's right. But he is doing what he can to make himself first citizen. Well, in any case, I have a question for you: remember our friend Gilbert?"

"Ah yes, your merchant friend. Very amusing."

"He thinks that Wriothesley is intercepting and stealing his merchandise."

"Illegal imports?"

"Of a sort. He thinks that Wriothesley has taken wormwood, lotus, that sort of thing. Expensive, small, easy to conceal. Probably destined for the late king's bedchamber."

"And?"

"Well, is he?"

"Is Wriothesley stealing? No doubt. Could we prove it? No. He has the finest forgers and fences in London in his pay."

"How do you know, then?"

"Because the Guards are sometimes co-opted. I have been

fortunate enough to avoid such duties, but there are a few who have done time on the wharves. They are told what to look for."

"Interesting. How does Wriothesley know which ships to target? Spies?"

"He must have his informers. But I do not know exactly. Your man Gilbert most likely has a spy in his own house."

"I shall break the bad news to him. It may just buy us a favour in the future."

"Master Strelley," Elizabeth says, looking up from her work. "I cannot decipher this."

They sit in a room unfamiliar to us, which is panelled in a dark oak that seems to pull the light into itself. The partial gloom is offset by Elizabeth's sky-blue dress, which envelops her chair to the extent that it is invisible beneath her.

"I have provided you with a crib, My Lady," Strelley says, gesturing in the direction of his morning's work.

"I know, but this is not Latin." She looks down at it again. "What is it?"

"A sort of Italian, Madam."

"Why have you presented me with a piece I cannot read?"

"I hoped we might learn something about politics. The author was a Florentine. I have another piece by a different Florentine which you might find equally instructive."

"I am glad that you still have *my* instruction as your goal, Sir. I had thought that my father's death might precipitate your removal into my brother's household." She smiles, for once genuinely warm and affectionate.

"Your brother's tutors are carefully selected by his Protector, Madam. As an unknown, I am deemed a potential threat, I think, and kept instead where I am able to do no harm to the machine of state."

"My father rated your opinion highly, didn't he?" Strelley offers a nod in reply, unassumingly candid. Elizabeth continues. "I don't understand why men such as Hertford, or Somerset as we must now call him, refuse the counsel of those such as you. Disinterested men."

"Men with nothing to gain or lose?" Strelley asks. Elizabeth's eyes narrow, but he speaks again. "With a few exceptions, the nobility see the common people, even the gentry, as footsoldiers and land-workers. Seymour does not always take account of the people's wishes, though he is better than some. Anyway, what right do the people have to determine how they are governed?"

"The people make the nation."

"You would do well to remember that, should you ever find yourself on the throne."

Elizabeth is just preparing what would doubtless be an acid

response, but Grindal comes back into the room, and his entry disturbs her thought. He leans over and looks at Strelley's prepared translation.

"The *Commedia*?" he says. "A difficult piece to read if you do follow the language. Nigh impossible if you don't."

Strelley sighs. "I had hoped to show the lady a little about its construction, the beauty of its conception."

"And no doubt some of the horrors it contains. You are not *just* to show the lady the works that fascinate you, Master Strelley. We are obliged to ground her in the great classics."

"She has had such a grounding, Master," Strelley replies, his deference just about disguising a little frustration. "The lady needs, indeed the lady wishes to widen her compass."

"To impress whatever foreign prince she marries?" Grindal snaps. For a moment, the tension is palpable. But Grindal sits himself down and smiles. "I apologise. To both of you. I find myself already a little weary of the requests of His Majesty," Grindal smoothes out a paper, "relating to the doctrinal education of My Lady." He watches as Elizabeth reads the note. "As you will no doubt recognise, your brother is prescribing your instruction. He names specific authors, and recommends that we study several of the Archbishop Cranmer's commentaries on various primers."

"Am I to be subject to the same rigours as my sister?" Elizabeth asks, without lifting her eyes. "It seems that Seymour is using his influence to ensure my conformity."

"Your sister," Strelley says, "is playing a dangerous game with the king and his Council. Might I offer my opinion? It is that if conformity is required, then conform. You can read Dante alongside Luther, but you must be seen to do what your brother asks."

"I shall consider your advice-" She is cut off by a knock at the door. A footman steps in and announces the Dowager Queen Catherine. As she comes over, Grindal picks up the piece of paper with Edward's note on it, folds it and drops it by the side of his chair.

Strelley and Grindal rise as the Dowager Queen approaches. Elizabeth offers her a nod. "Elizabeth!" she hails. "I have very much missed your company. Allow me this opportunity to apologise for my absence. Now I am returned." She wears a sumptuous black gown, with tasteful but expensive jewels arranged about her neck and fingers. Her mourning dress is dramatic, but her countenance is contented, even happy.

"Your Majesty," Elizabeth greets the queen, a little sullen. "I had not expected your company at my lessons."

"I shall be taking a much greater interest in your education henceforth. Your father was very proud of your learning, Elizabeth." The queen takes her step-daughter's hand between hers. "I shall continue his work, if it please you."

Elizabeth looks at the queen warily. She does not speak in reply, but her mouth curls slightly, unseen by Catherine who is looking at Elizabeth's hand between her own.

"Well," Catherine says brightly, lifting her eyes and failing to notice the rapid rearrangement of her stepdaughter's features, "proceed with your work!" She releases Elizabeth's hand, and sits back.

Elizabeth points to her manuscript. *"Lasciate ogne speranza, voi ch'intrate."* She reads slowly as Catherine watches and listens, her attention fixed on Elizabeth's struggle to pronounce the unfamiliar words. She waits to the end of the line, then turns to Grindal.

"Italian?" Catherine asks. "I do not recognise it."

Grindal frowns in Strelley's direction. Strelley offers him a dry smile in return. "Florentine Italian, about two hundred years old," he says, to Catherine. "It means, roughly, 'abandon all hope, you who enter here.'"

Catherine pulls in her breath through pursed lips. "I do not recognise it," she repeats.

"The Florentine was called Alighieri. He writes of a dream in which he visits Hell, Purgatory and Heaven with Vergil as his guide." Strelley picks up the crib and passes it across to Catherine, who begins to read immediately.

"I see," she replies without looking up from the crib. "This is your translation, is it? You shall have to let me borrow this, Elizabeth. Though I think Purgatory is a somewhat outmoded idea, is it not?"

"We do not refrain from reading Homer because we no longer believe Zeus to be real," Strelley says, quietly.

"Indeed." Catherine still does not look up from the translation. "Fascinating, Master...?"

"Strelley, Madam," he replies. At this, Elizabeth pulls a hectoring face, which Strelley and Grindal notice but Catherine again does not. Strelley suppresses the urge to admonish her, a hint of a smile flashing across his face. Grindal frowns, darting his eyes between Elizabeth and Strelley, then the moment passes.

Catherine puts the parchment on the table, again leaning in towards Elizabeth. "I have great hopes for you, my dear. You are a great asset to this nation and to your family."

Elizabeth looks back at her, head tilted. "I shall not be some heifer to be paraded before those with whom we seek an alliance," she spits.

Catherine adopts a conciliatory tone. "I did not mean to offend you, Elizabeth. You should not think that we regard you as a bargaining token."

Elizabeth bristles. "Then I shall be free to choose a husband for love, shall I?"

"Your future marriage is your in brother's charge, not mine. I had merely intended to offer a word of praise." Catherine's eyes flash, and she blinks to prevent a tear falling. "I have the greatest affection for you, and I take great care to look after your best interests. I hope you will come to understand that, in time."

"What do you mean?" Elizabeth asks, and the anger has left her voice.

"Your position as the late king's heir needs to managed with great discretion, as you no doubt realise. There are those who would seek to gain by association with you."

"That I know well." Elizabeth smiles. "Marry me, see off my brother and sister, and the throne is yours. I shall not fall for it. If I rule, it shall be in my own right."

"A noble sentiment, Madam," Catherine agrees. "But one that you must not speak of, nor should you anticipate it inwardly. The Duke of Somerset even now plans to secure the hand of the girl Queen of Scotland for your brother."

"Ah, my father's war is to be recommenced, is it? Master Strelley here was part of our last foray into Scotland." She gestures in Strelley's direction. He looks up and confirms with a nod, a mirthless, flat expression on his face. "I understand that it is not the easiest of countries in which to prosecute war."

Catherine folds her lips inwards, licks them, and sighs. "My Lady is knowledgeable on such subjects. I had rather thought her education might be focused on more liberal, humanist matters."

"With respect, Your Majesty," Grindal intervenes, "what could be more human than war?"

Catherine laughs. "You are correct, of course, Master Grindal. I see that the lady's education is in good hands. I hope you will welcome me on future visits," she says, rising. She bows to Elizabeth and turns to leave. Her handmaiden, who has waited at the door, eyes lowered away from the conversation, follows behind her.

Elizabeth looks from Grindal to Strelley and back again. "Well, gentlemen, it seems that we shall have the company of my stepmother the queen for our lessons."

Strelley smiles back at her. "We shall ensure that our instruction is to Her Majesty's tastes."

Five hours later, it is dark around Catherine's house. The household has largely retired to its rest, with just one or two windows visibly lit. The winter chill has brought a fine mist, but through it, just detectable by the glinting of their tack, a pair of horsemen ride across the grounds. Some way distant from the house, they dismount. One tethers the horses to a tree, and spreads a cloak on the ground. He sits on it, as the other looks out towards the house. After waiting a minute or two, the standing figure begins moving slowly across the gardens towards a lit ground-floor window. There is a postern door a few yards away from the window. The figure approaches the window closely and, for a moment, looks through it. From a distance it appears to be curtained, but something keeps his attention. Then he turns toward the door, walks over to it, and raps on it three times, tap, tap-tap. It opens without a sound, and he disappears within. Three minutes later, a third figure rises from the cover of the sculpted bushes. He has seen the two men arrive, and one of them enter. This third man withdraws around the house, moving silently to avoid being noticed by the remaining watcher.

Just before dawn, the postern re-opens, and out comes the unidentified figure, his gait and bearing announcing that it is the same man as before. He makes his way across the grounds, less discreet than before, rejoining his companion. They do not speak, but both mount and within half a minute they are gone, lost among the woods that surround Chelsea Manor, Catherine Parr's house.

Two days later, Edward Strelley rides out towards the palace at Whitehall. The king's flag flies above the highest tower, indicating the presence of King Edward's Majesty. At the gate, Strelley is challenged by a guard, but is able to enter as he is recognised by another of the Yeomen. He asks to see Longshawe, and is led to a long, low hall that serves as sort of recreational area for the guards. Longshawe is practising his fencing, and showing off to the other guards the sword he bought with Strelley from the merchant Gilbert.

"Toledo steel," Longshawe is saying. "Doesn't look so great, but much stronger than this shiny stuff." He points to the weapon his partner uses. The blades clash, then the fencers come apart. Longshawe runs a finger gently along his sword. "See!" he says, triumphantly, pointing to his own weapon's edge. "Not a mark on it. Yours is notched." It is true, his partner's sword has a nick in the cutting edge.

Strelley sidles up to him unnoticed. "Never one to miss the opportunity to show off, eh?" he says, laughing as Longshawe startles momentarily. "I need to speak with you. Alone."

They walk off along a series of corridors, eventually entering Longshawe's room, where there is little beyond a wardrobe and a few assorted arms. "The room of a soldier..." Strelley mutters as Longshawe sits on the simple pallet bed.

"What were you expecting?" Longshawe asks. "Four posts and a lion's skin for a coverlet?"

They laugh together. Strelley is the first to straighten. "I need to get some information to Protector Somerset."

"And? Write to him. You're good at that, aren't you?"

"It's sensitive."

"So are you. What's the big secret?"

"It concerns his brother."

"The Baron of Sudeley? Tom Seymour?" Longshawe raises his eyebrows. "Surely Somerset will be aware of what his brother is about."

"It's more *who* his brother is about."

"And who-" Longshawe stops as Strelley holds up his hand. He rotates it gently, telling Longshawe to think. "The queen?" Longshawe chews his lip. "But this is hardly great news, is it? They knew each other before she married Henry, didn't they?"

"Indeed. But the king has hardly been dead a month."

25

"So he pays his court. Just preparing the ground, isn't he?"

"And I would agree, if he visited her by day."

"She grants him an assignation!" Longshawe exclaims. "But..."

"Indeed. She still wears mourning for the late king."

"I should imagine that Edward Seymour will have trouble forgiving even his own brother for this..." he considers the right word. "Licence."

"And whilst I would not wish to bear bad news to the First Subject of the Kingdom, I would rather gain his favour by telling him than lose it by not doing so."

"I shall see what I can do."

"There's another thing."

"More state secrets?"

"Possibly. Remember the Earl of Southampton's light-fingered attitude to our mutual friend Gilbert's stock? I need to see his office."

"You don't ask for much," Longshawe replies. "Access to the Protector to pass him treason charges against his own brother, and just for good measure, a quick look inside the Lord Chancellor's desk drawers. Are you not satisfied with what I told you before?"

"I leave it to your ingenuity."

"No need." Longshawe is up and looking out of his small window. "That's Seymour now. He looks like he might be off to see Wriothesley. Shall we follow?"

Longshawe leads Strelley out into the courtyard, and they pass across into another part of the building opposite, following Somerset and his handful of retainers. Somerset strides along a corridor, turning sharply at a heavy oaken door and waiting as one of his men hammers on the wood.

The door opens, and Somerset is admitted. Longshawe and Strelley hang back at the end of the corridor for a short while, then they approach the door to Wriothesley's office. Some of Somerset's men recognise Longshawe, and tip their hats to him.

"I need to speak to the Protector, urgently," Longshawe says, putting on his air of leadership. There is a brief commotion among Somerset's band of men.

"His Grace the Duke of Somerset is in counsel with My Lord Southampton. He will be available shortly," one of the duke's men says.

"This is a matter that concerns the security of the Realm."

Longshawe acts his part well, emphasising carefully the words designed to frighten.

"I-" Somerset's footman begins, but Longshawe's scowl defeats him, browbeating him into submission. He opens the door.

Somerset half-turns, not quite facing them. "I had not expected to be intruded upon," he whispers over his shoulder.

"Your Grace," Longshawe announces, "my friend and associate has just ridden from Chelsea with news of great import." He ushers Strelley into the room, and closes the door behind them.

"Longshawe, isn't it?" The Duke of Somerset turns to face Strelley and Longshawe, folds his arms and tilts his head. "The late king trusted you, and so shall I. For now. Do not waste my time."

"I shall not, Your Grace." Longshawe bows his head. Strelley is looking around the room, before fixing his eyes on Wriothesley. Strelley smiles affably, hiding his usual shrewdness. Wriothesley does not return the gesture, taking no trouble to disguise his own wiles.

"What news, then?" Somerset asks.

Longshawe turns to look at Strelley, who has not responded to the duke. Strelley is still holding Wriothesley's gaze, and continues to do so for just a moment before he speaks.

"Your Grace," he says, turning to Somerset, "I bring you news of Dowager Queen Catherine."

"She is, by King Henry's will, still Queen Catherine, not a dowager." Somerset corrects Strelley. Strelley nods his head slightly.

"In either case, she does not observe the proper... exequies."

"Do not be cryptic, Sir." Somerset observes Strelley carefully. The young man does not flinch under the scrutiny. "I know you," Somerset continues. "You are the tutor's boy, are you not? You have taught the king himself once or twice. And you know full well that Her Majesty is granted the full rights of a queen." Strelley coughs gently in reply.

"Indeed, Your Grace," he says. "Her Majesty does not take her responsibility as queen seriously."

"Master Strelley, I forbid you to obfuscate any further. Get to your point, or I shall dismiss you," Seymour growls, his top lip curling.

"Very well. The queen resides at Chelsea Manor, as you no doubt already know, and she receives guests there..." Strelley pauses, sighs, looks at Longshawe, carefully building the tension. Seymour begins to shake his head. "Your Grace's brother has visited the queen. At night."

Somerset flashes forward. In a heartbeat, he has Strelley's shirt in his hand, holding a hunting knife withdrawn from the folds of his own clothes at Strelley's neck. "Slander and calumny!" Somerset shouts. "I shall have you hanged!" Longshawe's hand is on the hilt of his sword. Somerset sees and relaxes his grip, pushing Strelley away.

"What prompts this? The truth, or you shall wear your balls for earrings."

Strelley rights himself, dusting down his shirt-front and standing up straight. "Your Grace knows I am lodged at Chelsea with the queen and Lady Elizabeth. I awoke one night to hear a man leaving the house, and watched from the window as he joined another man, hidden in the grounds. I did not wish to accuse anyone without further evidence, so the following night I went outside and secreted myself in the bushes. I watched as a man entered the house by a postern, and left before dawn."

"And what evidence do you have that this was my brother?"

Strelley once again looks at Longshawe, before turning back to face Seymour. He pulls a scrap of cloth from a pocket. "This is your brother's, is it not?"

Seymour examines the piece of material. It clearly bears the Baron Sudeley's arms. "You could have got this anywhere." His voice is quiet, resigned, unconvinced by his own rebuff.

"And yet I did not. It is newly torn, as you can see. Your Grace will remember the queen's fondness for your brother before her marriage to the late king..."

"Who else knows of this?" Seymour snaps.

"No one, Your Grace. Just the four of us in this room, and any at Chelsea who have made the same discovery as I. Though I do not think the inference is a difficult one-"

"Hold your tongue!" Wriothesley shouts. "Do not speak ill of your betters in this rude fashion!" Strelley lowers his eyes. Wriothesley turns to Somerset. "What action, Edward?"

"None, for now. I shall speak with my brother. Gentlemen," he continues, his tone much softer than Wriothesley's, "your discretion in this matter is now of the utmost importance. Do not share your theory – for that it remains, Master Strelley, until proven conclusively – with *anyone*. Do you understand?" Strelley and Longshawe nod. "Then you are dismissed. Return to your duties."

Both bow, and leave. As soon as the door catches closed behind them, Longshawe breathes out dramatically. They walk away down the corridor, watched by the group gathered outside.

"What were you doing?" Longshawe asks. "You seemed to be trying to make him more angry!"

"Did I?" Strelley asks, his expression oblique.

"Some master plan, no doubt."

"Just making sure that Somerset remembers us."

"Was that scrap of cloth-"

"Yes. He tore his cloak on a rose-bush. Only someone with Tom Seymour's streak of vanity would wear a cloak with armorial bearings to an assignation."

"Does Lady Elizabeth know?"

"I shall do my best to find out. I suspect not. And if not, I should not be the one to inform her."

"Somerset will be furious with his brother. The king has hardly been dead a month."

"Equally with the queen, though he may not show it in quite the same way. If it is not treason, it is close. Regardless, it shows Sudeley's ambition."

"I thought they were in love?"

"That might be true. But why do you think Henry stipulated that she be respected as queen?"

Longshawe pushes out his bottom lip. "I don't know." As Strelley stops, a satisfied expression on his face, Longshawe shakes his head in frustration at his friend's scheming.

Strelley allows himself a moment for the sake of drama. "Because *he did not want Tom Seymour at his queen after he was gone!* If she is Queen Catherine, not Dowager Queen Catherine, then she is not free to remarry."

"But surely if she is widowed..." Longshawe asks without conviction.

"Of course she *can* remarry. It's just not what she *should* do. The king left her queen in his memory, so she can't properly take another husband. And the reason Seymour – Edward – is so furious is that it's a challenge to his authority as Protector."

"One more question. Why does this concern us?"

"Two things. One is that it is always wise to have a favour in hand from those in power, and the other is that Tom Seymour is a braggart and a fool who needs to be brought down a notch or two."

"I agree with Wriothesley. Do not speak ill of your betters!" Longshawe laughs. "Did you see what you wanted to?"

Strelley smiles broadly, before reaching into his pocket. "Even better." He says, unfolding a piece of paper. "This is the original manifest from Gilbert's ship. And this," he continues, taking out a clay bottle about two inches high, "is one of the items he took!"

"I did not have you marked as a thief. I shall watch you more closely in future."

"I'm not sure it's theft. After all, it was Gilbert's to begin with, and now it shall be Gilbert's again."

They re-enter the mess, where Guy Fletcher is oiling some leather tack. He rises and bows elaborately to his master and to Strelley, who replies in kind.

Strelley goes over to him and grabs him around the shoulder. "Master Fletcher!" Strelley cries, enthusiastically. "What a pleasure it is to see you! I hope you are keeping Longshawe here under strict control." He reaches into a pocket and pulls out a book and a couple of gold coins. "This is for you to read, and this for you to spend in whatever way you see fit."

"I thank you, Master Strelley," Fletcher says. "And no, I do not keep Master Longshawe under anything resembling control."

Longshawe looks at him, his head tilted to one side. "When I have a secret of yours to keep, Guy, you shall be assured that everyone in the palace shall know it!" he says, in a bantering tone.

Strelley turns to Longshawe, all seriousness. "Be careful, though, James. I should have thought that an illicit child would be a great burden to you." As he utters these last words, his face creases into a broad grin.

"Neither of you has a sense of adventure! In any case, I keep no mistress." Longshawe laughs. "It is the truth. Besides, the king, by which I mean Somerset, of course, is planning a sort of progress, so that eliminates half the opportunities. Although it might present others, I suppose."

"Does he intend to visit Chelsea?"

"To see his sister? I think so. I shall send Guy here to tell you. Perhaps he shall speak of other sensitive matters when he comes."

Strelley bids them farewell, and sets off across town. He follows the road that leads him towards Gilbert's warehouse, passing along the docks among wharves, and he arrives there perhaps an hour and a half later.

Gilbert sits at his desk, smoking. "Good day, my young apprentice." He smiles, showing teeth stained yellow by the tobacco.

Strelley shakes his head at the joke. "I have your proof."

Gilbert jerks forward in his seat. "Truly? I had not expected much from you, if I am to be honest."

"You dissemble. Nevertheless, I have what you want." He puts the clay bottle on the desk in front of Gilbert.

"This is good work, Master Strelley." Gilbert picks up the bottle. "It's a shame I can't do much with it. Wriothesley and his ilk have too much... *authority*. No one higher to complain to..."

"No." Strelley chews his lip. "Even Wriothesley has to be seen to obey the law."

"What do you mean? I can't march into the palace with this and confront him with it, can I?" Gilbert stares at Strelley. "What else have you got?"

"What would you give to ruin Wriothesley?"

"I am not a vengeful man, Master Strelley."

"But you are a man with a reputation to uphold."

Gilbert leans back in his chair, looking out from under his eyebrows. "I have enough credit, both monetary and otherwise, in this city, to survive a little altercation with the palace."

"Would it not redound to the credit of your name to come off best in this skirmish?"

"For God's sake, man!" Gilbert shouts. "Get to it!"

Strelley smoothes out the shipping manifest on the desk.

"This is brilliant!" Gilbert says, eyes wide. "How did you get it?"

"At great personal risk."

"You didn't break in to the Lord Chancellor's chambers?"

"Of course not! I am no fool, Gilbert. I created a distraction."

"What?"

"I had a tale to tell to the Lord Protector, and so caught Wriothesley off guard."

"A tale?"

"The Protector's brother is bedding the queen."

"Two extraordinary pieces of information in a minute." Gilbert laughs. "Are you sure you are not a spy?"

"No. But I trust that information will go no further, just yet. Do what you will with Wriothesley."

"What do you want for this?" Gilbert asks. His knuckles show white on the desk.

"Not money. I want your assurance, as you offered before."

"What?" Gilbert replies, unsure.

"That influence you wield... You know people, powerful people. Not lords and dukes, I mean."

"A good word with the underworld? You shall have it, but I know not what for!" Gilbert shakes Strelley's hand.

"Nor do I. Yet."

A week later, the household at Chelsea is preparing to receive guests of the highest honour and dignity. Great state rooms are decorated with all manner of hangings, gildings and display. A huge feast is prepared for the evening, and Elizabeth and her governess Kat spend all day about choosing her attire. Strelley and Grindal use the time to read for pleasure, something they manage infrequently when tutoring the lady. Queen Catherine bustles about the house, seeing that the reception will be magnificent.

It is early in the afternoon when a footman calls out that he can see the king's standard in the distance. Some half an hour later, with final touches applied to the house, the king's party arrives. Longshawe and another guard flank the boy King Edward and his uncle, who ride abreast at the head. As they approach, Seymour drops behind a little, gesturing to the king that it is he who should make the threshold first, in light of the dignity of His Majesty.

Elizabeth is in the front row of the assembled household. "Brother!" she calls, rushing up to Edward before he is even dismounted. Longshawe, a few yards behind, dismounts smoothly and quickly, positions himself at the flank of the king's horse, and helps him down to greet his sister. Elizabeth watches the manoeuvre with great interest. Seymour also dismounts and greets Elizabeth warmly.

"Sister!" Edward says, breathlessly. "It is the greatest pleasure to see you. I grow weary of my duties, sometimes."

Elizabeth takes his hand and holds it between her fingers. "The burden on you is great indeed." She says it quietly, and the king takes this to show her sincerity. Strelley, some distance back but carefully positioned to watch, notices that she lowers her eyes as she speaks. Jealousy, perhaps, or something else, but she dissimulates. As this moment passes, Edward Seymour glances in Strelley's direction. He sees, but does acknowledge him.

Later that afternoon, Thomas Seymour, Baron Sudeley, arrives with his party. They precede by a few minutes the larger entourage of the Earl of Shrewsbury, who comes with his son among a large party of gentlemen. Shrewsbury does not comment on the breach of protocol, but Edward Seymour takes his brother aside shortly afterwards. Their raised voices are audible, but their words are muffled by the heavy doors at Chelsea Manor.

Elizabeth is dressing. Her governess fusses about her, applying a white powder to her face to even her complexion.

"Why do you think men take precedence in the succession, Kat?" Elizabeth asks.

"I'm sure My Lady has read much about the laws of primogeniture. I do not pretend to understand it much myself."

"I do not mean, 'in what way is the succession codified into law?'. If I had wanted an answer to that question I should have asked Master Grindal, or Strelley. I mean to ask why it should be that being male is in itself enough to secure precedence. My brother, after all, is younger than Mary, younger than I, and yet he is my father's heir, despite his youth."

"Madam should not concern herself with the wherefores, rather she should accept her position as Lady of the Royal House of Tudor. Your brother may even restore your title as Princess. I think he was well-pleased to see you today."

"My brother...? If any change to my status is to occur, it will be at the behest of the Duke of Somerset, I believe."

"You have discussed these matters with your tutors? They tell you their opinions of the way Protector Somerset guides your brother the king?"

"I have asked for their opinions. They do not judge the Protector unfavourably, they simply acknowledge that the power in this realm lies with him."

"Protector Somerset guides your brother in the exercise of his power. When he reaches majority, Edward will be king in his own right."

"I know that, you do not need to explain further," Elizabeth replies, curtly. "Since your marriage to Master Astley, you have affected to be known as Astley yourself, have you not?"

"It is the custom, Madam."

"But it should not be so!" Elizabeth says. "A woman has just as much right to her name as a man. Were I to marry, my husband's name would not replace my father's."

"We have had this discussion over and again, Madam. Your future husband will be some great prince of a powerful nation, and it will not do for you to show such wilfulness."

"Were more of my sex to 'show such wilfulness', perhaps we should not have to bow to patriarchy."

"For heaven's sake, Elizabeth, do not speak so at dinner this evening. I do not want the Protector to think that I am encouraging these sentiments."

"I should be quite happy to tell him that far from encouraging them, you try to suppress them. Master Strelley is more supportive of me than you!"

"Madam!" Astley replies, pretending to be shocked. "I have had your care since you were a little child! Do not be so cruel. Besides, you talk too much of Master Strelley. He is a servant."

"He is a good man. His friend Longshawe..." Elizabeth giggles.

"I can see that there is no hope for you, My Lady. You must endeavour to find it within yourself to behave decorously." Astley is affectionate, but her fondness for her charge does not disguise her real concern.

"I shall have no difficulty displaying the airs and graces of a royal princess this evening."

As Elizabeth is talking, there is a knock at the door. Without preamble, one of the queen's maids, a child of about ten years, enters. She comes forward and bows.

"What is it, Jane?" Elizabeth asks.

"My Lady, the queen is here to see you." Jane stands by as the queen enters.

Elizabeth bows her head. "Your Majesty," she says, smiling.

"I'm glad to see you in a good mood, Elizabeth." Queen Catherine smoothes her hand over Elizabeth's dress. "I worried that I had upset you previously."

"No, Madam, you did not."

"Good. I know that I am not your mother, but you must believe me when I tell you that I will do anything for you that you might expect of a mother."

Elizabeth contemplates Catherine, who is awkwardly holding Elizabeth's shoulders. The grown woman and the young teenager share a brief moment of affection, then it passes. Elizabeth's lip curls slightly.

"I thank you for your kindness, Madam," Elizabeth says. Catherine is still holding her, as though expectant of something further. Elizabeth notices, but is unsure what to say. Catherine begins to say something, but stops. Elizabeth turns back to Kat Astley. "I shall see you this evening, then," she says to the queen, who delays a moment, thinking about saying something further, before instead turning to leave.

The evening's feasting is a credit to the queen's household at Chelsea. A vast range of dishes is served, each more delightful than the last. Eventually, everyone present is satisfied, and the servants begin to clear the food away. The young king and his Protector Somerset make the rounds of the assembled nobility, including our acquaintances the Earl of Shrewsbury and his son.

"It is to be war, then?" Shrewsbury asks, stroking his beard.

"Yes, Francis. We shall teach the Scots a lesson!" says Somerset. He puts his hand on King Edward's shoulder. The boy looks up to him. "We shall unite the two kingdoms once and for all, and finally England shall be free of its irksome neighbour to the north. You shall truly be King of England and Scotland! What say you, Your Majesty?"

Edward raises his eyebrows in a gesture calculated to look stately. "I shall have the child Queen of Scotland for my wife, and we shall beget the greatest royal household in Europe."

"It is well said, Sire," Shrewsbury replies, watching as the Lord Protector pats his young charge, half avuncular, half patronising. "But, as His Grace Somerset knows, an invasion of Scotland is no simple matter. Even your great father never fully brought it under control. My son was part of the last force that went north, and that army was sent back with its tail between its legs. I believe Your Majesty knows Masters Longshawe and Strelley? And your sister Mary's man, de Winter? Each took his part, and each could terrify Your Majesty with stories of backsliding mercenaries and wild country where whole armies disappear into the mist, only to return when you do not expect them." Shrewsbury hams it up for the child king, stretching out the words for dramatic emphasis.

Somerset looks aslant at him. "You doubt our capability, My Lord?"

"I do not doubt that you can win a victory of sorts, that at least you have shown before. Perhaps you may even achieve your goal of capturing the queen. But you cannot subdue the country. The people are rough, they are warlike rogues who will not know when they are beaten." Shrewsbury leans in to the king. "But with a leader such as Somerset here, anything is possible, Your Majesty." He looks up at

Somerset for a brief moment after finishing his blandishment.

Somerset bows. "I thank you for your confidence," he says, again putting his hand on Edward's shoulder. "Come, Sire, it is time for you to speak with my brother."

Somerset leads the boy away. Shrewsbury watches without speaking, until the king and his uncle begin their conversation with Thomas Seymour.

"Madness," he says quietly to George Talbot. "They would need an army of twenty thousand with money to buy the whole borderland to invade successfully."

"Perhaps Somerset has the will to create such an army," George replies. Then he contemplates for a moment. "I should like to see Longshawe and Strelley if they are present."

"This, then, is an excellent opportunity to present you to Elizabeth. Strelley is still part of her household here, I am told."

They stand, and make their way over to where Queen Catherine sits with Elizabeth, discussing the dances that are about to commence.

"Your Majesty... My Lady." Shrewsbury offers a deep bow. "May I present my son George?"

Elizabeth looks up at Shrewsbury, then over his shoulder at his son. The queen lowers her head to the young man, and addresses the elder. "Well met, both of you. It is good to see that the men my late husband held in such high esteem are gathering around his son."

"We are loyal subjects, Madam," Shrewsbury replies. "The king has need of those, I think."

"As does the Protector," Catherine replies. "You know the late king much desired to see Edward wedded to the young Queen of Scotland. It would be of great comfort to all Englishmen to know that the Scots were our allies, not our enemies. And it would greatly sting the French!"

"Madam, you speak as Henry himself did." Shrewsbury bows in compliment.

"Well then, Sirs, you must see to it that our expedition is successful. Protector Somerset tells me that he intends to take a force of considerable size, no doubt including such fine soldiers as yourselves."

George Talbot allows himself a wry smile at the memory of Ancrum, but says nothing. His father stands upright, considering the queen's words. "I had not anticipated going to war again," he says

38

simply. "I shall ready myself."

"Your Grace," the queen says to the older Talbot, half-laughing, "I had thought you a man of great perspicacity. Surely you divined the cause of this gathering. It is a part of a great council of war that shall include all England before it is done."

"It seems that we are perpetually at war. I had rather enjoyed the lull." Shrewsbury allows himself a smile. "But when the king calls, we shall answer. As ever it was. Madam." He bows and turns to leave. George Talbot steps forward and offers the Lady Elizabeth a gracious obeisance, turning his hand to accentuate the gesture.

"My Lady," the young Talbot says, "would you do me the honour?" He offers her a hand. She glances at Catherine, who nods.

"I would be delighted, My Lord." Elizabeth stands and accompanies George Talbot to the floor cleared for dancing, which is where we shall leave them.

Across the room, Longshawe is at ease in his best finery. Edward Strelley stands next to him, watching Elizabeth dancing with George Talbot.

"So you're going to war again?" Strelley asks.

"It seems that way. The king will remain in the south, but much of the household guard will accompany the Lord Protector."

"Somerset is allowed to take the king's personal guardsmen with him?"

"It would be foolish to leave us in London when the fighting is in Scotland." Longshawe laughs, enjoying the opportunity to condescend. Strelley shakes his head.

"Indeed. But the king does not cease to need protection because his minister wages war elsewhere. You are selected as elite bodyguards for His Majesty, not so that he can be abandoned as soon as there is a battle. Whatever the cause..."

"Well, Edward, I shall take great comfort in knowing that you remain close to the king. Perhaps Master Cheke will be able to assist you when the time comes to foil the myriad assassins that lurk waiting for our departure."

Strelley half-smiles. "I am not joking."

"Nor am I. The king is perfectly safe."

"Truly? With Seymour's brother left behind?"

"Tom Seymour is no threat to the king."

"No, but he is a threat to his brother's authority. I shall keep an eye on him."

"You promised not to involve yourself in politics." Longshawe raises his eyebrows.

"This isn't politics. This is..." Strelley searches for the right words. "National Security."

"I shall raise your concerns with the Captain of the Yeomen, if it will calm you down."

"It will. Who else is part of this invasion?" Strelley asks.

"No doubt Shrewsbury and George – Waterford, I suppose we ought to call him. Somerset says there shall be in excess of fifteen thousand all told. The Earl of Warwick is in the Shires mustering."

"Dudley was in command of the fleet at Portsmouth, you know?"

"I did. I met him. Seems a good soldier."

"But an earl? That is Somerset's doing."

"What does it signify? The king needs strong men around him, and if that means elevating Dudley, so be it."

"It is to be hoped that all these novitiate nobles do not seek greater power than has already come to them," Strelley says, frowning.

"No politics. You promised. And I need a dance." Longshawe casts his eyes around the room. Gathered around the queen are a number of Ladies-in-Waiting, and Longshawe strides off in their direction, leaving Strelley to his thoughts. As the music comes to an end, George Talbot leaves the dance, bringing with him Lady Elizabeth, and they come over to Strelley, both just a little warm and breathless.

"Edward!" Talbot greets him informally with a shake of the hand. "I had hoped to see you. The lady tells me that you are a wonderful tutor. It is a great pleasure to my father and I to find you hale, hearty and in good office."

"I cannot thank My Lords enough for their interest. My employment with the lady is fascinating." Strelley pulls his lips over his teeth in an expression calculated to say that this fascination is sometimes a little too exciting. Talbot snorts, then tries to disguise it with a question.

"You do not wish to join us in this campaign in Scotland, then?"

"No, My Lord, once was quite enough for me." He lays his

fingers on the back of his scarred arm. "I much prefer peace, and my books."

Elizabeth looks askance at him. "Yet it is not always a choice a sovereign is able to make, is it, to avoid war? Sometimes it is thrust upon him."

"Indeed it is, Madam. And in those times, I should be just as little use on a battlefield as I was at Ancrum."

"You have no sense of adventure, Master Strelley," Elizabeth replies with fake curtness. "I shall see to it that you are found some delightful commission in the Orient to shake you from your complacence."

"Madam is right to admonish, as always. Though I should like to visit the Holy Land, perhaps, when my time with you is over."

"A noble goal, Sir," Talbot says. He listens to the music for a moment. "Ah! My Lady, we must join this dance! And I have seen Master Longshawe over there. I would speak with him." He pulls Elizabeth back into the dancing. As she turns, she smiles broadly at Strelley, who shakes his head. He watches as she returns to the middle of the floor with Talbot, noticing that she follows with her eyes the young Earl of Waterford's gesture towards Longshawe, and that she stays focused on him for rather too long.

Some time later in the evening, the gathering continues even as the king, young as he is, has retired to bed. Elizabeth has finished her dance with George Talbot and sits with her step-mother, Queen Catherine. They watch as others dance. Elizabeth's eyes are now drawn in particular to Thomas Seymour, Baron Sudeley.

"Is that the Lord Protector's brother?" she asks Catherine, pointing. He notices, and looks over to them, then carries on dancing.

"Indeed it is," Catherine replies, her composure slightly, briefly, dented.

"I thought I recognised him. He has visited you here, has he not?" Elizabeth asks casually.

"Baron Sudeley is an old acquaintance of mine, Madam. I have known him for many years."

"Since before you became queen, as I understand it." There is a hint of malevolence in Elizabeth's voice. "It seems that you have renewed your *acquaintance* with him rather precipitously, Madam. Do you not think it might be more seemly if you refused to see him?"

"Do you suspect me of impropriety?" Catherine arranges her face to look shocked, eyes wide.

"I meant nothing of the sort. Though from your keenness to defend yourself..." Elizabeth half-smiles. "As queen, Madam, surely it behoves you to behave with the greatest dignity and circumspection."

"Elizabeth..." Catherine hisses. Her eyes flick from side to side as she tries to read the teenager, seeking confirmation of her fear. "I have done nothing that does not befit my station."

Elizabeth nods, apparently pacified. "I should like to dance," she says, scanning the room. A moment passes before she catches Strelley's attention, and beckons him over. "Edward," she says, "Will you ask the Baron Sudeley to dance with me?" As the words come out, Strelley looks at the queen for the briefest moment, then he nods and sets off to seek the Baron. Catherine's face remains emotionless. Elizabeth waits, watching as Strelley makes his way across the room. He approaches Sudeley, offering a curt bow.

"My Lord Sudeley," he greets him. "The lady wishes that you would dance with her." He inclines his head to where the queen and the Lady Elizabeth sit, both watching the exchange carefully.

"Truly? I would not have thought it politic for us to be seen together. Still, if Her Majesty commands..." He is just about to bluster past Strelley when Strelley speaks.

"Begging your pardon, My Lord, but I referred not to the queen but to Lady Elizabeth."

Strelley does not move, addressing his comment to where Thomas Seymour had been standing a moment before, so that Seymour has to turn and ends up looking at the back of Strelley's head. Seymour stops, angles his head. His eyes narrow, and his nostrils flare visibly.

"You are impudent, boy," he says, venomous. "I shall have you whipped."

Strelley raises his eyebrows, body still facing away from Sudeley but turning his head to make his reply. "With the greatest respect, My Lord, I do not understand you." He manages to set his face so that Seymour cannot tell if he is dissembling or not.

"No?" Sudeley spits. "Well, I shall make you understand soon enough. You would do well to remember yourself." Seymour breathes in and out, recovering his poise, then strides over to Elizabeth and

Catherine. Strelley watches him with a broad smile as the baron kneels before Elizabeth and asks her to dance. Catherine watches them, nonplussed, occasionally looking over to Strelley, questioningly, unseen by Elizabeth whose attention is wholly demanded by the blustering Tom Seymour. By now, though, Strelley has straightened his face again. Seymour and Elizabeth join the dance, as Strelley goes over to the queen.

"You wish to speak with me, Madam?" he says.

Catherine stares at him for some moments. "What did you say to the baron?"

"I told him that the lady wished to dance. He seemed to think that I meant Your Majesty."

"What did he say to you? When you corrected him, I mean."

"He called me impudent and threatened me, Madam." Strelley bows extravagantly.

"There is no need for that," Catherine replies, flustered.

"May I speak, Madam?" Strelley asks, leaning close to the queen and lowering his voice.

Catherine blinks, her face showing her frustration. After a moment, she nods.

"Madam," Strelley begins, in a whisper, "it is no secret that Seymour visits you. At night..."

Catherine's eyes widen. "How dare you-" she begins, but Strelley interrupts her.

"Somerset knows." He says, quietly. Queen Catherine shuffles uncomfortably in her seat. "When they argued earlier... It was not about the Baron's lack of respect for the Earl of Shrewsbury, as he will have told you."

Catherine is blank, uncomprehending.

"I tell you for your own good, Madam. The Protector knows of your assignations. It will be of no use to you to dissemble." Strelley leaves the words hanging.

"Elizabeth...?" Catherine asks.

"I know not. She knows that Seymour has been here, but perhaps not that he has visited you at night. In any case, it would be difficult to establish without risking her guessing. She is artful, as Your Majesty is aware."

"You will speak to no one of this matter." Catherine means it as

43

a statement of fact, but her tone is a mixture of imploring and threatening.

"Indeed not, Your Majesty." Strelley stands upright, lifting his gaze away from the queen.

"How do you know?" she asks, shaking her head.

"I am close to someone close to the Protector." He looks at her, measuring the effect of these words, chosen to disguise his own central involvement in the intrigue.

"Do not tease me with riddles, Master Tutor, else I shall find a way to have you dismissed." Her voice changes from sharp to despairing. "Am I so wrong to hope for discretion in mine and others' servants?"

"The Protector knows. That is what matters now."

"The king?"

"I'm not sure Edward would understand. He doesn't know, though. I imagine the Protector would guard his feelings by keeping him ignorant."

She looks at him. "I am lost," she sighs.

"No, Madam. You are still Henry's Queen."

"And what good do you suppose that will do?" Strelley does not offer a reply. "What do you hope to gain by telling me this?" Catherine asks, eyes aslant. "Do you take pleasure in seeing me suffer?"

"No, Your Majesty. Rather I seek to protect you from rumours spreading more widely."

"Then you would have my gratitude," she whispers. "Though I should like to know how Somerset found out."

"The Protector has eyes everywhere, Madam."

"It was you!" she hisses, realisation spreading across her face. "What do you hope to gain from this?"

Strelley leans in toward her, disguising the snarl in his voice from the roomful of assembled nobles and their entourages. "You are Queen of England, Madam, and your king has been dead no more than three months. Do you not think you owe it to him, to King Edward, to his sisters, to be a little more circumspect?" His splenetic cadence betrays him. He had not intended for the queen to realise that it was him who had made the revelation to Protector Somerset. Now that she has, he needs to rescue the situation.

"How dare you!" she replies. "I will not have my conduct

challenged by a peasant!"

"Then you would throw this country into civil war by marrying the Protector's brother, would you? It was better for England when Tom Seymour was in the Low Country, where he could do no harm. He is bad for this nation." His matter-of-fact tone elicits a high colour in the queen, who calculates her next move carefully.

"Speak to me no more, Master Strelley. I shall abjure from punishing you for your insolence in return for your future silence." She doesn't look at him as she speaks, and so misses the change in his expression from hard-faced to relieved.

Strelley breathes in slowly. "You have my word." He walks away, looking for Longshawe.

"You told the queen? I don't understand you sometimes. Actually, no, I never understand you. You said 'no more politics', and then this!" Longshawe drinks from a pewter cup, before turning back to Strelley. They sit apart from the other remnants of the party, which has long since broken up. A few other stragglers sit drinking. Longshawe continues, "I thought when we told Seymour we were trying to win a friend in a high place."

"We were." Strelley shakes his head. "And after a closer encounter than I had foreseen, I think we did."

"So why threaten the Queen?"

"I wasn't threatening her. I've already played my hand, haven't I? I didn't expect her to see so clearly that it was me. The Protector knows, and the queen knows that he knows. Beyond that, there's no one else other than you and me, and whoever Seymour and the queen have taken into their confidence. Oh, and Wriothesley. But Catherine does not know that."

"So you expect the queen to be your friend after this?"

"No. But at least it might take some of the swagger out of Tom Seymour's step."

"You've done this to get at him?"

"He's a danger to the king and the Protector!"

"He's got a lot more friends than we have. Honestly, Edward, I can't see this going well."

"We shall see. But if the queen found out that I had betrayed her secret, from anyone other than me..."

"So you felt guilty?"

"Perhaps a little. But she knows now."

"What do you have against Tom Seymour, anyway?"

"He's an arrogant bully. Amongst other flaws."

"So you've taken it upon yourself to bring him down? You don't seem to realise how easily all this could be taken away from us. One false step and you'll never see that lady you think is so precious again."

"You mean Elizabeth?" Strelley asks, taken unawares by his friend's assumption. "I have no special regard for her, beyond my respect for her eminence and her learning."

"You feel no particular loyalty to her?"

46

"On the contrary. She is more my patron now than Shrewsbury. I even expect that she might defend me to the queen. You may not agree, but this, this revelation to Catherine, this is for Elizabeth. She seems to have some affection for Baron Sudeley. Knowing that he and the queen have renewed their connection so soon should stop that."

"Edward..." Longshawe sighs. "You should not be getting involved. Imagine if one of the kitchen porters decided to tell me how to handle a sword."

Strelley laughs at his analogy. "I shall do my best not to cause any difficulties when you are away."

"Well, at least I shall be close to the Protector. I can put in a good word for you if one of your schemes goes awry." The two young men laugh together and continue their drinking.

The following morning cold dawn breaks to see the gathered soldiery already prepared. The body of men that accompanies the Protector, and of which Longshawe is a member, is formed up and ready to ride out. The Protector himself, garbed as part-soldier, part-statesman, rides to the head of the group. Some of the gathered nobility, including the Earl of Shrewsbury and his son, stand by as the company departs. Somerset calls to them from horseback. "Jedburgh, gentlemen," he reminds them. "You have three weeks to complete your musters." With that, he spurs his horse and departs at the gallop, his bodyguard following.

Strelley watches them from a half-hidden corner, arms folded. He turns to go back inside and is surprised to find that Elizabeth is standing near him, also watching. Unusually, she is alone, without Kat Astley, her usual chaperone. Strelley bows his head. "My Lady," he says, by way of further obeisance. She looks away from him at the departing army.

"The best men ride off to war again, Master Strelley. Yourself excepted, of course. I do not doubt your quality, nor your resolution on the futility of war."

"I do not claim to be great, My Lady," Strelley replies sheepishly. "In any capacity, least of all the prosecution of war. I am not even sure that I could claim to be a good man."

"You have committed some sin?" Elizabeth moves closer to him by a fraction, her hands jerking ever-so-slightly but not rising from their positions by her sides.

"Of sorts, Madam. I may not have served my friends as well as I ought."

"One can only do what one thinks best."

"Indeed, My Lady. I should go further and say one always ought to do what one thinks best."

"Do you think, Master Strelley, that God judges your actions, or your intentions?"

"I do not pretend to know the workings of the mind of God, Madam. But I do not think that God can condemn an action made in good faith for its bad consequences. I rather fear that I have acted from spite rather than conscience. Though I confess I do not know myself."

"You are not normally given to spitefulness, Sir." Elizabeth smiles at him, her face for a moment echoing that of her late father. "I would say rather that you are quite generous of spirit."

"I am glad that you say so. I worry that I have not acted with honour and dignity. That is sin enough in itself, but it might speak ill of my temperament, and so threaten my continued employment with your household."

"You should not trouble yourself on that score, Sir. My father himself left instructions about your employment."

"Truly?" Strelley's eyes widen. "I did not know that. I am a little relieved if a man as great as your father thought me a worthy character."

"You can speak truth to power, Master Strelley, although I wonder whether you shall ever have chance to speak truth to me in power," she sighs, looking off into the distance, focusing on nothing in particular. "I shall be married to some foreign prince at my brother's behest, and sent away to some foreign court."

"Madam, you are second in line to the throne."

"Indeed. But my brother is yet a child and has many years ahead of him. And his children shall inherit before me, as shall my sister."

"Your marriage shall be a great affair of state. You shall have your pick of the nobility of Europe."

"Inbreds and degenerates!" she says, rather loudly. "Would *you* marry a Habsburg? A Medici? A Valois?" Strelley shakes his head at the impropriety of the question. Elizabeth eyes him for a moment before picking up her thread. "The common people all wish themselves to be royalty, but what little comfort it brings, Master Strelley. I should much rather be you, or Master Longshawe. You are able to choose your life, as far as anyone might. Your friend marches to war, you stay here. You might choose a wife, or not. I have no such choice to make. I am a pawn, Master Strelley, in someone else's game of chess."

Strelley listens in silence to the harangue, and does not reply when it finishes. Instead he looks out with Elizabeth into the distance. There is a long silence. "Be wary of Thomas Seymour, Elizabeth," he says quietly. "He is no friend to anyone but himself." He walks away. The young woman remains, contemplating his words and watching him as he goes through the cold morning mist out into the grounds.

A band of riders makes its way through the parkland around Hertford House, heading toward the main building. At its head is small ensign flag bearing the arms of the late King Henry. The deputation is headed by our friend William Pike, who has the honour of leading the mustered men to join the army on its march north. As they approach the house, uniformed Yeomen form a line to welcome them. James Longshawe steps forward to meet his friend, and Pike dismounts elegantly to take the offered hand.

"James!" Pike shakes his hand firmly. "So we ride together again. I understand that your word to the Protector himself brought me here?"

"I just mentioned that a man of your precision with a gun might be useful in our campaign. He expects you to join his personal retinue, I think."

"Well, I thank you. I think." Pike waves his men to enter the courtyard, where the Duke of Somerset's men are making preparations for the march. "These men are mostly servant-boys and farmers, not trained soldiers," he remarks as the party goes past them.

"They practise their archery, don't they?" Longshawe asks.

"They're good at hitting a target. But there might be ten thousand half-rabid Scots in front of them the next time they have to shoot."

"Then they just need a bit of battlefield experience!"

"Like us not so long ago...?" Pike leaves the words hanging for a moment. "Their experience of a battlefield could just as well be from the flat of their backs as the world goes dark. War is not my favourite occupation, James. But one cannot pass the chance to be close to the Protector."

"Indeed. I wondered what had happened to you out at Hampton."

"Well, nothing, as you might expect. The Protector doesn't seem to think the Prince should be spending too much time out at the hunt, so we're redundant. As much as I enjoy my role, it doesn't do to be idle too often."

Longshawe claps his arm round the shoulder. "Let's see if we can get you an introduction to the Protector, then."

"Do you think he will remember me?"

"Seymour is good with his people. He might, you know." They make their way into the courtyard, out of sight.

"Master Longshawe." The Duke of Somerset looks up from his papers. "And...?"

"William Pike, Your Grace," Pike says, stepping forward. His accent, broad in comparison with his friend's and markedly different to the aristocratic duke's, seems to shock him as his eyes widen at his own voice. Seymour eyes him for a moment.

"You're the marksman, aren't you? Did your friend ever get you that smokeless powder?" He doesn't wait for an answer. "I understand from Longshawe that you are a master of the outdoors. I should like to have you as one of my outriders. Does this suit you?"

"It does, Your Grace," Pike replies. "Though I should prefer to avoid the front line of battle if I can."

"I admire your honesty, Sir, if not your courage." Seymour laughs. "Nevertheless, I understand your caution. One might catch a bullet in the teeth or an arrow in the eye, and bravery is no defence against either. If our Germans and Italians prove as effective as they're rumoured to be, it'll be the Scots stopping bullets." Somerset leans back and folds his hands behind his head. "War, gentlemen, is so much simpler than state-craft. Perhaps I shall retire as Protector and offer my services simply as a commander of the king's armies."

Longshawe and Pike glance at each other. Neither replies to the duke's speech. Seymour takes up his own thread again. "But for now, we shall lead the king's army as his Protector, and win him this girl-Queen of Scotland for his bride." He dismisses the two young men with a gesture, and returns to his papers.

Meanwhile, some three or four miles away at Chelsea, Elizabeth is with her stepmother and another girl of about ten years, whom we have met before as part of Catherine's household. Catherine is explaining patiently to the younger girl.

"Well, Jane, they're going to war to try to secure the Queen of Scotland for the king."

"For him to marry, you mean?" Jane asks. She is bright-eyed, enthusiastic, with the characteristic auburn hair shared by Elizabeth, and her father and brother. Jane has inherited it from Henry's sister, through her own mother, and is as such the great-granddaughter of Henry VII.

"For him to marry, yes," Catherine replies, patronising. Elizabeth's eyebrows rise just a little. Catherine, noticing her stepdaughter's expression, chooses to ignore it and continues the thought. "You see, the king would much rather have Scotland as an ally than as an enemy. Whilst ever the French are able to form alliances with Scotland, it is a threat to us in England."

"But she is just a little child, isn't she?" Jane asks, looking at Elizabeth, who pointedly ignores her, and then back at Catherine.

"A child, yes. But if she is brought to England and raised as the great princess she might be, she would be a fitting queen for your cousin when she comes of age."

"Mother told me I would be a fitting queen for Edward." Jane Grey copies Elizabeth's technique of turning her gaze to her work. Elizabeth herself suppresses a grin at her stepmother's dilemma.

"Jane," Catherine says, firmly enough to stop both Jane and Elizabeth writing, "you must not say such things. It is the greatest presumption on your mother's part to assume that the king might enter into marriage with you." Catherine tries but fails to keep a hint of frustration out of her voice. "You must be careful that you do not discuss this with others, or the king and his Protector may become very angry with your mother. Do you understand me?"

"I do, Madam," the child replies. "I understand you perfectly. Though I do not allow that the king should be angry with mother."

"Lady Frances is right to be proud of you, dear," Queen Catherine says, stroking her hair. "You are destined for a great marriage, no doubt. But the king must marry for England. And Mary of Scotland is the right queen for him."

Elizabeth leans in conspiratorially. "Besides, why would you want to marry my brother, Jane? He is ever so smelly!" She collapses in a fit of giggles. After a moment she composes herself. "Oh, Jane, it is not true. But you should not waste yourself waiting for marriage to make you, but rather make yourself what you wish to be."

"Mother said it is not a girl's place to elevate herself. A girl should honour and obey her husband." Jane recalls the words with suspicion, questioning them as she speaks.

Elizabeth looks at her, eyes narrowed. "When one has a claim to the throne of her own, Jane, one ought not to resign herself to the control of a man."

Catherine takes both girls under her arms. "Now, it will not do to be rebellious, my girls. Do not let's get all excited." There is a knock at the door, and a retainer announces Edward Strelley, whose face when he enters is a picture that says he was not expecting to be announced by name. He looks at each of the three before pacing across the room. He offers the queen a deep obeisance, Elizabeth a nod, and goes down on one knee for Jane.

"My Lady Jane," he says, "I had not known that you had joined us here at Chelsea. I thought-" He stops himself. Elizabeth has one eye closed as she watches, and Strelley pretends not to notice.

"Jane has joined us from Baron Sudeley's household for a period while the men are away fighting," Catherine tells him. Strelley replies with a questioning look. "The baron has not himself joined the campaign, but much of his household has. He sent Jane to us to partake of Elizabeth's education for a few weeks."

"Then My Lady has much to look forward to. I believe Master Grindal has something rather special planned for us today," Strelley replies. "Do you read in Latin?"

"A little," Jane Grey answers. "Though Master Aylmer says that one should learn Greek and Hebrew if one really wishes to understand the Bible."

"Ah, well, we are not studying the Bible today." Strelley smiles at her.

"No?" Jane looks at him through narrowed eyes. "You are not going to torture me with the Schoolmen are you?"

"Indeed not, My Lady," Strelley says, looking at Elizabeth. She is smiling. Catherine watches the exchange without expression. "Rather we shall be treated to Aeneas' story of the sack of Troy."

"Vergil!" Elizabeth exclaims. "You shall enjoy Master Strelley's reading of Vergil, Jane. He is a great performer."

Strelley smiles back at her. "One does one's best. Anyway, I came from Grindal to ask if Madam would like to join us at our studies." He addresses the queen. She looks up at him, searching him for a clue as to his intentions. Strelley does his utmost to arrange his features in conciliation and friendliness.

"I need to know," he says to the queen, "whether to prepare an extra manuscript. I should – Master Grindal should – very much like it were you to join us."

"Very well," Catherine says, "I shall. It will allow me to keep an eye on Jane here as you begin your lessons with her." Strelley nods and turns away. When he gets to the door, he gives each of the three women a little bow before he leaves.

38: Married?

"Married?" Lady Elizabeth Tudor's expression is wide with surprise.

"Yes, Madam. Married," Queen Catherine replies.

"Have you my brother's blessing?" Elizabeth asks, and her tone suggests she knows the answer already.

"I... We..." Catherine searches for the right words. "My husband assures me that the king approves."

"Congratulations. I think," the young girl says quietly. They sit in a withdrawing room at Chelsea Manor, bathed in the spring sun from the tall windows. Catherine waits patiently for Elizabeth to speak further. Elizabeth's face shows her thoughts as they progress. There is consternation, wonder, deep contemplation. After a minute or so, Catherine turns to Elizabeth and begins to speak.

"As you know, Madam, Baron Sudeley and I have long since been acquainted. When one reaches my age, one wishes for a companion to share life." Elizabeth's attention is caught only partway through the second sentence. Catherine chooses not to restate her case, instead continuing, "I shall be accused of marrying him too soon. I have no doubt of that. But as I say, Baron Sudeley has sought and received King Edward's blessing for this marriage. I am old, Elizabeth, and I want a child of my own before it is too late for me."

Elizabeth sits and listens to the queen's impassioned speech. At this last, she smiles. "My royal brother, my sister and I *are* grateful for your surrogate motherhood. One could only wish to be born your child." She speaks quietly and seemingly sincerely.

"I shall not give up your wardship, Madam. I shall be as much mother to you as I ever was. The only change shall be that My Lord Sudeley shall be equally responsible for you."

Elizabeth's expression does not change, but her eyes flicker ever-so-slightly. "I cannot be otherwise than grateful for your care." She stands and offers Catherine a deep courtesy, and turns to leave. "If it please Your Majesty, I should like to retire to the company of my governess."

Catherine nods, and Elizabeth walks out of the room, her breathing slow, deep and deliberate. She smooths her skirts as a footman opens the door for her.

Kat Astley is in Elizabeth's rooms, speaking to William Grindal and Edward Strelley. Strelley says something to her, so quiet as to be inaudible. She looks at him, one eyebrow raised. He nods his head in confirmation, and she thumps down into a nearby seat. Grindal remains standing, but Strelley kneels by her, still speaking.

"Elizabeth will know by now. I think the queen summoned her to tell her. She may be quite shocked at the news, and you must try to mollify her. It will not be good for any of us if Elizabeth gets angry with the queen."

"She has a right to be angry. Why did the Protector not put a stop to this?"

"He is away to war, as you well know."

"So Thomas Seymour should have been told not to do anything in his absence." Astley shakes her head, her voice sharp as she speaks.

"I have no doubt he was told exactly that," Strelley answers. Grindal watches the exchange without commenting. "But in Somerset's absence," Strelley continues, "Sudeley has acted."

"Does the king know?" Astley asks.

Grindal takes up the conversation, weary with the politics of it, which comes out in his voice. "Sudeley has put it about that he has the king's blessing for this marriage. I do not doubt that he has spoken to the king of it, but I wonder whether the king offered a true and disinterested assent to this, or whether the baron has bribed him with promises."

Strelley looks round at the older man. "Promises? You suspect the baron of... What?"

"I do not know," Grindal says.

"It is no secret that the Baron would replace his brother if he could," Strelley says, making explicit something that Grindal has chosen not to reveal. "I wonder if Thomas has sweetened the king to this course by promising to govern him in a more amenable manner," Strelley ventures. Both Grindal and Astley nod their heads at this suggestion. As they do, a retainer announces the Lady Elizabeth. Strelley leaps to his feet. Kat Astley stands and arranges her dress. Grindal swallows hard.

The young girl strides into the room, her face red with anger. "My father would not tolerate this insult to his memory!" she shouts, throwing herself into the chair recently vacated by Astley. "My brother has not sanctioned it, I'll warrant. Seymour will have blustered and bedevilled him, most likely confounding the poor child until he did not know what he was allowing!" She screws her face into her hands, and Astley stoops beside her, offering a cambric handkerchief to dry the tears.

"Master Grindal," Astley says quietly, "perhaps it would be better if you and Master Strelley left us."

Elizabeth is quick to intervene. "No, I should like them to hear what I have to say. As my allies in this household, it is better that they know than that they don't." She has recovered something of her composure. "I shall write at once to my brother the king, with your help, gentlemen. I shall demand of him whether he is party to this abhorrence, and that he puts it right immediately."

Grindal throws his head back, and draws breath before he speaks. "With the greatest respect, Madam, if the marriage is contracted, there is little that even the king can do to annul it."

"Master Grindal," Elizabeth says with the hint of a sneer, "my brother is the king, and a Tudor. He can do whatever it is in his mind to do, as my great father showed."

Grindal bows his grudging assent. Elizabeth turns her eyes to Strelley, her chest rising and falling rapidly as she struggles to maintain control of her anger. She searches him, questioning with her expression. He looks out from under his eyebrows, and thinks for a moment.

"With the Protector away," Strelley says, "there is little to be done. Even if you could persuade your brother... He does not govern, in reality." Strelley speaks slowly, weighing each word carefully. "Madam should not show the queen your... distaste... for this marriage. It would not be politic."

"Ever the pragmatist, Master Strelley," Elizabeth replies. "Should I always hide my feelings thus?"

"I speak not about 'always', My Lady, only on this occasion. You would be unwise to sever your bond with the queen."

"Even if she shows such disrespect for my father?" Elizabeth jabs her fingers at Strelley, who does his best to remain in a posture of quiet gravity.

"My Lady, your interests are best served by Catherine's guardianship."

"Is there no shred of nobility in that black soul of yours, Edward?" she cries. Astley half-swoons. Grindal cocks his head, but remains aloof. Elizabeth continues her attack on Strelley, vituperative. "Would you know what a principle is?"

Strelley leans in towards Elizabeth, meeting her angry outburst with steady calm. "One can die for a principle, holding course whatever befalls, or one can choose to run before the wind," he says, fixing Elizabeth with earnest eyes. "You have difficult waters to sail before you are ultimately free to choose your own path. Were I you, Madam, I should take any protection that others could offer, most of all that of the queen. To Somerset and his ilk, you are, as you frequently bemoan, a pawn in a game of international relations, not a person. The queen, whatever her choice of new husband, loves you for yourself."

Her eyes flick from Astley to Strelley. "Thank you for your concern, Master Strelley." Her tone is even and controlled. "I will see you at our lesson tomorrow." She dismisses the two men with a gesture, and they turn and leave.

As they pass the threshold, Grindal says, "you are a braver man than I, Edward."

"Or more foolish?"

"Perhaps." Grindal agrees. "But she needs more than ever someone foolish enough to tell her what's really happening. Just be careful."

"I shall do my best," Strelley answers. As he passes a burning brazier in the corridor, a tear is just visible on his cheek.

Thomas Seymour arrives on horseback at Chelsea the following day, with a small entourage of gentlemen. His countenance is satisfied, smug even, a permanent grin of victory etched in his eyes if not always his mouth. Even when he sees Strelley, who has chosen to busy himself at his reading outdoors, he does not lose his look of triumph. He rides over, separating himself from the group, approaching Strelley who sits quietly on a bench. Strelley flicks his eyes up toward the baron as he comes, but returns them to the paper in a calculated gesture of defiance. Only after Sudeley has noisily brought his horse to a stop and waited several moments does Strelley acknowledge his presence, rising slowly and deliberately. Strelley offers the merest of bows, and mouths more than says, "My Lord."

"I assure you, Master... Strelley, isn't it? Yes, be certain that it is with no great pleasure that I find you in this household. But my wife tells me that you have your advantages, even if respect for your betters isn't one of them."

Strelley watches as Baron Sudeley speaks. He does not reply, other than to repeat his cursory bow. Sudeley's eyes narrow.

"Listen to me," he hisses, "you ingrate pleb! You may have risen above your station, but it is more than within my power to reduce you to the gutters where you clearly belong. I shall find my opportunity some day soon."

Again, Strelley absorbs the harangue without reply. He glances to his papers, which he holds in his left hand, making sure that he doesn't catch the baron's eye. Sudeley glares at him, but Strelley holds firm. The contest of wills is ended when Sudeley decides it is time to speak.

"Do not fool yourself into thinking that you have stung me, you cave-dwelling savage. I shall not trouble myself over you." With that, he turns, and rejoins the group of riders. He mutters something at which they all laugh, too loudly. They disappear around the house towards the stables. Strelley continues to read until they are out of view, then stands and walks quickly back into the house. As he does so, he passes a footman very close, nearly knocking into him. The retainer steps back, in expectation of an apology, but Strelley marches past him, slamming the door to his room behind him. His curse, the foulest he can conjure, is just audible through the old oak.

The following day, Strelley sits sulking across the table from Grindal, who is doing his best to engage Elizabeth in a Cicero oration, and not meeting with much success. The girl is distracted, occasionally flushing a deep red which does not suit her auburn hair and pale complexion, but more often breathing steadily and deeply, as one who struggles to control her anger. After a minute or two of silence, Grindal stands unsteadily.

"My Lady, please do excuse me. I do not feel at all well." He disappears through a door that is not closed behind him. Elizabeth follows him with her eyes, and looks down the corridor for a moment before turning to Strelley.

"Your face is like thunder this morning, Edward." For the first time, her lips break into a smile. "I should like to know what it is that ails you. I wonder if we share a common... illness?"

"Of that I have no doubt, My Lady. But your case reflects the fact that you are still second in line to the throne of this country. Yours is a malady of frustration, is it not?" Elizabeth neither confirms nor denies, but opens her hands to suggest that Strelley can carry on with his exegesis. "You are angry at the queen for marrying Sudeley so soon after your father's death. That is understandable, and the fact that they have waited until the Lord Protector has ridden away to war doubles your grievance. Further, you perceive that the one person who has really loved you now has someone else to occupy her thoughts."

"You speak with great freedom to me, Master Strelley."

"Madam did not stop me."

"Indeed I did not. You are right that I am angry at this marriage." She looks down, away from Strelley, who is watching her carefully.

"But not about your worries over the queen?" Strelley asks, his hand twitching as though he thinks of reaching for hers and taking it.

"Master Strelley... I do not really remember my mother. My father never spoke of her to me, and I was only young when she..." Elizabeth finally looks Strelley in the eye. "There has not been a day when I haven't wondered about her. I have read what letters and reports I could, of her and those who surrounded her. Her genius was to make my father wait, and grow more eager in the anticipation, but I suppose it was my birth, and my failure to be the son that he – that they both – wanted, that undid her. After me, none of the children lived, did they?" She taps her fingertips lightly against each other. The angry redness of earlier has left her, replaced by a sort of resigned calm, reflective and sad.

She continues after a moment. "I did not have a mother, in the sense that Mary had hers. Though I suppose my brother lost his mother even sooner than I. But my father *loved* Edward's mother to the end. And beyond. He still loved her when he married the others. Edward has never understood that, nor that he, as the son, is the one child my father ever truly wanted. Mary has wrapped herself up in her religion. Her piety is her armour against the harsh reality that she, more even than I, is an unwanted bump in the succession. God forbid that either of us should ascend the throne."

Strelley leans forward. "You would not wish to be queen? In your own right, I mean?"

"What would that mean? No queen of England has managed to reign in her own right. Besides, the nobility would not allow it. There would be nothing but 'to whom shall we marry her?', night and day. No peace nor rest for Queen Elizabeth."

"My Lady has the heart and stomach of a king, if not the body."

"But this weak and feeble body is put on Earth to bear children," She replies, sharply. "That is what I am continually told."

"Madam, you do not believe that yourself."

"It is a saw put about by men, no doubt. Though I think that I have read it many times in the Bible."

"Which was written by men!"

"I do not think it is your place to encourage me to blasphemy, Edward." She smiles at him. "But you may be right. I do not think it fair or just that I should defer to my brother just on the grounds of our respective sexes. But that is how ever it was and ever shall be."

"Do you know about Eleanor of Aquitaine? Or Isabella of Castile?"

"A little, Master Strelley. Neither ruled without a husband."

"Perhaps not, but these are the messages of history."

"The message I understand from history is that Livia Augusta had to beg Claudius to deify her as she was so afraid of the punishments awaiting her in the afterlife! That she prostituted herself to Caligula for her own ends. No, you shall not persuade me of this, Edward. My mother was sacrificed – to her death, you understand, not just dishonour or demotion, though God knows there was a great deal of dishonour heaped on her – sacrificed, I say, on the whim of a man who wielded the royal power as an instrument of his own personal aggrandisement."

Strelley considers an interruption, but thinks better of it. Elizabeth takes up her thread. "Don't think I am unaware of the failures of my father's reign, Edward. I know more than most the consequences of his..." she waves her hand by her ear, indicating her frustration, "compulsions. I am the result of one. That I am an orphan at fourteen is another."

"Your mother was not the demon she has been painted to be."

"I know. Nor was she the angel that Mistress Astley would have me believe, in her weak moments. She knew more about running before

60

the wind than you, or I for that matter, but that did not avail her in the end. That is what I fear."

"So you would rather die for a principle?"

"For what principle should I die, Master Strelley? I am not a man, to be sent to the stake for my religious beliefs. My sister is the proof of that, even now in her defiance of my brother. I cannot ride to war to find death on the battlefield. I am more likely to meet God on my back, screaming to push out some Spanish prince's child. I have no illusions, Edward. I am as I say, a pawn in a game played by others."

"It is a feeling I know," Strelley says. "I am afraid of Sudeley."

"You have counselled me to be so as well. He is a braggart, but is he dangerous?"

"I think he is vindictive. And I have insulted him."

"Truly? You are no fool, Edward."

"Not usually. But I was. And he wants me to regret it."

39: Of Fathers and Sons

A bright June morning sun rises above the hills and valleys that surround Sheffield. The castle and its grounds are thronged with men coming and going, and surrounded by a camp of many hundreds of tents. There are perhaps eight hundred or a thousand men gathered, many more than the area is used to. Children stand about watching the activities. Longbowmen practise at the butt, challenging each other with escalating feats of marksmanship. One or two of the soldiers are checking exotic-looking firearms, but these are rare among the men. More occupy themselves with fettling tack or honing the edges of weapons.

The Earl of Shrewsbury stands with his son George on his left, surveying the muster. "It is an impressive band, this," he says. "Our contribution to the Protector's war effort will please him."

"This army is smaller than the one that was beaten at Ancrum," George replies.

"Indeed, but this is no more than a tenth part, if not a twentieth, of that which Seymour is gathering. And this time there shall be guns, George. Heavy cannon!" The earl sounds quite proud of the Protector's plans. "I cannot help but feel this campaign has been thought through more than your raid of three years since."

"But even if we win a victory, the Scots are too diffuse to bring under control, aren't they? Let's say that we capture this infant queen, and Edward marries her. That's the strategy, isn't it?" His father nods. George carries on. "So all that we could possibly hope for comes to pass, and even then, do you think the bearded savages that inhabit the land will submit to the king? I would hardly say that royal authority even extends throughout Hallamshire."

"Indeed not, but the political will to invade... That comes from the nobility, not the men on the land. Seymour wants to eliminate Scotland as a threat, particularly because they tend to ally themselves with the accursed French."

"So it's not about control of the land?"

"Not as far as I can see."

"So why not *persuade* the queen to marry Edward?" George claps politely as a nearby archer makes a tough shot.

"Queen Mary is little more than an infant, so it is not her we must persuade. It is her nobility, the men – and it is men – who govern her, that must be persuaded. Her mother, despite her apparent power as regent, is as much a figurehead as our own king. These men do not submit to the gentle cajoling of diplomacy."

"But surely we could offer the Scots a deal, something to make it preferable for them?"

"I too wonder the same, but I think the depth of their antipathy makes it unlikely. Mary's mother is French. Thoroughly French."

"So the Protector has settled on war as the most likely way to bring about this new alliance." George Talbot shakes his head. "We force the Scots into an alliance by killing as many of them as we can."

"His Grace Somerset thinks that this marriage will allow us to concentrate our diplomatic efforts on the continent. One swift campaign, the goal achieved, and we are relieved of our rebellious neighbours to the north."

"We just have to secure that victory, then."

"Which may prove a difficult matter, as your previous experience shows. The Scots might be a fractious and unruly bunch, but when it comes to defending themselves, they seem a sight more focused. I hope we can bring about a decisive engagement, as a long campaign does not suit such a large force as ours. I understand that Seymour has bought a large contingent of mercenary Germans and Italians to bolster our levies."

"Professionals? We shall be invincible!" The son's bluster is obvious, but his father still frowns at him.

"Do not allow yourself to think it. No force is invincible, George," Shrewsbury says.

Later the same day, a sentry calls that Protector Somerset's standard is approaching. With him marches a huge column of perhaps ten thousand soldiers and their followers, that stretches out of sight and kicks up a cloud of dust visible for miles around. At the head rides the Protector himself, his standard borne at the moment by his friend and compatriot John Dudley, the Earl of Warwick, whom we have encountered at play with the late king. Seymour and Dudley chat as they approach the Castle gate, and their column scatters behind them to make its camp, surrounding and swallowing that already in place. In the retinue of mounted soldiers, a couple of ranks behind these most important men in the state, ride James Longshawe and William Pike, kitted out with the green-and-white of the Tudor household guard, arms and armour gleaming. George Talbot notices them immediately, but hangs back a moment or two out of respect for the duke and the Earl of Warwick. As soon as greetings are exchanged, he slips behind the front ranks and approaches his former companions.

Longshawe leaps down and embraces Talbot. "Well met once again, Sir!" he cries, pushing the young Earl of Waterford away from him, taking a long look at his face. "It seems you might be in danger of growing up! Hardly the jejune youth of our last campaign..."

George Talbot allows himself a smile. "A little soldiering and you think yourself rather fine! I remember that we both turned tail together last time we were in Scotland." He laughs as he speaks. "Although flight is the refuge of the wise, I reckon."

Pike jumps down to join the exchange. "Indeed. There is no renown in an unmarked grave in defeat."

Talbot takes Pike's hand and shakes it vigorously. "It is good to see you both again. This time it seems we shall be a little better-equipped than before."

"It seems that Somerset has gathered a rather impressive battery of cannon," Longshawe confirms. "Though I doubt that half-a-dozen field pieces would have had much of an effect last time."

"At least we shall have a chance of winning a siege, should one arise," Pike says. "I would rather sit at the back somewhere, out of range, and perhaps fire the occasional warning shot. Although these cannon of ours look rather more dangerous for those standing next to them than for those on the other side of the battlefield." He laughs, and it is taken up by the others only after a moment. "It seems," he says, gesturing around him at the assembled army, "that this is rather a force gathered with a pitched battle in mind."

"There must be ten thousand in your column," Talbot says, impressed.

"Something like that, yes," Longshawe answers. "Though quite a few are mercenaries, rather than levies. The Protector expects to pick up more on the way north. A lot of the Borderers will involve themselves, no doubt."

"Perhaps we shall meet de Winter's Buccleuch? I wonder what he would have to say to us now." Talbot moves to lead Longshawe and

Pike away, but Longshawe holds him a moment. From out of the press of bodies, Guy Fletcher makes his way through.

"Guy!" Talbot exclaims. "So you haven't managed to find yourself a proper job, yet? Still following this blackguard around?" He nods at Longshawe. They laugh again. As they pass forward, Dudley and Seymour are discussing the arrangements of the camp with the Earl of Shrewsbury.

"We must make our march as soon as possible," Dudley is saying. "Any delay will only result in a loss of initiative."

"You can't think we're going to surprise the Scots?" Shrewsbury asks.

"No." It is Somerset who speaks. "But with these ten thousand, we need to make our move as quickly as we can. They will get bored, or worse, hungry and thirsty, should we fail to keep them occupied!" He laughs heartily at his own joke. "This is an army with a purpose, gentlemen. We shall bring home that girl for our king and unite this island."

"I hope your confidence isn't misplaced. We shall gain nothing if the child-queen escapes us." Shrewsbury looks out over the enormous body of men that is still just beginning to arrive. "All this will be to naught if she does."

Dudley snorts. "We shall blockade the ports, surround the towns and flush her out like a beast."

"Have you been to Scotland, Sir?" Shrewsbury asks pointedly.

"I have. I fought there before Ancrum."

"Then you will know that even with an army of a hundred thousand, one cannot force an encounter, nor can an army of even modest size survive out in the wilds for more than a week or two."

Dudley's head tilts, his right eye narrow. "You do not foresee success? I have not heard these objections previously." Dudley's physique is that of a professional soldier, his body hard and strong, his face weathered but still displaying some of the signs of youthful handsomeness. Shrewsbury looks at him, sizing him up both as a man and as a leader of men, before making his reply.

"I simply remind you young, bellicose men that no amount of desire to fight with these barbarian Scots will get them out in the field on your terms. And even with this fine body of men, we shall be hard-pressed in the wild lands. The queen – her servants – know every hill and valley, every stream and forest."

Dudley taps Somerset's shoulder. "Do not allow the earl to address the troops, My Lord Protector. He shall have them deserting in their thousands!" Somerset and Dudley laugh. Shrewsbury tries to force a smile, but it is watery and unconvincing.

A few hundred yards away, Longshawe seats himself in front of a tent, one of a ring of six, and points George Talbot to a spot opposite. Pike positions himself next to Longshawe, and they start to ask him about what has befallen him.

"My wife has finally joined me at the castle," Talbot answers. "We were married when we were very young."

"Hmm!" Longshawe harrumphs. "And are you not still very young? You are, what, nineteen now?"

"But you are only a very little older yourself, *Master* Longshawe." Talbot stresses the form of address. "In any case, I shall be a little disappointed to leave her behind, but, as we know, campaign is no place for a lady."

"You shall meet ladies to suit all tastes, young lord," Pike interjects. "I had not realised how many souls an army dragged along with it. Our last expedition had barely a wagon. If we are ten thousand fighting men there must be another five thousand mouths to feed each day."

"I have no interest in the harlots that accompany an army." Talbot sounds genuinely hurt. Longshawe laughs out loud.

"You say that now, Your Grace. But your wife is less than a mile away. In a fortnight, when the most attractive thing you've seen all day is the back of Pike's head, these painted whores might just appear a little more appealing."

"You do not patronise whores, James," Pike says, definitely.

Longshawe laughs again, leaning in conspiratorially. "I don't have to!" he says, followed by a half-minute of barely controlled convulsion. Talbot and Pike have the good grace to join in, although less enthusiastically. As Longshawe calms himself down, Talbot starts to speak to Pike.

"I would not have expected to see you joining an army again, Will," he says. "I thought the idea of fighting had lost its appeal."

"It never had much of an appeal to me, Sir. But I had grown a little restless at Hampton, and there seemed little possibility of making a name any other way. James remembered me to his master, and here we are."

"Will needs no introduction from me," Longshawe objects to Talbot. Turning back to Pike, he adds, "Seymour is more than aware of your skills with a gun."

"Then perhaps he will value those skills enough to station me some distance from any actual fighting."

"You can handle a sword, though...?" Talbot half-asks-half-states. "I remember you being rather able."

"Give me three heartbeats to aim and fire, Sir. Much more civilised than all this hacking and slashing." Pike smiles at Talbot. "Though I concede there is more elegance in the longbow than a musket. And a lot less cleaning up afterwards."

"You can't think that a lead ball is more civilised than a sword!" Longshawe shakes his head. "Centuries of the finest warriors stride in to battle and meet their enemies eye-to-eye, testing their strength and skill against each other. And you'd spatter their brains to the four winds when they were still thirty yards distant."

"I would. I have no wish to be measured against another man's strength or skill. I would rather survive the encounter than prove myself inferior, no matter how glorious the challenge."

"That's the difference between men like you, Master Longshawe, and men like us," Talbot adds, pointing at Pike. "You would see Hector or Achilles on the field and make direct for him, where we would take the opposite road."

"I did not think you a coward, Your Grace," Longshawe replies.

Talbot sighs theatrically. "Prudence is not always a failing, James. You would do well to remember that. Or do you have some ill-starred wish to die a hero's death?"

Pike looks at Longshawe, whose head hangs a little at the last words from the Earl of Waterford. After a moment, Longshawe makes a little noise to signify some sort of assent.

"Master Longshawe is always a little moody when we get near home, Sir. He finds the proximity to his father rather suffocating. It brings out the heat in his humours."

"You didn't mention him before," Talbot says.

"No. He isn't my favourite topic of conversation."

"Then I shall leave it be." Talbot raises an eyebrow.

Longshawe stares past him into the distance. "We do not share views on the roles of sons and fathers. Perhaps he *would* rather hear of my celebrated death than endure my continued presence on this Earth. If he had his way, I would be at Longshawe, wasting away."

"My commiserations," Talbot says with sympathy. "Though you *are* quite the soldier now, aren't you? Despite my bluster earlier on."

"I suppose I am. Perhaps I should go to see him when we return from this campaign." Longshawe looks over his shoulder at the hills between Sheffield and his family seat on the road to Hathersage. Then, watched by Pike, his head turns again in the direction of the home of the Baron of Sheffield, George de Winter's father. His gaze remains trained thus for some moments. There is silence between them, none knowing how to end it. Eventually it is broken as Guy Fletcher returns and throws some loaves of bread at the three young men. A second youth follows him, perhaps a little older than Fletcher himself. He is dressed smartly, extravagantly perhaps, not a soldier but a nobleman. He steps out from behind Fletcher and bows rather curtly. Talbot leaps to his feet, recognising him.

"Gentlemen, I present to you Robert Dudley, Viscount Lisle's-" he corrects himself, "-the Earl of Warwick's son." Dudley nods his greeting to the two soldiers.

"I asked your lackey if I might meet you, Master Longshawe. I have heard Mistress Elizabeth speak of you, and wondered if you were as impressive as she seems to think."

Longshawe is totally bewildered for a moment. Pike understands, and puts his arm around Longshawe, a broad smile breaking across his face. Realisation comes to Longshawe. "*The* Lady Elizabeth?" he asks. "The princess?"

Talbot shakes his head. "Master Longshawe, you know we are not to style the lady 'princess', on account of her late father's wishes." He barely stifles a laugh as he speaks. "Although when one has made an impression, one does not quibble over a word such as that. When the lady is of the Blood Royal..."

The young Dudley bows his curt bow again. "You are indeed fearsome, Master Longshawe." He smiles wryly. "The defence of king and Protector is in safe hands."

"Although," George Talbot says, an edge of aggression

perceptible in his tone, "the thoughts of a lady are not safe in your rough hands."

Dudley's right hand rests on the pommel of his sword. "You test my patience," he says, quietly. Longshawe and Pike rise from their seats.

Pike moves to stand before Dudley, hand half-raised in pacification. "Now, My Lord, we shall have enough to deal with when we get to Scotland without cutting holes in each other before we even depart."

Dudley spits elaborately. "Your father is weak, Talbot, whatever the provenance of your title." He turns and disappears amongst the throng.

"What a charming young man!" Guy Fletcher rolls his eyes as he sits down. "He did not seem so impudent when first he spoke to me. I would not have led him here had I known that this would be how he behaved."

Talbot replies, "I should not antagonise him so. Though there is sport enough in it!"

"It's an odd thing to come to see a man just to insult him, though," Pike says. "Perhaps he really is convinced that there is such a thing as noble blood, and doesn't like to see Elizabeth's head turned by someone as common as Longshawe." He ducks to avoid a playful blow aimed at the side of his head by Longshawe, who anticipated the joke.

Talbot draws breath, thinking. "Do not dwell on it. There are only a few of us with land and titles, but it is always the ones newest to the fold that are the most concerned with it. Nobility, blood, all that nonsense. I was lucky to be born to my estate, nothing more. There is no difference between us, in the end. We're all born, we all fuck, we all die." The silence that had built as he spoke is shattered by Pike, Longshawe and Guy Fletcher descending into roaring laughter at the coarseness of the young nobleman's words.

William Paget and John Cheke stand facing each other, as the young king busies himself with his papers. There is tension between them, some unresolved matter that has caused the one to look sternly at the other. Paget, after a moment or two, breaks the accusatory silence.

"I should think that you of all people, Master Cheke, would realise that a public rift in the Royal Family would be..." he searches for the appropriate word, settling on "abominable."

"Then Mary should conform. Then there is no conflict, no secret, no dissembling." Cheke raises an eyebrow. Paget glares at him. Edward flourishes a signature as he does so, not looking up.

"But two years ago, Master Cheke..."

"An age, it seems, Master Paget."

Paget bristles. "You know very well to address me as 'Sir'."

"Perhaps, Sir, we should agree to let the king himself express his opinion to the lady."

"I will not risk the disruption of the realm with the Protector away in the North." Paget shakes his head vigorously. "You are a tutor, Master Cheke. An academic. You should not play at politics."

"I might return the same criticism, *Sir*. You are an accountant, not an academic. You should not involve yourself in matters of doctrine. Matters that are beyond your-"

The king holds up his hand. "Enough, gentlemen." His voice is still some way short of breaking. His pale Tudor complexion emphasises his youth, as does his exuberant clothing. "*I* shall speak with my sister, and she will see the error of her ways." His tone suggests that he believes wholeheartedly the words he has spoken.

Both of the men begin to speak. Cheke starts with "Your Majesty, she will not-"; Paget tries "Sire, I would counsel you-". Both are stopped by another gesture from the young Josiah.

"I would remind you, Sirs, that God speaks very clearly to me in this matter." He looks up from his work, turning from Paget to Cheke then back again. "I would have the company of His Grace of Canterbury. Please see to it that he is summoned before my sister arrives."

Paget bows his assent, and leaves, still throwing aggressive glances at Cheke, who chooses to say nothing to his student. The king signs more papers, but after a few minutes he turns to Cheke.

"Master Cheke, Sir," he begins, definitely. "You must not persist in arguing with Sir Paget. He is representative of My Lord Protector Somerset in his absence. Even if you do disagree with his counsel."

"I am shamed to be rightly admonished by my student, he of such few years." Cheke does his best to sound sincere. "Your Majesty must act as his conscience dictates, of course."

"I have made no secret of my concern for my sister. Every day that she refuses to abandon her frankly heretical mode of worship she exposes herself to the risk of everlasting damnation. Until she changes her ways, she is beyond the protection of God. And of me." His supercilious tone is emphasised by this last addition. Cheke struggles to arrange his features in a suitably serious way. The boy is in absolute earnest.

"Your Majesty is right," Cheke says, "that the current learning suggests the Lady Mary to be in error. But she is a good woman, Sire, and God will not ignore that-" Cheke is stopped by Edward's hand again.

"You must not mince your words, Master Cheke, nor must you equivocate regarding Mary. My sister is damned should she not see the light of the new teaching. His Grace Cranmer shall prove the matter to her."

"With all respect to the archbishop, if it were that simple, all Europe should have converted itself to Protestantism. It is not so."

"Then all Europe may be damned." The boy's eyes burn with fervour. "I pity them."

The silence grows for a moment or two, and is broken by the announcement of the Archbishop Cranmer. He enters, his archiepiscopal robes catching the air and billowing impressively. His presence seems to calm the king's zeal. Edward welcomes him with a nod, and he bows before the king.

"Your Majesty," Cranmer says, "I understand that your sister Mary is to attend you this morning."

"It is true," Edward answers. "I had hoped that with the help of yourself and Master Cheke here, we might begin to persuade her to adopt the correct manner of worship."

Cranmer looks to Cheke briefly, seeing the exasperation in the tutor's expression. Cranmer rises from his bow before making his reply. "Your Majesty is good to care so for his Sister's soul. Though I perceive that we shall not have an easy time of making the case."

"You share Master Cheke's pessimism in this? I am disappointed. I had rather hoped that you of all of us might be possessed of such arguments to steer her back to God from her errant path. As the chief churchman of the realm, is it not your responsibility to show her the truth?"

Cranmer again looks first to Cheke, who, standing behind the king, is able to reply with a shrug of the shoulders. Cranmer gathers himself again. "I shall do what I can, Majesty. Though you must not be disappointed or indignant with your sister, nor with us, should our arguments fail to persuade her."

For the first time, a flash of anger clouds Edward's features. "If my teacher and my archbishop are unable between them to bring my sister out of her outmoded, Spanish nonsense, then I despair for the realm. You are supposed to be the finest thinkers in the kingdom, and you – without even making the attempt – state that you will not be able to bring round one ignorant woman from her apostasy. What chance is there of me leading this realm into holiness if my advisers are so impotent?"

Neither Cheke nor Cranmer reply. Cheke is still in the advantageous position of being behind the king, and he points at Cranmer, placing the responsibility with the churchman. Cranmer frowns.

"Your Majesty must understand that his sister's teachers have had more than thirty years to indoctrinate her. No matter how just the cause, it will take a little more than an hour or two to alter her thinking. She sees it as a matter of conscience just as you do, and she is equally persuaded as Your Majesty of the rectitude of her position." Edward shapes to speak, but Cranmer silences him with a gesture. "Please listen to my counsel, Sire. It is to Your Majesty's credit that he thus pursues the spiritual welfare of his sister, but you must not allow it to become consuming. Your sister has powerful friends outside this kingdom, who might not take our attempt to achieve her conformity in the spirit in which in is intended. They do not share our convictions, indeed they share your sister's, and she may yet find friends to back her."

"What do you mean, Your Grace?" Edward folds his hands over

his lap, an exaggerated gesture that he has learned from older men.

"I mean that your sister still corresponds with her cousin. And no doubt seeks his assistance in this matter. Your Majesty cannot afford a war with the Emperor."

"God will dispose." Edward's eyes are fixed on Cranmer's. "Or do you not have faith, Your Grace?"

"God does not intervene in matters of diplomacy between his realms on Earth," Cranmer answers, a stern edge to his tone. "The Exchequer is bereft. The coin is all but worthless. We cannot prosecute a war. Not with Spain."

"And yet my Protector is in Scotland even now, with a proud army at his back." Edward smiles as he perceives victory in the argument. "But we have no money?"

Cranmer sighs. "I should not, had I been asked, have supported the Protector's designs on Scotland, Sire. But that expedition is a trifle compared with a full scale war on the continent. It is a campaign of which the scale is in our control, not the enemy's. And it may, should it succeed in securing the Queen of Scotland for Your Majesty's bride, make defending your realm considerably easier."

"If I understand you correctly, *archbishop*," Edward stresses the word excessively, "then I should allow my sister to continue in her heresy, forgo my prerogative as king to order her to conform, and for this the reason is that she might write a letter to a distant cousin and invoke war on her own nation?"

"Your Majesty should not trivialise. But yes, that is what I counsel you."

"You do not think that it is my burden to bring my sister out of her sin of pride?"

"When your Majesty has an heir of his own, and can take for granted the succession, and is of age to govern, and the future of the nation's religion is assured, then we shall conquer your sister's adherence to Catholicism. Until then, there are too many reasons for us to hold our peace."

"Do you agree with the archbishop, Master Cheke?" Edward narrows his eyes first at Cranmer, then turns the gesture on Cheke.

"He is wise, and what he says is just, Sire." Cheke looks away from Edward at Cranmer for the shortest moment partway through.

"Then you are both the worst kind of politicians. I had hoped that there might be a fibre of moral worth among you, but it seems that you would bend before the wind. That Italian was right, about you two in any case. I, however, cannot divorce my own conviction from the fact I reign." Edward raises his chin a little as he finishes speaking. Cranmer once again looks to Cheke, but neither of them can think of anything further to add. Edward returns to his papers, calling for Paget to assist him in his work.

A little later, the young king is still at his work, with Paget over his shoulder. Cheke has disappeared, but the Archbishop of Canterbury sits across the room, reading papers of his own. A footman enters and announces the king's sister, Lady Mary. Mary enters with a small entourage, which includes her friend Susan Clarencieux, and our friend George de Winter. There is a wary caution about the group surrounding the lady, expressed in frowns and mutterings that are partially concealed but still perceptible.

Edward doesn't look up at his sister. Instead he continues with his work for a moment or two, before ostentatiously handing Paget a bundle of papers. "Please be kind enough to send for Master Cheke, Sir," he says as he dismisses Paget with a wave of his hand. Cranmer, having risen at the Lady Mary's entrance, shuffles himself around so that he can see both of their faces. Mary is flushed, fighting to keep emotion back. Edward is apparently a model of practised cool. He repeats his earlier raise of his nose, and observes his sister with pursed lips.

"Lady Mary," he begins, "I had rather hoped that we would not have to have this conversation." His voice is a little higher and more strained than it has been previously. "It cannot escape anyone's attention that you persist with a way of worshipping that has been shown to be false." He puffs his breath out, convinced of his rectitude. "As your king and your brother, it is my responsibility to ensure your well-being in matters of religion. As your brother, I thought you might see the error of your decisions, and I might guide you to the right path. As your king, I am disappointed that you continue to foment rebellion in my people with your disobedience." He leaves the words hanging in the air. Mary masters herself, forcing back the urge to lose her temper at him.

"Your Majesty," she says quietly, "our great father the late King

Henry, who saw matters more clearly than either of us, defended the sacraments, even as he rejected the authority of the Pope. I do not see that you, as a young boy not yet of age to rule, can overturn that statute."

"Our father rejected the authority of a church that is mired in ancient dogma. He may have had his personal beliefs, but God has shown me the true path."

Mary turns as John Cheke enters the room. His eyes widen at the sight of the group she has with her. He makes his way over to the Archbishop of Canterbury, and several faces follow his progress minutely. The moment of silence has disrupted the king's flow. Mary speaks.

"Your tutors, who were chosen by the Dowager Queen Catherine, are the ones who have instructed you. Your stepmother has made certain that you follow in her ways. Nothing more supernatural than this has occurred." Mary glances over her shoulder. Susan Clarencieux takes her hand and presses it between hers. De Winter stands a little closer than before, his shoulders tense and raised.

Edward sneers back at his sister. "I admire your conviction, sister, but I pity your lack of vision. You cling to the old, outdated and superstitious ways that your mother taught you, but you forget that God has chosen me as rightful heir to my father's throne. If that is so, even you should see that this is a message from Heaven." He sits back against his chair, and it accentuates again how small he is. He waves vaguely at Cranmer and Cheke. "These men," Edward continues, "are in support of my arguments, even if they are in fear of the consequences of decisive action. I shall make my request politely but firmly. You are to stop practising the old ways."

"I repeat my earlier refusal," Mary says, reddening. Her voice has a forced evenness that betrays her anger. "Your Majesty is not yet of age. I do not accept your request, as you do not have that authority."

Edward leans forward, and his feet dangle six inches above the floor. He clutches the arms of his chair tightly, his knuckles showing white. "You make me very angry, My Lady. The Lord Protector is away to war, and he does not need to be troubled with such matters. Sir Paget-" he gestures to the door, indicating the absent Secretary, "-can issue such an order if you wish it so. They rule by my authority, not my father's, and they do as I request."

"Do not test the Secretary, Majesty," Mary says, with a soft smile that looks genuine. "He has matters of much greater significance with which to deal. He would seek the confirmation of the Protector in any case, and Somerset would not give it." The smile broadens, victory in sight. "They both know the danger to your realm of persecuting me. Neither wishes to attract the attention of my nephew, the Emperor."

"You threaten me with foreigners! I had thought you above such tactics, Mary. It saddens me that you reject my care for your soul. However, I see that you are unshakeable. I shall speak with the Protector, and the archbishop, and I shall prepare what is required to govern this realm, and *all* of my subjects. Make no mistake, I shall have your obedience, or I shall have your head."

Mary stares at the young king, as does each member of her retinue. After a moment, Susan Clarencieux takes Mary in an embrace, and tries to steer her from the room. De Winter, with marked coolness, takes half a step forward and bows to the king.

"Your Majesty," de Winter begins, "has upset the lady with his talk of death. I trust that you will consider this carefully before next you address your sister."

"My sister is disobedient, headstrong and wilful. She must learn to behave herself." Edward turns his nose up at de Winter and those behind him. "And that means that she must conduct herself in a manner becoming to an heir presumptive to the throne. Though there will come a time when she is no longer heir."

There is a murmur of voices from Mary's group of followers. Her friend Clarencieux continues to console her, offering a lace handkerchief to dry the lady's tears of anger and frustration. Mary cranes over her shoulder. "My brother will break my heart if he continues to threaten me so. I wish that he would consider me as his sister rather than his subject."

Edward is about to speak, but Archbishop Cranmer puts his hand on his shoulder. "I shall speak to His Majesty in your absence, Lady Mary. It is not now the right time to settle these matters. Though I counsel that, just as you make your request that the king treat you as his sister, you remember that your brother is the king."

De Winter aims his bow somewhere between the king and Cranmer. "Your Majesty, Your Grace," he says, by way of a leave-taking. As he turns, he widens his arms to usher the lady out of the room. As the door closes behind her and her followers, the king throws whatever paper he had in his hands, and begins to cry tears of hot anger.

George de Winter rides alone in the direction of Chelsea Manor. It is the end of summer, and he wears fashionable light riding clothes, picked out with fine details such as the red-and-white rose of Mary's Tudor household on the breast. There is a series of crosses down the arms, signifying piety. His mount is fleet and strong, picked no doubt to impress his importance upon the subject of his visit. As he approaches, he slows, and as he emerges into view from the house he presents a rather dashing figure, the lone horseman with the important charge.

He is welcomed brusquely to the house by a footman, who has immediately recognised him as coming from Lady Mary by his clothes and manner. The footman takes the bridle and leads the horse away, pointing de Winter in the direction of the door, which is attended by another retainer. De Winter approaches, and announces himself.

"I am George de Winter, son of the Baron of Sheffield. I am sent by My Lady Mary Tudor with a message for her sister Elizabeth."

"Good day, Sir," the retainer answers with a slight nod of the head. "I was not told we were expecting visitors."

"I come not as a visitor, my man." De Winter comes closer to the retainer, baring his head with a flourish. "I come only to deliver my message."

"Well, I can see to it that it arrives in the lady's hand."

"You misunderstand me, Sir." De Winter smiles gently, but he continues with a firm tone. "I must pass this message to the lady herself."

"Then you must consent to wait as I seek the lady within. She may not wish to receive you. What did you say your name was?"

"De Winter," he repeats. "I am sent by the Lady Mary. I am a friend of Edward Strelley's."

"You are Master Strelley's friend?" the doorman asks, but de Winter waves him away. He stands facing away from the house as the man rushes inside. A moment later the door opens again, but it is not the footman.

"George!" Strelley cries, embracing de Winter. "To what do we owe this unexpected pleasure?"

"A grave matter between Lady Mary and her sister, I am afraid." De Winter shakes his head dramatically.

"A matter which you do not wish to share? Or you have not been sanctioned to share?"

"The latter. My instructions are to deliver the message to Elizabeth herself. It is not written for its contents are perhaps inflammatory."

"Perhaps the Lady Mary sends to her sister that Baron Sudeley is a blackguard? That is inflammatory, if not particularly informative."

De Winter laughs quietly. "If only it were that simple. We are all at the mercy of the twist of fate, and a nine-year-old boy sits on the throne, his Protector absents himself in the arse of this island chasing a baby for a bride, and the heir..." He stops himself. "I speak out of turn. I should like to speak with you after I see the lady, but of other matters than this. More pleasant matters...?" He tails off. The silence, only a moment long, is oddly tense as Strelley's eyes search for an answer to his unasked question: what is de Winter's message. The footman returns.

"I shall take you to the lady at once," he says. "She states that she will receive you only with her maid, Mistress Astley, and her tutors Masters Grindal and Strelley as her company." He notices Strelley as he finishes. "Ah, that is one accounted for. Will you show Master...? Never mind, if you are his friend you will know how to announce him."

De Winter shakes his head at the man's absent-mindedness, and follows Strelley inside. As they walk through the corridor, Strelley appraises his friend. "You have dressed as though you come to woo the lady, George. I doubt *that* is your object..."

"I have learned too much through your mistakes and my own, Edward, to break my peace with the powerful. I shall keep my counsel, and whatever your thoughts, you should keep yours."

"I bow to your wisdom, George," Strelley replies with half a smile. De Winter makes a show of returning it, but without success, instead appearing blank in the depths of his concentration.

They approach Lady Elizabeth's receiving room, within her apartments at Chelsea. It is unguarded, and Strelley knocks firmly to indicate their presence. Kat Astley's voice issues from within.

"You may enter!" she shouts. Strelley opens the door, and shows de Winter into the room, bathed in the late summer sun.

"Master George de Winter, Madam," Strelley says, bowing neatly. "Sent from-"

"My sister, I know. De Winter was one of your soldier friends, wasn't he?" She looks him up and down. "I see my sister has a little more income to outfit her retainers than I have here. Master Strelley does not follow the fashion., Sir. Master Grindal does not seem to be aware that it exists."

"I thank you for the compliment, My Lady." De Winter bends himself double. "Though I would ask that you reconsider your decision to receive my message in the company of others. Your sister, Lady Mary, asks that only you should hear it."

"Then that would mean that my sister is impossibly naïve, and I don't believe it. Whether they hear it from you or from me, she must know that I would share her message with my advisors."

De Winter suppresses a laugh at the word. He looks pointedly from Astley to Strelley and back again. Elizabeth watches as he does so.

"Do you not think my maid and my tutors worthy of giving me advice, Sir?" she asks, more than a little sharply. "At least I can trust that they have nothing of importance to gain from my decisions. Which is not something that can be said for my sister." She makes a fuss of closing her reading-book, and putting it to one side. "Now," she says decisively after smoothing her skirts, "tell me this message. Grindal shall have to hear it second-hand."

De Winter widens his eyes at Strelley. "You will not reconsider your decision?" he asks the young girl, without taking his gaze away from his friend. Strelley holds it, still trying to read the intention in de Winter's countenance. "No? It is brief, but solemn. She asks that you no longer accept the tutelage of those chosen by the dowager queen. She asks that you consider leaving this household, as it is a place of iniquity and it will lead you to endanger your soul. She asks also that you consider the welfare of your brother, who, she says, is already far down a path of wickedness and injustice. She shall guide and protect you if you wish it."

"I thank you for delivering this message," Elizabeth says, looking down, "though I profess that I do not like its contents. As a friend of Master Strelley's you are welcome, but you do not bring a message of peace to me. Rather you counsel me to abandon those I trust, and moreover my brother the king, whom we all serve. You may return this message to my sister: I do not accept her proposal. I shall continue to make my own choices, though I thank her for her advice. Please tell my sister that I love her and shall always do so, but I will not follow her in this. It is treason, and she will lead herself to the block if she pursues this course of disobedience."

De Winter nods his head. "Then I shall take my leave." He turns and walks out of the room. Strelley looks to Elizabeth as he does so, and her nod is her consent that he may follow.

He chases de Winter down in the corridor. "I understand your reluctance to speak before me. Did the lady choose those words herself?"

"With the utmost care."

"She can't have hoped for success."

"She hoped, but did not expect." De Winter sighs, his shoulders visibly dropping. "The king threatens her openly. Her conscience will not allow her to obey her brother, but her reason tells her it is not safe to defy him."

"Would she not be better abroad?"

"I have suggested it, but her counsellors say that such a move would be to abandon her claim to the throne."

"Surely she does not take seriously such a possibility." Strelley's cadence suggests a question, though he intended a statement of fact.

"Oh, but she does. And as heir presumptive, it only wants for an accident or the plague to elevate her."

"You ought to keep that thought close, George. Do not share it with anyone else. You know where it leads."

"It is not my thought. It is hers."

"Then you must protect her from herself. She will be no queen if her head is separated from her neck."

"Indeed not. I shall do what I can to keep her safe." He takes Strelley's hand. "Be well, Edward. Goodbye." He opens the door and shuts it again behind himself, and is gone. Strelley returns to Elizabeth's room, where the lady and her maid are already deep in discussion. He looks at them, but they continue their conversation. He edges over to an unobtrusive location, then listens intently without interrupting.

"You must cleave to those who hold your best interest dear!" Astley says, holding Elizabeth's hand. "Your brother and the queen share your beliefs. Your sister... She seeks your support for her own ends."

"You may be right. Though I think Mary truly thinks she is looking after me. That she is protecting me from Edward's and the queen's desire to reform religion. Protecting me from damnation." At this, Astley's face twists into an admonitory frown. Elizabeth ignores her, continuing instead, "she didn't hold with my father's ideas, nor those who have come after him."

"Your father, Madam, was not quite so clear in his thinking as that."

"What do you mean?" Elizabeth asks, head tilted in accusation.

"Well... there were times, such as when the king was with your mother, that he seemed to favour the reformists. Then there were times when he was more conservative in his thinking."

"You mean that he wavered." Elizabeth is curt, final.

"That is not the right word, My Lady, but your father had such great matters on his conscience, and he considered with such devotion, that his mind could change."

"There is no need to flatter him, Mistress Astley. He is gone, and you cannot commit treason by criticising him now. He found the path of reform when he wanted to marry my mother, and he left it again when he began to fear his own death. He had Queen Catherine choose my brother and me reformist tutors, but at the end found himself in great fear of abandoning that which his youth had taught him. I do not think any the less of him for it. Nor should you."

"My Lady is perspicacious as ever," Astley says, accepting the rebuke.

"Not especially. What is more concerning is this between my brother and my sister. Master Strelley, you are the strategist. What would Odysseus do?"

Strelley pretends to notice that he has been addressed, and joins the conversation. "Madam?" he offers, stalling, allowing himself to consider for a moment. "Odysseus himself would struggle with this. I am no gambler, especially not with stakes such as these. But here are your choices: On the one horn, you have the choice to abandon your brother and your stepmother, join with your sister, and adopt the Catholic faith. A risky choice, as you distance yourself from those currently holding power; but should your brother die before he has issue, especially if it is soon, when he is still young, one which you shall be glad to have made. The alternative is that you forswear your sister, and this choice seems to me less risky. She has no temporal or spiritual power in the realm, and it is more than likely that your brother will have a long reign and many children."

Elizabeth waits until he finishes, then sighs emphatically. "You do not have a clear preference then. What about Mentor?" she asks as Grindal walks into the room.

Strelley stifles a laugh at the epithet. "I doubt that Master Grindal will have much time for this, My Lady."

"We shall see," Elizabeth replies. "Master Grindal, my sister wishes that I should abandon the queen and have nothing to do with her. She thinks that Catherine is responsible for my descent into spiritual oblivion, and this decline must be arrested at once."

"Does My Lady wish me to recommend a course of action?" Grindal asks, buying time to think. Elizabeth nods in agreement. Grindal's eyebrows rise, and he gives a little shake of his head as he makes his reply. "I do not see why she should ask such a drastic course of you."

"She is being bullied by my brother, and wants an ally," Elizabeth offers. "Not that this should sway your choice. Do I back my nine-year-old brother, so young that he isn't actually allowed to rule the country for another nine years, or my sister, who binds herself to an Italian degenerate who made his own grandson a Cardinal at fifteen?"

"My Lady offers a very stark choice," Grindal ventures. Strelley looks down to hide his smile at her use of the word 'degenerate' to describe the Pope.

"No, Master Grindal," Elizabeth answers him, "I offer no choice at all! I do not wish my sister ill, but I would that she could leave me out of this. It is not my place to intervene in her spiritual quarrel with my brother. Certainly not by taking her side against him. But I have no doubt that the next letter I receive from him will be equally vituperative. Edward will seek my assurances of loyalty to him and to the new religion, and I shall have to give them to escape his attention." She grunts in frustration, stands, and flounces off from the room. Astley follows her, leaving Grindal and Strelley alone.

"So it seems that there is a rift in the royal family," Strelley says wryly, enjoying himself a little too much at Grindal's upbraiding by Elizabeth.

"Indeed," Grindal replies. "I have a job for you." He hands over a handwritten list.

"These are to be bought from Gilbert? What are they for?"

"Do not trouble yourself with that which does not concern you."

"Master Grindal, these are for some sort of poultice. Who is ill? You?"

"Possibly. Do not press me on the matter, for if I am it shall only make it worse."

"I can help, if you would describe your symptoms."

"I trust to my own learning on this, Edward," Grindal says, laying his hand on the young man's shoulder. Strelley holds his gaze for a moment, before breaking off and leaving the room.

An hour later, Thomas Seymour, Baron Sudeley, approaches the house. He has been hunting with his retinue and they carry slung between them a large hart, lolling upside down as the horses rise and fall. The herald announces them, and the household staff begin to prepare for his arrival. A uniformed retainer meets them, and stable boys are summoned. They enter the house. As they progress towards the hall, they encounter Elizabeth walking primly in the opposite direction.

"My Lord Sudeley." She courtesies as she welcomes him. He stands over her, breathing rather loudly.

"Elizabeth!" he shouts, unnecessarily loud. Her eyes narrow at the unwarrantedly familiar use of her name. "How is my bonny girl?" He lays his gloved hand on her shoulder. "It is good to see you, My Lady. It seems you are growing up rather fast." His eyes flick down to her neckline and then back to her face. She reddens slightly, and does not say anything. He pats her gently on the backside and walks away. One or two of the men who follow him do not hide their own visual interest in the lady as they pass, but though Elizabeth's eyes are wide, they are fixed on the stone floor.

A hundred leagues away, Longshawe and Pike ride just behind the Duke of Somerset and the Earl of Warwick. The huge army, as much as twenty thousand strong now, follows in their wake, kicking up a cloud of dust that announces their presence as they cross the border into Scotland. Their coming has roused the villagers of the region to watch as the progress, always keeping a safe distance on ridges and hills. Longshawe turns to Pike, and says, "I wonder what my father would say if he were amongst them."

"He would remark on your proximity to the leaders. Perhaps your rather spectacular uniform?" Pike smiles.

"Perhaps." He looks behind them, surveying the army. "I am sure he would find something not to his liking."

"When did you last speak with him?" Pike asks. "Did you see him after Ancrum?"

"I never went. I stayed with the earl."

"Why not?"

"I have no desire to be told all of my failings."

"Does your father really press you so hard? I never saw him being so harsh with you."

"I might be a little less vulnerable to it now. Seeing what I have, and all. In any case, I have resolved to visit him when we return from this campaign." He gestures about him. The column stays within sight of a fleet of ships that bring provisions and carry the artillery, and the wind off the sea is damp and cool enough to carry off the heat of the closely pressed bodies on the march. He continues, "These are pleasant enough conditions for campaigning, but unless we are quick, we shall have to return to winter quarters before we have achieved anything."

"Surely Lisle – Warwick, I mean – and Somerset know what they are doing."

"We do seem to be serving with more capable soldiers than last time, don't we? I think they mean to go north, sack Edinburgh, capture this queen and be back in London before Michaelmas."

"Good. I don't relish all this soldiering. I can't fathom how you persuaded me into this again."

"Because you have that desire to shoot things, and it doesn't matter if they are man or beast!" Longshawe laughs, drawing the attention of those around him. "Who shall be the first to bring down a Scot?" he calls out, relishing the moment. "Who, I say?"

A cheer goes up from the soldiers around him, which spreads to the rest of the column. Twenty thousand or so men, with their followers, send up a bellicose shout. As it dies away, Pike is shaking his head.

"I shall do my best to stay out of any actual fighting. I never was much good with a sword."

"No, Will, but that long gun of yours might just save my life, or the Protector's."

"There are fifteen hundred hackbutters with us. I doubt that my bullet will be the key one."

"I shan't be standing next to fifteen hundred Germans and Italians. I shall be next to you. As shall Seymour, and Dudley. You would trust me with my sword-arm, would you not?" Pike nods his agreement. "So I trust you with that musket."

"If we're lucky, the foreigners will do the bulk of the fighting before we're even close," Pike says, uncertainly. "Seymour won't commit-" He stops. An outrider has returned to the front of the column. The drums sound the halt, and the column stops.

The rider, dusty and sweaty, dismounts and kneels before the Lord Protector. Seymour looks as though he is about to ask him to rise, but thinks better of it. "Well, then?" Somerset asks. "What news?"

"The Scots army, My Lord. They've reached Edinburgh."

"Will they march to meet us?"

The rider nods, adding, "they'll be at Musselburgh tomorrow. If they get further, they'll cut us off and trap us on the spur."

"We need the artillery for this." Somerset turns to Warwick. "We must double the pace!" The drums strike up again, this time with a much quicker rhythm. The marching column resumes, faster than before.

That evening, the camp is alive with bustle. Soldiers sit outside their tents by fires, sharpening weapons and checking the straps on the few bits of armour they carry. Some test the mechanisms of their guns, and there is the occasional report of gunpowder as the fire takes. In the commanders' tent, the Duke of Somerset and the Earl of Warwick sit at table. Their guests include the young George Talbot, the Lords Grey and Wilton, and sitting either side of Talbot, Masters Longshawe and Pike. Neither Longshawe nor Pike looks comfortable with this arrangement, both out of their depth in this social setting, despite their familiarity with the people. Pike hardly eats, afraid to commit some act of barbarism. Longshawe is a little less stiff, filling his plate at the first opportunity, and occasionally asking Talbot a question.

The talk turns to the campaign. Somerset, in his element as both the military commander and the ranking nobleman, speaks boldly of his previous victories.

"We took Boulogne with a much smaller army than this," he is saying to Warwick. He gestures around the table. "But the cause! When Henry spoke, men listened. John," he says, putting his hand on Warwick's arm, "I wish he were here to lead us now."

"But the men look to you now, My Lord Protector." Warwick smiles back at him. "Your authority is that of the king, Your Grace."

"I would not be a king, John. I would not be a king for all the riches in the kingdom."

"And yet..." Warwick says. His smile has faded, replaced by a stern expression that is difficult to read. The conversation around the table happens to have quietened. Those sitting around it settle their attention on the two leaders. Seymour raises an eyebrow.

"And yet what?" he asks, trying to sound good-humoured.

"It is you who are the Lord Protector, Edward. The king does not come of age for many years. It is *your* campaign that we fight now."

"Do you truly think that?" Seymour asks, a note of real surprise in his voice. "This is what Henry wanted, you know. The Queen of Scotland for the boy's wife. A united island, so that we could live without the threat of invasion from the north. And as it seems we can achieve it, so we should."

"So you have no ambition of your own outside of that?" Warwick asks. He takes a drink as he finishes, hiding from the fact that he has broken protocol with this most direct of challenges.

"I do not, Sir." Somerset is firm. "I have only the king's and the realm's interests as my guide."

"I am impressed by Your Grace's conviction," Warwick says, his dishonesty not quite disguised. "We must make it our business to secure the bride His Majesty desires."

"Indeed," Seymour says, finishing the exchange. He then turns to Talbot, deliberately changing the focus. "I understand that you have campaigned in Scotland before, My Lord?"

"I have. Accompanied by these men. I should say led by them, in truth, for they knew much more than I at that time. And no doubt they still do." Talbot smiles first at Pike, then Longshawe. Seymour looks at them.

"I remember you," he says. "You," he points at Pike, "are a fine shot." He looks at Longshawe. "And you... You fought on the Isle of Wight. When Henry was king. He thought well of you, I remember. You reminded him of his youth."

Longshawe nods but doesn't reply. There is a moment as Seymour waits, then he realises that Longshawe does not know what to say. Seymour smiles at him. "Men such as the earl and I, we very rarely get to stand at the front, doing the fighting. That's not what we're there for. Henry wanted to do that, to stand toe-to-toe with the French and give them all hell. That's why he liked you. But he was jealous, did you know that? That you could fight unburdened by a thousand counsellors. He thought that they would be the end of him, all the urging and cajoling away from what he wanted most."

"Our late king," Warwick interjects, "liked nothing more than fighting and fucking!" He roars with laughter. A few others join in, but Seymour's face remains impassive, even a little sad.

"He wanted England to be great, John," Seymour says quietly. "As should we. A man's choice of wife or mistress are little to the point."

"Except they were with Henry, weren't they?" Warwick laughs. "That whore Boleyn had him break with Rome. And Catherine Parr-" Warwick is interrupted by a movement from Longshawe and Pike. "Gentlemen?" he says, unsure.

Longshawe raises his eyes, holding Warwick's gaze. It costs him great effort to keep calm. "Her Majesty, Sir. It is wrong to impugn her honour."

Warwick snorts. "It must be wonderful to have such loyalty."

"It is not my loyalty to the woman, Sir, but to the dignity of her rank." Longshawe now looks away as he speaks, focusing on the wine in his cup.

Warwick shakes his head. "The throne is a prize. Make no mistake about that. Henry's father took it with the blood of his soldiers from that crooked devil Richard. But he took it. Do you think God ordained it so? That thousands of men might die so the son of a bastard son of a royal widow might become king?"

Seymour stares at him. "Do not speak such treason," he snaps. "You would do well to keep your counsel in your cups, John."

"It is not the wine that makes me speak the truth, Edward," Warwick replies. "You lack the courage! It is a simple enough matter, should you wish it."

"I do not wish it. I have told you that," Seymour answers flatly. "I wonder that you think you can say such things."

"And what would you do, Edward? Have me arraigned for treason? Are we not a little beyond that now?"

"If it is treason you plot, then you shall be stopped." Seymour bristles. There is silence. It is broken by Warwick's barking laugh.

"I am your loyal servant, Your Grace, just as I am the king's! I do not want any part in this game of power." The Earl of Warwick is still laughing as he drinks deeply from his cup. Seymour watches him, eyes narrow. He does not return to his food for some minutes, even as the others continue their repast.

An hour later, the gathering breaks up, and the various guests begin to leave. Talbot leads Longshawe and Pike with him, and they walk away from the Protector's tent, finding a space near a large fire that is surrounded by chattering soldiers. The noise allows them to exchange their whispers without being overheard.

"Do you think that Warwick is truly loyal?" Talbot asks the other two. Pike pouts his bottom lip to indicate that he is unsure. Longshawe tilts his head in thought. Eventually, the latter replies.

"I don't know, but he is a true master of sowing doubt in the mind of the Protector."

Pike nods in agreement. "But what does he gain from Seymour thinking he is disloyal?"

"Nothing," Talbot says. "What he gains is if Seymour himself thinks of disloyalty."

"What do you mean?" Longshawe asks.

"Seymour is the arch servant," Talbot answers, picking his words carefully. "He does not seem to seek to aggrandise himself, beyond his station, at least. So a man such as Warwick, who stands to gain much should Seymour fall..."

"You think that Warwick would claim the throne for himself?" Pike suggests.

"He has no claim. But he could marry the boy to one of his daughters. Or marry his son to Lady Mary, or Lady Elizabeth. He could have Edward meet with an accident."

"You exaggerate, George!" Longshawe hisses. "Even Dudley wouldn't stoop so low as to murder the king, whatever he says about Richard and Henry."

"Worse has happened, if we are to believe the rumours," Talbot says. "Richard Plantagenet was no heir to the throne either. People speak of the murder of those two boys."

"Even I know that they died of the sweating sickness," Pike replies. "It was Henry's father that put that rumour about the Richard had them murdered."

"You would trust a hunchback who could take the throne by such action? That he would not be tempted?" Talbot asks, shaking his head. "You are credulous, Will. Seeing the good in folk when it is not there. Too trusting by far!"

Pike pushes his palms into his eyes. "I am tired," he says, "and we shall need our wits tomorrow, even if Warwick is prepared to abandon his to the wine."

"We shall," Talbot says, clapping him on the back. "Goodnight, gentlemen." He leaves, disappearing along an avenue between tents. Pike and Longshawe watch him go. Before they resume their conversation, another voice that the reader will recognise joins the exchange.

"I reckon it was Tudor himself that had them killed," Guy Fletcher says. "But then, to say that is probably treason." Pike and Longshawe laugh at his joke. They walk off into the camp, their young lackey between them. Longshawe hands Guy a cut of meat, which he has sneaked out from their meal with the Protector, and Guy takes it and eats enthusiastically.

Dawn comes early, her rosy fingers lighting the camp, warming the tents and rousing the thousands of soldiers. Not much time passes over breakfast, with quartermasters distributing bread and calling the march to begin in less than half an hour. The English army, all twenty thousand souls, is assembled in order of march before six o'clock, and on the move only a few minutes later. A nervous two hours is spent some distance inland, with the ships' masts just visible over the horizon in the early morning mist. Strategy demands that the army is at Musselburgh before the Scots can cross the Esk in numbers, and speed is of the essence.

Ahead, a column of smoke is clearly visible, rising from some place as yet hidden from view. The outriders again return to the head of the column, addressing Lord Protector Somerset. The first among them dismounts and kneels as he delivers his message.

"My Lord, the Scots are entrenched on the Esk. They have a few field-pieces, which are stationed to fire on our ships if they come close to shore."

Somerset strokes his chin. "Hmm. Then we shall get ourselves up those hills and see what they do next." He points to a low brow a mile or two distant. "We can defend that." He does not look round to seek the approval of the Earl of Warwick, whose eyebrow rises almost imperceptibly at the lacuna. The movement of soldiers is efficient, no man moving further than he has to, without any obvious battle-fever. The wide range of languages in which orders can be heard confirms the partly mercenary nature of this army, although a good half of the men are English levies, drilled in the use of their longbows as men have been for hundreds of years. The formation is neat and secure. No Scots army could approach without dread.

Longshawe and Pike sit in the saddle just behind the Lord Protector, at full attention behind the main line of English troops. This impressive array is made up of a large number of pikemen and longbowmen, and a smaller but significant contingent of gunners, mostly foreign. The cavalry sits at the wing, with Lord Grey's pennant standard fluttering high in the late-summer breeze. The Scots army waits on the other side of the river, apparently waiting and watching, just as the English have set themselves to do.

It is after perhaps half an hour of this standoff that there is movement on the far bank of the Esk. A large body of the Scots cavalry, with the Earl of Home's standard flying, breaks off from the main army and crosses the river. The rest of the Scots remain where they are. Warwick signals from his flank to Seymour, the message advising simply that "we are ready." Seymour returns only that the infantry should "stand firm until further orders."

Home's body of horse halts a mile or so distant, and a detachment of twenty or so begins to approach the English line. Seymour immediately calls out that no man is to fire upon them, or loose arrows. This is diplomacy, not some lunatic charge, as the pace of the small body of riders slows to little more than a trot when they come within hailing distance. Home himself approaches at the head of his band, riding an enormous destrier, rather unlike the other Scots whose mounts are lighter and quicker. He calls out, positioning his mount side-on, looking over his right shoulder.

"Englishmen! If you are men of honour, I call on you to fight! There are fifteen hundred Scots-" he points behind himself "-all willing to face the same number of yours. Let us settle this as men of valour should!" He wheels his mount around, all the while making it rear and snort, but the effect of this is diminished by distance and the vastness of the English army. Before twenty thousand of them, it is a gesture either of great bravery or great folly. Seymour signals to the cavalry to accept the challenge, and nods his head to Home. Less than a minute is required for the English to be ready at the charge, and Home is barely back with his small company before the two forces begin to close. The Scots horse, suitable for running battles and guerilla warfare, are no match for the heavier and better-armed English, and it is only a few minutes before the force under Home turns tail, fleeing back towards the river. As the bridge is blocked by the first wave, and Grey and his men are chasing hard, many of the Scots flee inland, but the disorder and confusion means that most of them are caught and cut down. Only a few English casualties remain on the field, but between prisoners and the dead, less than half of the Scots cavalry return.

The evening after this initial cavalry encounter sees the English in bullish mood. The men drink and sing, buoyed by the success of their horsemen. As the sun sets, Seymour sits down to eat outdoors, making a grand show of his optimism and ease. Longshawe stands at one end of the table, dressed in his cleanest and most striking uniform, at the rigid attention demanded by the show. The gleam of honed and polished weapons in the low autumn sun adds to the impression of power and invincibility.

A few minutes of twilight pass in this confident mood. Slowly a noise builds, a commotion of men mumbling, whispering and some shouting to summon their friends to witness whatever extraordinary scene is taking place. A single messenger in Scots colours rides through the camp, his eyes fixed forward, ignoring the agitation he has caused. His horse whickers and neighs, snorting blasts of hot air at those approaching it too closely. No one hampers its progress, though, and soon it approaches the outdoor bench of the Lord Protector and his closest companions. Longshawe and the other guards step forward and display their weapons.

Seymour raises a hand to stop the hostility. "I would hear whatever it is you have to say," he says, his confidence in the situation clear in his tone.

The messenger dismounts elegantly, and steps up to the table. There is a moment when the guards do not part to allow him to approach. Seymour coughs pointedly, and a gap appears. The line of green-and-white soldiers turns about and closes, hemming this Scotsman in.

Slowly, emphatically, the messenger removes his helmet, revealing a rugged man of about twenty-five or twenty-seven years, who has a bearing rather of a nobleman than a messenger. He removes his riding gloves, transferring them into his left hand and regarding them with casual interest.

"I am addressing the Lord Protector Somerset?" he asks. His voice carries the merest hint of a French accent in amongst the thickly guttural Scots. Edward Seymour nods. The Scotsman eyes him, weighing the leader of the English army. "Then I ask you to rise, Sir."

Warwick, seated next to Somerset, laughs at this suggestion.

"How dare you-" but he is cut off by Seymour's hand across him.

The newcomer watches this exchange between duke and earl intently, an eyebrow raised. "We stand," he says, "before each other, Master Seymour, each of us with a nation at his back." Seymour pushes back his chair and rises, but still says nothing. "Good," the Scot says, "so we begin to understand each other."

Somerset puts his hands on the table leaning forward over his wine cup. "I want the girl, Hamilton."

"I have thirty-five thousand across the river who will stop you."

"You exaggerate."

"Perhaps I do. But are you willing to gamble this fine army you have assembled to find out?"

"You would not be here if you did not fear defeat." Seymour frowns. "What is it that you want?"

"These men need not die for your old master's ambition. Why not settle things the honourable way?" He throws his right glove down on to the table between Seymour and himself.

"What?" Seymour spits. "You want to put this to a trial of champions?"

"Well, My Lord Protector, as we are both champions of our young monarchs..."

"I do not accept this impertinence!" Seymour shouts, jabbing two pointed fingers at the Earl of Arran. "You do yourself no honour, nor do you serve your queen well, My Lord."

"Then you must do your best on the field tomorrow. I am disappointed in you, though. I had hoped that you might spare your men this hardship." He turns. The line of guards this time parts without hesitation. As Arran rides away through the English camp, the hubbub starts up again. Pike walks over to Longshawe from among the throng that has gathered to watch the exchange.

Longshawe shakes his head as he sees his friend approaching. "Balls of solid rock on that one," he says, his voice shot through with awe.

"Or the total departure of his wits," Pike answers. "Battle it is, then. I would have given up my salt to see those two fight."

"I don't think Seymour thought he would win," Longshawe whispers, conscious of how close the Lord Protector is to them. "I wouldn't have bet against Arran. I might have backed myself against him, though!" Pike laughs out loud. Seymour eyeballs them both, clearly flustered.

"Stand your men down, Master Longshawe. I am away to bed. We shall have to be up early to steal the march on these Scots bastards." Seymour waves the guards away, and stares out into dusk as they leave, across the river towards the waiting Scots army.

Dawn comes early to witness fervid activity on both sides of the river. The Scots are already pouring across the Esk, frantically trying to draw the English into a pitched battle on their terms. The English are more circumspect, arranging themselves defensively around their guns on the slopes of Inveresk. The reason for this is apparent soon after the Scots begin to advance. The English ships have sailed into the mouth of the Esk, and the cannonade batters the Scots closest to the sea, out on their left. The guns fire repeatedly, tearing apart the body of soldiers, ripping great bloody holes in the formation. As the English watch, these men begin to break, fleeing across the line into the middle of Arran's troops, disrupting that disposition as well.

On the other flank, English cavalry hurl themselves forward. The Scots pikemen, ready for the charge, dig in and the horsemen are halted abruptly, some impaled on the pikes, others thrown from their mounts and battered to death by the front rank of Scots infantry. The cavalry, Lord Grey's pennant still flying, turn and flee. The English foot move forward, filling the gap left by Lord Grey's butchered cavalry. The lines close, and soon it is almost impossible to tell one army from the other.

In the English front rank, Longshawe cuts, thrusts and bludgeons the unfortunate enemies before him. His sword rises and falls, drops of blood flinging from its tip and edge. Among the front ranks of the Scots, a hole begins to form as the soldiers steer clear of this deadly foe. A quarter minute passes with a gap between the two lines, as Longshawe and those around him taunt the Scots. The noise is punctuated by the report of firearms. As the shouting rises, one crack is followed by a quiet grunt as Longshawe falls forward on to his knee, clutching at his chest. The men around him haul him up and push him back through the bodies, towards the back of the formation. A moment later, another shot crashes from the middle of the English rows. A man falls in the third or fourth row of the Scots, the same man who shot

Longshawe a moment before.

As Longshawe's stricken frame is hauled out from the back of the English division away from the fighting, a young man of fourteen or so years charges forward from the hill where he has been watching the battle. Another soldier pushes his way backwards through the line, erupting from the press into the open with a loud cry. The young man is, as we might anticipate, Guy Fletcher. He runs to where Longshawe is lying supine, and drops down to crouch over his master. The other soldier, the one whom we saw firing the shot that hit Longshawe's nemesis, is William Pike, who has also forced his way back through the ranks to come to his friend's aid. Pike stands upright behind Guy Fletcher, markedly pale and breathing heavily.

Fletcher claws at the leather thongs that hold Longshawe's armour, freeing them only after a distraught two minutes of pulling and swearing. Pike goes round to Longshawe's other side, kneeling by his friend and brushing his hair off his forehead, cradling his head in his hands. Longshawe is white, almost blue, coughing and groaning. The armour comes free, the light showing the hole where the ball has obliquely struck, cleaving the metal and leaving it bloody from the flesh underneath. Longshawe lets out a cry, a mixture of relief from the pressure of the bent metal and pain as it tore at the edges of his wound coming free.

Fletcher pulls Longshawe's padded under-jacket away from him, revealing the raked gash underneath. White bone shows under the leaking blood. "This will hurt," Fletcher says quietly, pouring a stream of light-yellow liquid from a leather hip-flask. Longshawe roars with the pain, creasing about the middle.

"Hold still," Fletcher says, and Pike pushes Longshawe back down, rolling him on to the other side so his wound is up. He pours again, and Longshawe closes his eyes, mouthing silently in searing agony. "Your rib is broken. But I don't think you've lost your lung."

Longshawe breathes loudly, deliberately, trying to master his excruciation. He returns a wordless "Hnnh!" to Fletcher, who offers him a watery half-smile. Pike looks from one to the other, then to Longshawe's wound. He flinches, seeing the three inch split gaping under Longshawe's left breast. Longshawe sees his face contort, and laughs weakly.

"That bad?" he says.

Fletcher shakes his head. "Worse. The ball is wedged under your rib."

"Oh," Longshawe says. "Worse."

Fletcher hands Longshawe the flask. "Drink. Not all of it." Longshawe does, looking into Fletcher's eyes as he gives him it back.

"This will hurt," Fletcher says again. He wipes his fingers over his britches, then pours a little of the liquor over his index finger. "Really hurt." Longshawe looks into Fletcher's eyes, seeing in them fear, but also a calm that has fallen through an act of considerable will on the part of the teenager.

Fletcher hovers his finger over the wound. "As quickly as possible, then." He breathes in, biting his bottom lip. Longshawe lets loose an animal bellow as Fletcher digs his finger into the gash, then falls silent as the pain overwhelms him. Pike looks on nervously for the half-minute that Fletcher spends twisting his finger, trying to free the bullet. Eventually it thunks quietly against the soil. Blood follows, but it is clean and red. Fletcher closes his eyes briefly, pouring the last of the liquor over the wound.

"We need to get him away." Pike says, clasping Fletcher round the shoulders. They stoop and heft Longshawe up, dragging him away from the battle. The English are pushing the Scots back, and after only a minute or two a whoop goes up as the Scots begin to break and flee. The English give chase, a group of cavalry reforming and joining the harrying of the retreating Scots, and the noise recedes as the fighting, if it can be so called, moves away north. Pike and Fletcher are busy with their friend, the battle coming to its conclusion without diverting their attention away from him. Fletcher binds Longshawe's wound tightly with torn strips of cloth, doing his best to keep it clean, soaking the pieces of bandage in more spirit taken from Pike's flask.

"If it festers, he will die," Fletcher says flatly to Pike. "It must not fester."

"No," Pike answers. "It must not."

"You shot the man who-" Fletcher begins, but Pike cuts him off.

"I did..." Pike closes his eyes and shakes his head. "The Italian. The one we fought with at Ancrum."

"Lorenzo?" Fletcher exclaims, turning to stare at Pike. "*That* Italian?"

"Him. Yes. I'm going to look for him." Pike stands. Fletcher nods his head.

"I can look after James." He watches as Pike heads off across the battlefield, now almost deserted of those still standing, then he returns his gaze to Longshawe. He is pale, almost blue, still. "Fight, damn you!" he hisses at Longshawe.

An hour or two later, Pike is still scanning the battlefield, looking for Calonna. He sweeps his eyes up and down, trying to find the familiar face with its scars, or some other recognisable token. It is forlorn, though, as the bodies lie thickly strewn about. Many are cleft apart, limbs scattered. Some are headless or have been torn open. Many of those further away are wounded through the back and over the top of the head as they have been chased down by the horsemen. The mud is ruddy with the spilt blood.

Pike continues to trudge across the field, turning over some bodies that wear similar clothes to those he remembers Calonna choosing. But, despite the efforts of his search, he does not discover the Italian. Others are engaged in a similar pursuit, perhaps searching for friends. Some butcher the wounded. A few, macabre though it seems, go about the battlefield taking the valuable possessions of the dead, even knocking out teeth and collecting them in cloth sacks. Pike cannot hide his disgust as one of these ghouls passes before him, carrying off the grisly treasures of the lifeless. He goes over to a familiar place, where Longshawe was felled by Calonna's bullet. He looks over, trying to replay the scene in his mind, picking a direction and walking across the churned mud to a point perhaps thirty yards away.

Pike stands tall, breathing deeply. He drops down on to his haunches, picking up a pinch of the earth and rubbing it between gloved fingers. As he looks through the hole made by finger and thumb, he notices a familiar face. Calonna lies on his back, motionless, dirty with mud and blood. Pike rises, goes to him, and kneels.

"Guglielmo..." Calonna murmurs. "You shot me..."

"You shot Longshawe. And you yet live." Pike shows no emotion.

"He died?" Calonna asks, sadness in his voice.

"No. Not yet, at least." He blows out his cheeks. "You didn't know it was him?"

"I did not. I do not know what I should have done if I had. Did you-"

"No." Pike looks at Calonna for a moment. "But I would have shot you anyway!" He laughs loudly. "Where did I hit you?"

"Over the shoulder." Calonna lifts his left arm, pointing to his right shoulder. It is a ruined, bloody mess. "Didn't kill me, though. Not such a good shot after all, eh?" Calonna laughs as well. "Will you help me up?"

"I shall, since you're my prisoner," Pike says. "Let's see how Fletcher is getting on with Longshawe." He hauls Calonna up, holding him so that his wrecked shoulder and arm are supported. Their progress across the battlefield is tortuously slow, but after a while, they can see Fletcher, who is still kneeling over Longshawe, who lies still on his back. As the Italian approaches his erstwhile colleague, he frowns.

"The ball-" Calonna begins to say, but Fletcher stops him.

"I have it." He holds it up between his fingers. "He fainted with the pain..." Fletcher pushes the hair from Longshawe's face. Longshawe's eyes are closed, but his chest rises and falls. "When I got it out, I mean. His rib is broken, but he'll live."

"You're a chirurgeon now, Gui?" Calonna half-laughs, half-coughs. "Perhaps you will mend this..." He points to his shoulder-wound. The look on Fletcher's face betrays the seriousness, the monstrousness of the damage. "Ah, you understand. I do not think I will last the day."

Fletcher stands and looks more closely at Calonna's wound. "Will, fetch me water. And liquor. I used the last of ours on James." Pike, fascinated by the exchange, takes a moment to register the request, but he disappears as soon as he comprehends it. Fletcher, watching him go, says, "I will do what I can."

Calonna laughs again, this time without the cough. "Thank you for your optimism, young man. But I have seen many men die of such wounds as this."

"Then we must trust to God. And God saw fit to bring us together today. Sit." Guy points to the ground next to Longshawe. Calonna looks into Guy's eyes, earnest as they are to help. Then he sits as he is told. "This wound needs to be clean. It will hurt."

"I know pain, Gui."

"We shall see," Fletcher answers. Pike returns with two small leather-bound flasks and a large water-skin. As soon as he does,

Fletcher washes his hand with the spirit, and prods at Calonna's wound. The Italian winces but does not make a sound. A moment later, Fletcher pushes against an exposed bone with his finger. Calonna's eyes narrow for a few moments, but he still maintains his slow, steady breathing.

"The ball is gone. But the collar bone is broken. I must put it straight or it shall never heal."

"This is going to hurt?" Calonna asks, knowing the answer. He closes his eyes. Fletcher bites his lip and forces the bone straight. Calonna lets out an agonised yelp, but doesn't fall into unconsciousness. "You were right. That did hurt."

"It's not over. Hand me that flask, Will." Pike passes the spirit to him. "Ready?"

Calonna shakes his head in amusement. "If I survive this, I will be your slave."

"Don't make promises you won't keep, Lorenzo," Pike says. "The boy knows his surgery. Edward taught him from that book. *Weasel* or something similar."

"Vesalius," Fletcher corrects him. "Stay still." He pours the contents of the flask over the wound. Calonna first grits his teeth, then yells, then falls over backwards senseless.

Pike stands by him. "For such brave soldiers, they can't handle their liquor, can they?" He laughs nervously. "Will they live?"

"Longshawe should. The rib is broken, but I don't think his lung is punctured. Calonna, perhaps. His shoulder is very badly injured. The wound is deep, right into the flesh. But..."

"That sounds more hopeful."

"Perhaps, as I say. Pray for them both."

44: In which we lose two of our oldest acquaintances

The battle of Pinkie Cleugh ends in a resounding defeat for the Scots. There are perhaps ten thousand of them dead on the field by the end of the day, their flight before the English cavalry littering the Esk and its banks with dead. But the reader will no doubt wish to learn the fate of just two of those who took part in it.

It is morning, and the watery Scottish sun lightens the English camp. Victory has been achieved, and at the cost of but a few casualties, numbering in the low hundreds. Calonna has found his way into the makeshift hospital that flanks the tent city, and is sitting up, using his good arm to swig from a leather-bound flask. Standing by him is William Pike, and they both look over to the next pallet, on which Longshawe is recumbent. His face, green-tinged, is slack and unmoving. Guy Fletcher stands over him, holding one of Longshawe's wrists, feeling for a pulse.

"He lives," Fletcher says, quietly. "For now."

Calonna bares his teeth, sucking his breath in. "I am sorry."

"James wanted war. He wanted to serve his king and gather glory to himself." Pike puts his hand on Calonna's good shoulder. "You bear no fault for that."

"That does not mean I am not sorry for him," Calonna says.

Fletcher frowns at the two of them. "He is not dead. Of all of us, he is the strongest. Do not give up hope." He comes over to Calonna. As he raises the dressing from Calonna's wound, his face contorts.

The Italian catches his expression. "A little blood did not bother you so yesterday, Gui," he says. His eyes narrow slightly.

"Indeed. Will," he says to Pike, "Come with me. We need to find the cleanest water we can."

Pike and Fletcher walk away from their two injured comrades in the direction of the Esk, a fair walk away. Pike eyeballs Fletcher as soon as they are out of earshot. "What did you see?"

"Lorenzo's shoulder... It has started to fester. I cannot save him."

"How long?"

"Days... Hours if he is fortunate."

"Do you wish to tell him?" Pike asks. They stop walking for a moment.

"No. But he must be told."

Pike nods slowly, but says nothing.

An hour later, Pike and Fletcher return to the hospital. Longshawe hasn't moved, but his chest still just about rises and falls. Fletcher checks his wound, satisfying himself that it has not worsened, and has perhaps improved. He then turns to Calonna. The Italian is still sitting upright, but he is noticeably uncomfortable. His face is a little less composed.

"Lorenzo?" Fletcher says, tilting his head. The Italian looks down at the ground. He has vomited, and it contains blood. "Your wound..."

"My wound. I know. It shall not heal. It stinks."

"It has festered as I feared it might," Fletcher says.

Pike steps forward, taking Calonna's hands into his. He kneels before him. "It is my turn to say that I am sorry, my friend. I had no wish to kill any man, but least of all my colleague-in-arms. Make your peace with God, Lorenzo. I shall have to make mine with him over you."

"God will forgive you." He makes a supreme effort. "William," he says, slowly and deliberately, finally finding the correct pronunciation. "As do I."

Fletcher hands Calonna another flask. "This will ease the pain." Calonna takes it and drinks deeply.

That afternoon, Longshawe's face has regained some of its colour. He has moved, his mouth no longer slackly unconscious, but rather a little more animate. Fletcher sits by his side, reading to him from a little leather-bound printed Bible. He recounts the story of Lazarus from John's Gospel. Behind him, Calonna lies on the pallet-bed, sweating and groaning. As Calonna coughs out his life, Fletcher raises his voice a little.

"I am the resurrection; and I am the life," he reads. "He that believes in me, although he be dead, yet he shall live. And whosoever lives and believes in me shall never die." Calonna doubles up, hacking and wheezing. Fletcher looks to him, and continues with the passage. "Jesus wept."

A few moments later, Calonna falls back on to his death-bed,

102

lifeless. Fletcher carries his Bible across and stands over him. He flicks the page. "I am the way, the truth and the life. No one comes to the father except through me. If you know me, you will know my Father also. From now on you do know him and have seen him." Pike takes him by the shoulders and turns him away.

"Look to the living, now," Pike says, nodding his head towards Longshawe. "Lorenzo is in Elysium, the beautiful Blest Isle. I hope he is happier there."

As night falls, Longshawe shows a little more colour than earlier, and his breathing is stronger. His fingers twitch a little, and his face grimaces once or twice. The fire that Pike has built burns strongly, keeping him warm in the late summer evening chill. Calonna's body has gone, removed to one of the mass graves dug by the English for the thousands of Scots corpses. Fletcher returns from whatever errand he has been on carrying two small pots. He digs into one with his fingers, removing a greasy, strongly-smelling substance which he puts on Longshawe's wound.

"This balsam should help," he says, "though I had to swap my Bible for it."

Pike returns a watery smile. "I wish that you had had it to treat Lorenzo."

"It would not have been enough. The wound had been exposed for a long time before you found him."

Pike shakes his head. There are tears in his eyes. "Of all the terrible things that could befall... I told him. I am no killer."

"No. You are a brave man in service of his king and his country."

"It does not feel like that now," Pike whispers. He sniffs, trying to regain control of himself. As he does, a pair of soldiers in the characteristic green-and-white uniform of the King's Guard appear from the morass of soldiers, surgeons and other camp followers. They half-push, half-intimidate their way and stand to full attention before Fletcher and Pike, a little way separated as if to leave a path between them. Their object is soon revealed, as the Lord Protector himself strides up between them.

"Master Pike," he greets, as Pike rises to his feet a little unsteadily, "I heard our mutual friend was wounded. He looks to be through the worst...?" Seymour asks the question with a cock of his head. His confidence is betrayed by his raised eyebrows as he sees the open wound on Longshawe's chest.

Pike cannot find the words. Fletcher steps forward and bows his head to the Duke. "Your Grace," Fletcher says, "Master Longshawe is grievously wounded. I think he will survive if I can keep his wound clean."

Seymour purses his lips as he looks at Longshawe's supine form. "What is that?" he asks, pointing at the grease.

"A balsam, Your Grace," Fletcher answers. "It keeps the wound from festering."

"Hmm." Seymour shakes his head. "I did not know that you kept a surgeon for a lackey, Master Pike." He smiles. "You are?" He turns to Fletcher.

"Guy Fletcher, Sir. I first served with Master Longshawe and Master Pike at Ancrum."

"Ah, yes. We prefer not to discuss that encounter." Seymour claps his hand on Fletcher's shoulder. "It seems you have done much to save your master's life. I shall see to it that you are rewarded."

"If it please Your Grace..." Fletcher ventures. "I should like to have my Bible back. I exchanged it for this unguent, but it is very dear to me. Another friend of mine gave it to me."

"Then it shall be arranged," Seymour tells him. He gestures to the men following him to see to it. "I shall return in the morning to check on his progress. Do not let him die, Master Fletcher, he is one of the best soldiers I have in this army." Pike turns his head away, screwing up his eyes to stem his weeping. Seymour notices, and casts him a quizzical glance. "He is not dead, young man, and the master Chirurgeon here says that he shall not die."

Fletcher answers him. "Please forgive Master William, Your Grace. He has seen another of our friends die today."

Pike stands. "Do not make my excuses, Guy. I killed him myself."

Seymour tries his best to smile warmly, but it does not break the tension. "Men die in war, Master Pike. I am sure that you did as you thought best."

Fletcher tries to cut in, starting to say that "he fought with the Scots," but Pike doesn't let him make his point, stopping him with a gesture. Instead, Pike replies to the Duke of Somerset, his voice choked. "I am no soldier, Your Grace. Give me leave... Not to have to fight again."

Somerset stares at him, calculating his reply. "You have my leave. Do not throw away your life, though, Master Pike, as even if you do not value it, others will."

Pike dips his head in obeisance. "I will away, then." He turns, and with a brief glance over his shoulder back to Longshawe and Fletcher, disappears into the camp.

It is deep in the night when Longshawe finally awakes. He looks about him, struggling to throw off the stupor of his long unconsciousness. Fletcher sits by him, head bowed. As Longshawe begins to move, Fletcher cries out in gratitude and relief.

"Master Longshawe! You live!" he shouts. Longshawe coughs a little, trying to raise himself. Fletcher continues, "I would stay lying down if I were you. The ball broke your rib. It will sting a little for a few weeks."

Longshawe's hand moves to the site of his wound. It is dressed cleanly, the bandage showing no sign of blood. "It didn't kill me then?" He asks. Fletcher shakes his head.

"No. Apparently not. You will be weak for a while, but you will recover your strength."

"Where's Pike?" Longshawe again moves to lift himself but gasps in pain as he does so, falling back down on to his bed.

"I don't know." Fletcher's voice has a touch of desperation about it. "He asked the Duke of Somerset for leave earlier and I haven't seen him since."

"Leave?" Longshawe's tips his head back.

"Umm... He said he didn't want to fight again."

Longshawe's eyes dart around. "And you haven't seen him since? He's probably just looking for some wild animal he's heard about."

"I don't think so, Sir." Fletcher does his best to sound deferential and apologetic. "He... Well, the man who shot you..."

"Pike got him, did he?"

"Well, yes. But you see, we knew him," Fletcher says, looking away. Longshawe's eyebrows arch as Fletcher continues. "It was the

Italian. The one we served with at Ancrum and Wight. He shot you, and Pike shot him."

"Calonna?" Longshawe cries. Fletcher's head nods back and forth, but his eyes remain fixed.

"He died. We found him alive, but I couldn't save him."

"Calonna was here? Then he must have been..." Longshawe's tired mind catches up. "He was the one that shot me?"

"Yes. And Master William shot him."

"Oh." Longshawe's realisation cuts through. "Pike killed Calonna. Now I see. And he's gone? We must hope and pray that he returns to us."

"I have prayed for that just as I have prayed for your deliverance."

"I am tough enough without God's help." Longshawe smiles weakly. At that moment, the Duke of Somerset arrives, accompanied by a large party of retainers, and the Earl of Warwick. They look at the wounded soldier with sympathy.

"Master Longshawe," Somerset says, leaning over him, "I hear that you stopped a Scots ball yesterday. How imprudent of you to stand before such a shot." Longshawe closes his eyes for a moment and reopens them, blinking.

"I seem to have survived, though."

"Yes," Somerset replies, "thanks to your Barber Surgeon. Fletcher, isn't it?" He turns to Guy Fletcher. "If I'm ever wounded, I shall apply first to you." He turns back to Longshawe. "You have a good lad here, Longshawe. Look after him, because he's looked after you." Somerset takes out a gold coin and presses it into Guy Fletcher's palm. "For your service, Master Fletcher. I shall see you in London, no doubt, after all this is over." With that, Somerset turns and leaves, talking animatedly to the earl. They disappear too quickly for us to follow their conversation, but it begins with the words "the child Queen of Scots".

Longshawe turns to Fletcher. "Rather a promotion from lackey to Barber Surgeon, Guy. I thank you for what you did. I know I would be dead without it. You must ask for whatever it is that I can do for you."

"I think what I want most is to go home to the Palace and read my books." Longshawe laughs heartily in response. Fletcher frowns at him, then continues. "I don't think war is for me."

"No. Nor for Will, nor was it for Strelley. I'll take you home, Guy, but I've got to go somewhere on the way. Get me better, and I'll release you from my service when we get back."

Fletcher nods his assent. "So we are going to see your father?" he says.

"How-" Longshawe stops himself. "Yes, Guy, we are going to see my father. Amongst others whom I must see. I do not relish it, but I must. He will be insufferable, but I have the consolation that I didn't die as he said I would."

"Others?" Guy says.

"One other."

Longshawe stands in the early-morning sun, looking out across the battlefield. The autumn dawn chill leaves wisps of mist in the air, giving an ethereal quality to the macabre view, littered as it is with the already-decaying bodies of the recently killed. He stares out without focusing, contemplating, for several minutes. Guy Fletcher stands a gun-shot away, watching him with narrow eyes. George Talbot, neatly-shaven and beautifully clothed, walks over to Fletcher, greeting him with a warm smile.

"How is he?" Talbot asks. "Somerset told me that he had been wounded. He looks to be over the worst."

"He is. But Pike has gone."

"Gone? What do you mean?"

"He's not in the camp. We don't know where he's gone." Fletcher shakes his head.

"Oh. Perhaps he has..." Talbot is lost for words.

"He killed a man we knew. The Italian, you remember?"

"I do. Calonna was fighting for the Scots, then?"

"Yes. And it was he that shot Longshawe."

"I see. Is it wise for me to speak with him?"

"He would be glad of some kind words, Sir," Fletcher says. Talbot turns Fletcher towards him, taking him by the shoulders, gentle but nevertheless firm.

"If *you* ever find yourself looking for a position, Master Fletcher, I would welcome any application you might make to me." Talbot claps his hand over Fletcher's shoulder twice, smiles, then heads off towards Longshawe.

Longshawe shows no sign of noticing the young Earl of Waterford's approach. He simply continues to stare out unfocused, not taking in the view, not blinking. Talbot stands by him, almost doing the same, but his eyes move around the scene, surveying the human cost of the battle. After a half-minute, Talbot speaks.

"Master Longshawe... James. I am glad to find you well."

"I am not *well*, My Lord. I can stand, but I won't be able to fight again for a long while."

"But you are not dead, James, and that is what matters." Talbot makes a gesture, indicating the strewn bodies. "You don't mourn them, do you? I don't think you even mourn Calonna. For the first time, you've felt fear..."

Longshawe turns to him. "They say that a brave man is one who feels fear and masters it. I am not, then, a brave man. I have just failed to realise the truth. That I might die at any moment on the battlefield. That I might catch a bullet not even meant for me, and die unlamented on some foreign field for a king – or his Protector – who will mourn only the loss to his cause of my prowess, not my passing."

"And...? God puts us on this world, and he takes us from it. You might catch plague, or worse in some bawdy house, and die unlamented in the Thames. We all have to die, James."

"That is true. But perhaps I might prefer to die old in my bed, like Ed Strelley said."

"You are one of the best fighters I have ever seen, James."

"Then I have but little choice in my career," he says, shaking his head. "I don't see what else I might do."

"Perhaps you should take a lesson from your friend."

"I couldn't read a hundredth-"

"Strelley is good at reading. You are good at...?"

"Fighting. You said it yourself."

"And which fighting men avoid the battlefield?"

"I had wondered if I might miss out on the melee as part of the King's Guards. But I think Somerset had need of us."

"The king." Talbot inclines his head. "I shall talk to Somerset. I have an idea for you."

"What is it?" Longshawe calls, but Talbot has turned and is walking away.

"You shall see!" he calls back.

"A fencing master?" Longshawe exclaims, head to one side as Talbot raises his eyebrows.

"Not just *a* fencing master, James. *The* fencing master. *The king's* fencing master. You would never want for work again if it were known that you were engaged by the king."

"The king is barely ten years old!" Longshawe snorts. "And I imagine that M'Lord Seymour – His Grace the Duke, I should say – has no intention of letting him anywhere near a sword."

"His Grace the duke is rather keen that the king should learn to be a man. He fears that the late king did not allow Edward the licence to... grow." Talbot smiles at Longshawe, who is still shaking his head in response to the suggestion.

"But to engage a failed soldier as the king's fencing master... Does that not seem a little-"

Talbot interrupts. "No, you are not a failed soldier, James. You are a soldier who has served his king and country, and it is your experience and not your wound that brings you to this position."

"The king need never know...?"

"Know what? That you have lost your nerve?"

Longshawe frowns. "That is not quite true, My Lord. I have just lost my..." He thinks for a moment. "I have lost my innocence, I suppose. I am frightened to go into battle now, and I wasn't before. I have not lost my courage, I have just understood what there is to lose."

"Then you need not dissemble. There might be a time, when you are healthy again, that you want to go back into battle."

"Perhaps. I have had my fill for now."

Longshawe sits on a rock, chewing on a piece of black bread. His lackey, Guy Fletcher, bustles around, clearing up pots that have been recently used for a meal. In front of them, a large portion of the force that fought at Pinkie begins to strike camp and make its way home. Some of the army has been dismissed, no longer required. Some of it is detailed to march west with the Protector and his lieutenant, the Earl of Warwick, to try to secure the person of the young Queen of Scotland, Mary. George Talbot, the Earl of Waterford, emerges from the press of men, and approaches.

"You are resolved, then?" Talbot asks.

"Indeed. I am done with this *rough wooing*. Perhaps the king should look closer to home for his wife? Or to France, perhaps..."

"Protector Somerset sees the value in pacifying the north. And since the barbarian tribesmen that live up here refuse to be beaten by force, we must conquer them with a little diplomacy."

"Slaughtering ten thousand is hardly diplomacy." Longshawe smiles uncomfortably.

"Well... They weren't listening before, were they?" Talbot laughs, but he is disguising his own disquiet. "The battle is won, James, and we make our disposition from there."

"Do you think you will find the girl?"

"No. When Arran came out with his forces, he will have sent the girl the other way, if he had any sense. Whether he expected to win or not, he will have made his contingencies."

"So this might well have been for nothing?"

"Do not be so melancholy," Talbot says, coming a little closer and putting his hand on Longshawe's arm. "My father told me that war is very rarely successful in bringing about its ends." He forces another unconvincing laugh. "I will find you, when we return from this..."

"I look forward to it. Henry – before he died – told me to serve his son as best I might. This way I might serve the king well, by being near him. I shall always be grateful to you and to your father."

Talbot turns and heads away, disappearing quickly into the swarming throng. Longshawe bites his bread again, watching Guy Fletcher. After half a minute, Fletcher notices how closely he is observed, and stops his work, standing up straight and facing his master.

"Sir?" he says.

"Guy... You've seen battles. How do they make you feel?"

"I am no front-line fighter."

"Perhaps not. But you have been there and seen what we do. You must have felt something."

"I have always had faith that you would deliver me." Guy lowers his head as he says this.

"And now?"

"If I were behind the line and you were at the front, I think even now you would beat every enemy that stood before you."

"I thank you for your encouragement. I don't think you're quite right, given this blasted hole in my side!"

Fletcher peers over. "Your wound heals well. You are lucky."

"In one way, I suppose."

"How many of the lackeys on this field do you think would have saved you?" Fletcher smiles. "You have Master Strelley to thank for the knowledge I gained from him of such matters."

"Yes, Edward did talk about his experiences with the barber-surgeons. I am lucky that you learned so much. But there were only a few hundred dead on our side!"

"Well, if you will force yourself to the front... There is some merit in discretion."

"You sound like Strelley!"

"There is much to be learned from him and from his books, even in the art of war."

"That may be true. And I am grateful to you, Guy. For your... work..." He stands, awkwardly hefting his weight upright. His eyes narrow in a wince of pain.

"You must be careful!" Guy calls out.

"I shall introduce you to my father. You two will get on." He shuffles over to Fletcher and puts his arm around his shoulders. "That is where we shall go now. Back to Longshawe. I think perhaps I ought to stand before him and reconcile my differences with him."

"Your father? I didn't think you had much time for him, or his opinions."

"Well, Guy, I don't. He and I do not agree on... most things, I suppose. But in particular on how I should spend my time."

"He didn't want you to be a soldier?"

"No, because he thinks it is a fool's job, and the only outcome is death."

"So you have come to see things more from his perspective?"

"We shall not be telling him *that*, Guy. He shall be unbearable if he thinks that I've conceded that he was right all along. In any case, he isn't right, is he? We're not dead, thanks to you and Strelley's mystical books."

"They aren't mystical. They're just written by wise men who aren't Christians. So the Church-"

"Just be careful, Guy, because there are many who would find Edward's choice of reading matter rather worthy of their attention."

"His books are hardly heretical. Medicine, hunting, fencing, perhaps, but not much on religion. Then there are those old stories..."

"Those are the ones he has let you see, remember! He is being judicious, perhaps, in keeping the more dangerous material away from you."

"I should think Master Strelley knows a great deal more than these rabid zealots who go about burning people."

"And that is why, if any of them come asking, you should keep your counsel!" Longshawe shakes his head. "These people – these *rabid zealots*, as you so mockingly call them – are the ones who hold the power. Dying for what you believe in seems a great waste. Better to live, eh?"

"Do you say the same to Master Strelley?"

"When I get the chance, I will. He is lucky enough to have the ear of some powerful people. Although he does have a few enemies, as well," Longshawe adds, almost to himself. "No doubt he is plotting their downfall even as I speak."

"Strelley is not a vindictive person, is he?"

"Well... No, because that makes him sound cruel and evil. But he does hold a grudge!"

"He has formed a grudge against that Seymour, hasn't he? The one who used to be involved with Queen Catherine."

"He has. I would not like to number Ned among my enemies, you know. But sometimes having him as a friend is just as dangerous!" At this, Guy Fletcher falls about laughing. Longshawe is more restrained, and there is the slightest hint of a frown on his face as he watches Guy recover his composure.

Let us leave them to their conversation, for they make no further insight into Strelley's condition. It will suffice for our purposes now to say that they soon set off for home, leaving behind the vast army assembled for the conquest of Scotland, and heading south towards the Derbyshire seat of Longshawe.

46: How, whilst considerably incommoding himself, de Winter begins to achieve his goal.

Stephen Gardiner, the now-deprived former Bishop of Winchester, sits in a cell in the Fleet prison. He scratches a quill-pen across a sheet of paper already covered with his elaborate script. His dress, while understated, has a few hints of the episcopal robes he has recently forfeited. His face is set in a look of firm determination, and he frequently looks to the heavens for his inspiration as he writes. There is a knock at the door.

The turnkey opens it, and allows three hooded figures to enter without announcing them. Gardiner looks up from his writing. The first of the three figures, tallest by a foot and evidently that of a male by the shape of his body and the manner of his gait, throws back his cowl. He thus reveals himself to be our old friend George de Winter. Gardiner shows a sign of recognition, but cannot place the face, and begins to speak.

"Master...?" he says. "To what do I owe the pleasure of this visit? Who are your companions?"

"De Winter, My Lord. I have brought you one who is in need of your guidance, both spiritual and temporal."

Gardiner rises from his seat. With a sidelong glance at one of the two hooded figures, both shorter and slighter than de Winter and female, he steps forward.

"Your Highness!" he exclaims and falls to one knee. "I did not expect your company in my... current situation."

"Your current situation," Mary says, pushing her hood back and revealing face and her untied hair beneath, "is little different to mine. We are both prisoners of the king, My Lord, although he has made your imprisonment more worldly than mine."

"He does not allow you to worship as your conscience dictates?" Gardiner rises, and crosses his hands in front of himself.

"He tries to force the new learning on me and my household. I have tried to find ways of hearing the Mass, of preserving the true ways, but he, and that bulldog of his, persist in their threats. I fear I shall not long be able to do as I feel I ought."

"So you seek my counsel?" Gardiner's voice shows that he is already thinking out the possibilities.

"I have spoken with my friends, but they are few. Susan and I thought that you might help us to see the right path."

"Indeed. Have you sought the advice of the Emperor?"

"I fear that my correspondence is read by the Protector's agents. I have not written to my cousin."

"That may be wise. Could you send him a letter that made your position clear without appealing directly for his assistance in it?"

"I shall try to compose such a letter. I fear for its consequences."

"Do not fear, My Lady. The Emperor is a powerful man, and the king and the Lord Protector fear him greatly. His influence extends throughout Europe and affects our nation even in times of peace, through his power over the ports of the low countries. Were we to engage his assistance in this matter, we should greatly improve our position."

"He must already know of the king's preferences," Mary says.

"Ah, yes, but his ambassador may not have made it clear how serious your plight now is. And I wonder whether my imprisonment would have come to his notice." By his half-questioning tone, Gardiner seeks to focus Mary on his situation, but his speculative plea for recognition goes ignored.

"I see," Mary replies, thinking only of her own affairs, "so I must write only what is true, and allow him to make his own conclusion?"

"For now, that is as it should be. Who are your allies at court?" Gardiner gives up the attempt to bring matters around to his own imprisonment, seeing that Mary is firmly diverted.

"They are few. Norfolk is still in prison as you are, lucky to escape the headsman's axe and saved only by my father's death. Cranmer's word is final in matters of worship, and Edward is staunch in his beliefs. My sister runs before the wind, it is impossible to read her and she is no ally of mine. Indeed, she is more a politician than you are."

"You must do your best to avoid court, then. Angering your brother will make matters worse. If you can find a way to make yourself of no consequence to him, then you will be safest. Trust in God, Your Highness, and he will deliver. This is sent to test us, his faithful servants, but our triumph will come, and we shall return this nation to its right and proper religion."

115

"I thank you for your counsel, My Lord Winchester," Mary says, and bows her head. De Winter once again steps forward, making his wish to speak plain. Mary gestures that he should do so.

"My Lord Bishop, I have suggested to My Lady that she ought to remove herself from this land whilst the heretic king is on the throne. I fear for her safety, and I fear lest she be implicated as a figurehead of some imagined plot against the king. Moreover, there are those among our supporters who may not be careful enough to distance her from their own plotting. The Lord knows that the king is unpopular with his people, and the Protector even more so. There may be those who would think it astute to conspire against the king, perhaps with the goal of elevating the lady to the throne... But those thoughts, those whispered words... They may be the end of us."

Gardiner looks long at de Winter. "Your caution is judicious, Master..." Gardiner has forgotten the name already. "I agree that the lady's safety is paramount. But she must not be seen to be forgoing her claim to the throne by fleeing the country. If that comes to pass, we are lost altogether. God will restore his people to power, so we must trust in him."

"How, then, shall we ensure that our supporters do not involve us in some intrigue that might give the king pretext?"

"Be strong in your faith," Gardiner says, ignoring de Winter's question. "You will not serve God by running from this conflict, but you may serve him best by doing what is necessary to ride out this storm. God will recognise his own."

Mary turns to her hooded companion. "Susan?" she asks. "What think you to the bishop's words?"

"I am resolved, Madam. I will be strong in my faith that England will see its rightful queen take up her throne."

"I wish I had a sign," Mary says. "I pray every day, My Lord Winchester, for a sign or an omen, and I am denied."

"My Lady must not despair," Gardiner says, mustering his most ministerial tone. "These trials are sent by the Lord to test us, and we must not falter."

"No, My Lord, we must not," Mary replies. "I shall be strong, then." She and Susan Clarencieux turn to leave. As they pass the threshold, Gardiner calls back de Winter.

"Young man," he says, "you must arrange... the sign that our lady requires... However you should choose, but you must do it. If she leaves England, she shall not be queen. She must believe that she shall ascend the throne, or we are lost and this realm will fall forever into heresy. She cannot, she must not lead a foreign army against Englishmen!" Gardiner hisses the words out, face stern. "Do you comprehend?" he spits. "Everything depends on it."

De Winter nods. "I comprehend, My Lord Winchester. I shall see to it that Mary is shown the future she so desires."

"Do not fail, or we are lost," Gardiner says. "There are few enough loyal servants around Mary. I would not have chosen you for this task, but it seems rather that God has." He dismisses de Winter with a wave. He watches him go, then sits back at his desk and resumes his scribbling.

De Winter catches up Mary and Susan Clarencieux part of the way along the dim corridor. Mary is speaking.

"The heretics, for that is what they are and that is what we must call them, will send Bishop Gardiner to the stake for his beliefs!"

Clarencieux takes her mistress's hands, stopping them walking. De Winter slows his pursuit and stands a few paces away in the corridor, watching and listening.

"Madam," she says, "My Lord Winchester is subtle enough to avoid such an end."

"You should say rather that Archbishop Cranmer does not have the courage of his convictions to have Winchester executed. I cannot stand his equivocation. He knows not his own mind!"

"We faithful have the advantage of knowing our doctrine," Clarencieux says enthusiastically. "And if Cranmer wavers then at least it preserves the good bishop. It is those great men of our Church, the holy men who guide us from history, it is they that knew God!"

"But God does not speak to me! I should hear his voice..." Mary's eyes glint in the light of the flickering torches. "I have found his abandonment of me quite testing."

"I know, Madam," Susan Clarencieux replies, "but we must do as Bishop Gardiner says, and have faith. God will deliver us." They continue their walk through the Fleet, surrounded by imposing doors that separate sections of the prison, barely lit by torchlight. De Winter follows, deep in thought, barely noticing the grim surroundings.

Mary kneels before the rood at Great St Bart's. She prays earnestly. Outside, the light is fading in the late autumn evening. The church is otherwise barely inhabited, the scar of its encounter with the late Cromwell still showing clearly in its part-finished western nave. In the cloister, Susan Clarencieux, divested now of her hood, stands by and watches. She passes her rosary beads through her hands as her friend and mistress goes through her devotions. The confessional curtains are closed, and although the conversation of priest and confessor is muffled and indistinct, it is possible to hear that something is passing between them. The reader shall no doubt excuse the intrusion of the blessed sacrament of confession, so we shall join our friend inside.

De Winter is stroking his moustache. The priest, hidden in the opposite half, is intoning drearily. "One cannot repent of a sin not yet committed, my son." He has a slightly pompous air, as though the request is not only inadmissible, it is moreover somewhat undignified. "If you are aware that the commission of such an act may be a sin, or indeed you are already convinced that it is a sin, you should not thus act."

"I am not sure whether you misunderstand me, or if I have failed in my exegesis. The Bishop of Winchester himself has ordered this act, and it is my commission today to lay it before God that I do it in Lady Mary's blessed name, even though it is deception of she for whom it is done."

"To deceive may not be a sin in itself." The priest dwells over each word, as though he is making some profound theological discovery in his speech. "But to prophesy that which you cannot know, and to deceive by means of dissembling to speak the words of the Lord himself..."

"I do not propose to elevate myself to the status of some messenger angel!" de Winter hisses. Outside the confessional, this impenetrably muffled exchange draws the attention of Clarencieux, but not Lady Mary. De Winter breathes deeply in and out several times, composing himself, before continuing in a more measured tone. "I shall not masquerade as the Lord's voice. But I shall allow the lady to think that God has spoken to her. It is for her own benefit. It will be for yours, I might add, as you will find yourself with no church at all, rather than just half as it is now, if Seymour and Cranmer continue as they have begun."

"I remind you of where you are, and the sacramental nature of our conversation. I will not hear your confession if you persist in your aggression towards me."

"Novit enim Dominus qui sunt eius."

"I beg your pardon?" The priest's monotonal equipoise deserts him as his voice rises in pitch.

"I am more a servant of our God than you at this moment. If I have to disavow my religion, I shall do as I think best, as my conscience dictates. Perhaps God will recognise me as his own."

"Beware of such blasphemy. You risk the fires of eternal damnation if you ignore the wishes of God."

"And you speak the wishes of God to me, do you? I risk the fire if I ignore the demands of what is right, and what is demanded by your superior within the Church!"

"You speak of Gardiner again? He is deprived, as you know, and he has no authority."

De Winter sighs deeply. "You realise that if Mary goes abroad, that is it. No Catholic heir, no buffer against this tide of reform that threatens to sweep away everything we hold dear? Can you not see that God would have it this way? Our greatest thinker shows you how it might be done, and you tell me that it is a sin too far to beguile the lady with a little trickery?"

"You must not impersonate God, Sir. Whatever the cause."

De Winter laughs loudly. The unusual sound of it in the confines of the church causes Clarencieux to turn away from Mary and walk towards the booth. Mary herself glances over her shoulder but returns quickly to her prayer. Before Clarencieux has got there, though, de Winter exits the confessional, shaking his head.

"I shall be outside," he says, indicating the door with a pointed finger. "God, it seems, is finished with me, if not with our Mistress."

A few minutes later, Mary leaves the church with Clarencieux close at her shoulder. "I would thank you in future to remember your decorum, Master de Winter," Mary says, without humour, brows knotted in frustration at her servant's lack of respect for the sacrament.

De Winter nods slowly, accepting the rebuke. "I apologise, Madam," he says, but his thoughts are already elsewhere, reflecting on his conversation with the priest, perhaps, or plotting the intrigue to which he has already confessed.

De Winter walks in to a richly decorated office, with walls covered in brightly coloured tapestry and finely carved wooden panels, which match the equally impressive furniture. Before him sits a man dressed in the half-ecclesiastical garb of the ambassador. His name, as we can see from the portrait that shares his face hanging behind him, is Van Der Delft. A Dutchman by his appearance, with wispily blond hair and pale colour, he scratches the back of his hand as he looks up at this new entry.

"You are?" Van Der Delft has the peculiar vowels of his countrymen. De Winter, off guard, takes a moment to register his question.

"De Winter, Your Excellency. From the Lady Mary's household."

"I have not been told to expect you."

"Indeed not. Lady Mary does not know I am here."

"I should warn you, Master..." he casts about for the name, before finding it again. "Master de Winter, that I am not given to intrigue and I am not open to bribery."

"I do not expect you to engage in intrigue. And I do not have enough to bribe you."

"Then what is it you want?"

"Lady Mary has the support of the Emperor in her claim for the throne, does she not?"

"My master would see a staunch Catholic on the throne in England."

"Good. Mary's nerve is not as strong as it might be. She must know of his support."

"I am not sure I follow." Van Der Delft leans back in his chair, eyes bright. If he does not follow, his face suggests otherwise.

"Mary may not remain in England unless she feels she will inherit the throne. I do not counsel murder... But I say that if Mary flees, she shall never be queen."

"That is true enough, and you have not come to my office to tell me that. But the Emperor is not in a position to commit to a war to enthrone her." Van Der Delft smiles wryly.

"We do not need war. We just need Mary to feel that if there was a war, Charles would be on her side."

"You do not expect him to intervene?"

"Not now. If it comes to it, perhaps in the future."

"You said you do not come from Mary."

"I did say that. However she comes to feel it, Mary must feel as I say."

"I shall see to it." Van Der Delft scratches a pen across some scrap of paper. "You must keep me informed, Master de Winter. I would value your perspective on events."

De Winter sniffs a sort of half-laugh. "I'm sure you would!" he says, then he flounces his cloak as he turns and leaves, smiling to himself and smoothing his moustaches as he strides confidently through the ambassador's residence and back out to the street.

A few hours later, we find de Winter sitting in a dimly-lit inn, which is noisy enough to disguise the content of any conversation, but quiet enough to be heard without raising the voice much above a whisper. Across the table from him, without a drink, is a monk of some sort. He wears the simple robes of a pilgrim, cowl down off his head and around his shoulders, revealing his tonsured crown.

"I am recently returned, yes," he is saying.

De Winter swigs from an earthenware cup. "Good. You are to do a great duty."

"I am ready to do my duty to God, Sir." The monk is earnest, showing his devotion through his tone of voice but also through his movements and gestures, giving a little bow of his head as he speaks of God.

"This duty is to England. And to God." De Winter raises one eyebrow as he speaks.

"I'm not sure I follow."

"Allow me to explain, then." De Winter sits back in his chair and smiles. "The Princess Mary is a devout lady. She finds God distant from her, testing her. She needs to know that God is with her."

"Then she should pray." The monk, clean shaven around his chin and visibly marked by the smallpox, flicks his eyes around the inn.

"She has prayed. Endlessly. *You* are her salvation."

The monk begins to respond. "But-" de Winter raises his hand, foreseeing the objection.

"Before you begin with your questions, I should make myself clear. I am the agent of God in this matter."

"That is blasphemy." The monk raises his hand, almost literally fending off de Winter.

"No, brother. It is the truth. God speaks to me on behalf of the lady. But she does not listen to me. At least, she does not think I speak with the voice of The Lord. I am not a man of God. You, on the other hand, fit the part rather better. Wouldn't you say?"

"God speaks to you?"

"Yes. I have prayed with Mary, and though she does not hear the voice of The Lord in reply, I do. She needs to know that she shall be queen. Do you understand? That this vision has been put before me. She shall be England's queen, and there shall be a return to the Papal fold under her. She shall succeed."

"How can you have such confidence?" The monk shifts about in his seat. His nervousness reveals itself in his eyes and his face.

"I don't think you understand me. I have spoken to God, and this is what he tells me." De Winter notices the raised eyebrows of the monk. "What is your name, brother?"

"My name is Benedict, Sir."

"For your order?" de Winter asks. The monk nods. "Well then, Benedict... This is your chance to be a part of the restoration of the rightful Catholic faith of the nation. Do you think that God does not want this?" Benedict shakes his head. "Indeed. And you are wary of me, because I do not fit the picture you have of a chosen confidant of God. And yet here we are."

"Why would God not speak to me directly in this matter?"

"The Lord speaks in many ways. He is speaking to you now. Through me. Or are you *faithless*?" De Winter sneers the word, emphasising it cruelly.

Benedict shakes his head. "I must tell Mary that she shall be queen."

"You must tell Mary that she shall be queen. Anything you might do to persuade her will be generously rewarded. In Heaven, I mean." De Winter smiles. "Though the lady will of course be keen to remember those who have seen her through her ordeal, and her rewards will be of a manner more temporal, perhaps."

Benedict rises. "I think I understand. Where and when?"

"You remain here, Benedict. I shall return tomorrow, and I shall tell you exactly how it shall be."

It is early morning. Elizabeth is in her room, being dressed by Kat Astley, who pulls a gilt brush through the teenager's tangled auburn hair. Elizabeth, not yet dressed, fusses over her choice of jewellery, choosing carefully to enhance the look of her pale decolletage. The beginning of her passage into adulthood is apparent in this change of her body. She is no longer the girl of twelve we first met two years ago, her face having lost some of its girlish plumpness, now showing a slender neck and elegant chin. Her alabaster skin is set off by her deep-brown eyes and her hair, the same auburn red as her brother's and her late father's.

There is a thumping knock at the door. Both ladies turn to look, surprised. Without further preamble, the door opens and in strides the Baron Sudeley, fully dressed in rather fine fashion, calculated to impress. He thrusts his leg out, ostentatiously showing off the cut of his breeches.

"Good morning, dear Elizabeth!" he booms, his strutting and his unnecessary loudness quite out of keeping with ablutions and dressing. "I see that you are not yet out of your bed-clothes." He smiles as he says it, looking for much too long at the young girl's slight, pale form in her night-shift. She is discomposed, embarrassed. Kat Astley frowns at him.

"Sir!" she shouts. "This is most improper!"

"How can it be improper, Mistress? She is my ward, and she does not object to my presence." He waves away Astley's protests with a gesture, swaggering close to Elizabeth and angling his head as he again looks at her for too long. He purses his lips appreciatively. Elizabeth draws her arms around herself, but says nothing.

"My Lord Sudeley!" Astley shouts, with some venom. "I must insist that you remove yourself until the young Mistress is ready to receive you!" She bustles around him, desperately trying to interpose herself between the girl and the baron. After a moment, he seems to think better of it and turns to leave.

"I shall expect you to dine with me this evening," he says, leaning over and whispering, "enjoy your day." The baron sweeps out of the door and is gone as suddenly as he arrives. Elizabeth throws herself bodily on to the bed, bouncing on it several times, letting out a little grunt, possibly of irritation, possibly something else.

Astley stands over her. "What impertinence! A grown man to inveigle himself into your chamber!" She puts her hand on Elizabeth's shoulder. "We must speak to the queen."

"Don't be so ridiculous, Kat," Elizabeth says, turning her head up where it lies on the bed. "Catherine does not need to know of such trivialities."

"Trivialities? You are of the royal blood, young lady, and you must know that this is an outrage against decency." Astley is hot with anger, flushed about her face, all her movements jerky. Elizabeth shakes her head, then buries it in the coverlet and shouts with frustration. After a moment, she turns back to Astley and speaks again.

"Kat... You must not be angry on my behalf. I do not complain of this visit, do I?"

"It seems not!" Astley says. She sits on the bed, beside Elizabeth's prone body. "The baron is your guardian, not your father. He is a man, just like any other."

"What do you mean to suggest? That the baron somehow has designs on *me?*"

"Well... no... that would be ridiculous..."

"Then we shall hear no more of it, Mistress Astley." Elizabeth sits herself upright, pertly arranging herself. "I wish to be at my very best today. I understand that Marquess of Dorset's daughter is joining me at my lessons. Again."

"Ah, little Jane..."

"She is not *that* little any more. She has had her tenth birthday and approaches her eleventh." Elizabeth frowns at Astley, remonstrating with her for her affection for the girl.

"Madam must remember that Jane is here as the ward of the Baron Sudeley, not as a playmate – or a plaything – for you... And keep in mind that the young lady has her own claim, distant though it is, to your father's throne."

"No doubt we shall hear of it from Jane herself. I reckon that her father thinks she shall be Edward's wife."

"Yes, but Somerset and his lot will prevent that, won't they? Edward's marriage is far too valuable thing to be cast away on some English girl." As she speaks, Astley pulls a red dress over Elizabeth's head.

"Her grandmother was my father's sister. She is not just *some English girl*, Kat."

"No, but she *is* English. And these royal marriages are always made for reasons of state..."

"Yes, we have discussed this before."

"And we shall discuss it again. Madam must remember her place. If the king wishes that she marry some dashing French prince or some wealthy Italian duke, she must."

Elizabeth sighs. "I shall marry an old man, no doubt, and it shall be without charm or romance, and certainly without my consent."

"Do you think that you should be able to marry for love?" Kat Astley seems genuinely surprised to be saying this.

"My father did. At least twice." Elizabeth, knowing the challenge that she puts before Astley, tilts her head, awaiting the poor maid's response.

"Do not speak so flippantly, Madam. Your father was a great king!" Her tone is one of awed reverence. "You do not have those advantages of position."

"No. But I do, as you so frequently remind me, have royal blood running through these veins." She shows the insides of her forearms, indicating the blood she speaks of.

"It signifies, in who is eligible to even think about making a suit for you. You shall marry royalty."

"I shall marry whom I chose, Mistress Astley."

"You should be careful to whom you speak thus, Madam. The wrong ear might hear it as treason against your brother!" She laughs, and pats Elizabeth's shoulders. "You look wonderful, my dear. Now rise-" Elizabeth stands, admiring her own figure in the looking glass, "-and glide across the room..." This action Elizabeth performs admirably, a picture of youthful nobility.

We, however, shall leave these two in the midst of their lesson on deportment, and join our old friends Masters Edward Strelley and William Grindal, who are breakfasting in another part of the house.

Strelley, whilst reading from a parchment letter spread out on the table in front of him, pulls apart a small loaf, tears a lump off with his teeth, and chews vigorously. As he does so, he shakes his head and speaks, his mouth full and thus his words rougher than usual.

"Well, Master, it seems that they won the battle. James was hurt, and-" he stops, mouth open. He swallows, and resumes in a more measured tone. "It seems that one of my old acquaintances lost his life in the battle, and another of them was lost altogether."

"Lost altogether? They couldn't find his body?"

"From the letter, it sounds as though he disappeared after the battle had finished. But that he was very much alive when he did so. The lost one was the agent of the death of the other."

"Your friends fought for opposing sides?"

"Lorenzo was a mercenary whom we fought with when we campaigned in Scotland. He shot Longshawe, it seems, and nearly killed him, then my friend Pike – do you remember, the marksman? – he shot Lorenzo. Guy's writing is still quite hard to follow, but he seems to be saying that Pike just left the army and headed off into the wilderness." Strelley pauses, looking up at Grindal. "I hope he's safe and well."

"We all lose friends, Edward," he says, looking down into his own meal of porridge. "I do not know any who have reached my age that have not had to look down upon the cold corpse of a friend and wish him Godspeed on his journey."

"We were lucky to all survive our first campaign. I did try to persuade James that the life of a soldier was brutal and short, but I don't think he really understood."

"No, but then, do you? Have you mourned the loss of a dear friend? A brother? Seen your own life hang in the balance as the ferryman watches on, waiting for his fare?" Grindal takes a mouthful of his breakfast, and Strelley watches him, silent and engrossed. "You are a young man, and your sense of death has not yet been sharpened by its pointless and random action."

"What do you mean?"

"Well... Do you think that God watches each of us, and chooses when to bring us back to him?"

"I – well, no. I think that God watches each of us and lets the world take its course with us."

"That is rather brutal. God allows the infant child to grow sick and die of brain fever? And He does not intervene? Surely He is calling the chosen back to him."

"Yes, but He does not intervene to stop bad men from their sins. Take Nero or Caligula. Where was God then? He did not rain fire to prevent the Romans' leaders from murdering the first Christians in their hundreds and thousands."

"God moves in a mysterious way." Grindal's face takes on a look of contemplation, as though he has offered some profound and unassailable truth.

"I sometimes feel as though God does not move at all." Strelley, by contrast, has a canny, almost mischievous cast to his features.

"You have lost Him?"

"I'm not sure I ever found Him. I have read Hesiod, I have read Vergil, I have even read the Moslems' sacred texts. And I see no difference between those and our Bible."

"Then perhaps it is time that you find your way back to God." There is an edge in Grindal's voice now, willing Strelley to cease this line of thought.

"Don't you follow?" Strelley asks, then realises his mistake. "Ah, you don't wish to follow. I am content to be a heretic, or an atheist, or whatever it is that the men of the cloth might call me. I don't see anything in what they say to show me I am wrong."

"I shall lose my patience with you, Master Strelley, if you persist. Cleverer men than you have weighed the same words, the same arguments and evidence of natural and revealed religion, and have believed. Is that not enough for you?"

"I should not wish to be part of something that I myself could not understand, but could only be told of it by cleverer men than me."

"I see. Well, you must resume your study. If you cannot find what you seek, then perhaps attendance at Church might help? I note your absolute failure to attend. And so does the baron. Mend your ways, young man, or you shall find yourself without this cosy employ that you esteem so high. And I shall not be able to protect you."

Outside the door of the room that Elizabeth takes her lessons, a younger girl of ten years stands, smoothing her skirts. She has a hint of the Tudor about her as well, although her hair is less red than Elizabeth's, her nose less pronounced on her face. She is altogether different to the confident hauteur that we have seen in her distant cousin. She knocks on the door timidly. It is opened by Edward Strelley, who bows a little and ushers her inside. Before crossing the threshold, she courtesies, and does so again when she sees Grindal seated in his chair. Elizabeth is not yet present. The two men share a knowing look, and Strelley returns to a simple wooden chair beside the writing desk where the lesson is to take place.

Strelley offers a welcoming smile. "Lady Jane... We have prepared some text for you here. Master Grindal thought we might start with a little of Caesar's commentary on his Gallic campaigns."

"Caesar?" the girl asks. "I am familiar with some of his writing."

Grindal's eyebrows raise. "Already?" He shows some surprise. "It is well. Who has been your tutor?"

"Master Aylmer, Sir. He has given me a grounding in the classical languages." Jane Grey is demure, rather prim in her manner. She looks from Grindal to Strelley, pleased with the effect that her claim to prior knowledge has had on the tutors. Strelley eventually replies after a brief pause, during which he scrutinises the girl with his head tilted.

"I knew Aylmer at Queens'. He taught me some of my Greek and Hebrew. A good man."

"A good teacher," Jane Grey says, flatly. "I know nothing of him as a man." Her eyes are dead level in stark contrast to Strelley's, and she fixes him with a flinty stare that, given as it is by a ten-year-old girl, almost pushes him into laughing at her.

Grindal decides to intervene, just a hint of a smile on his face. "I can say with great confidence that he is a good man, just as he is a good teacher. But now, to our lesson."

Jane Grey reads the Latin of Caesar's Gallic War fluently. When called on to construe, she is confident in her grammar, if lacking a little in the vocabulary. Grindal pushes her on with a few hints, and she is making rapid progress when, perhaps fifteen minutes later, the door opens and Kat Astley announces Elizabeth.

It is clear that Elizabeth's lateness has been caused by an extended effort to create the right appearance. She is made up more heavily than usual, dressed, as we have seen, more finely than would be customary for her lessons, wearing an extra jewel here and there. She makes a careful play of removing her white gloves and looking down her nose, chin raised, at Jane.

"Good morning, My Lady," she says. "My father spoke very highly of your Grandfather. It is a pleasure to welcome you formally to this household."

Jane Grey returns the look, lifting her chin. There is a hardness to her smile, which doesn't quite suit her young face, as she appraises Elizabeth showing off with her rich attire. "It is my great pleasure to be here," Jane replies.

Elizabeth sits herself, forcing Jane to move her chair slightly to accommodate her at the desk. She looks over the work. "Caesar?" Elizabeth sneers. "Have we not moved on past this, gentlemen?"

Strelley closes his eyes for a little longer than he needs to. Grindal breathes in sharply. It is Grindal who replies, in his most soothingly diplomatic voice. "My Lady, it would be a shame to miss out on the thoughts of one of history's greatest leaders, would it not?" He looks between the two girls. "You are the daughter of a king, Jane is the great-granddaughter of a king. You must be educated not just in the language-"

Elizabeth raises a hand. "If it please Master Grindal, may we concentrate rather on the text?" She glances across at Jane to see the effect of her display of power. Jane sits, cool, impassively watching the exchange.

Elizabeth reads over the portion of text that Jane has already translated. Her own translation is rather quicker and more flowing than Jane's, but it is marred by the odd mistake from not concentrating carefully enough. As she comes to an end, she casts another superior look at her young cousin. Jane is nodding slightly, but her eyes remain indifferent. "You see," Elizabeth says, "I do not think that Caesar is much of a stylist in his writing. Great commander he may have been, I think he was rather rough. Was he not?" She directs the question at Jane, but Grindal does not leave her a chance to answer.

"Let us rather discuss the text, as the lady herself requested," he says, a little flustered by Elizabeth's showing off. Strelley watches him, an easy smile playing about his features. This sort of rancorous behaviour is obviously unfamiliar to Grindal, and Strelley seems to be enjoying his discomfort.

Jane Grey has the practised, studied intonation of one who sits carefully at her lessons and learns them well. Her translation is methodical, clear enough but lacking in expression. Elizabeth is more flamboyant, more confident in herself and able to find some fitting phrase for all but the most challenging of the Latin. It is Jane who reads the following phrase:

"Erant in ea legione fortissimi viri, centuriones, qui primis ordinibus appropinquarent, Titus Pullo et Lucius Vorenus. Hi perpetuas inter se controversias habebant, quinam anteferretur, omnibusque annis de locis summis simultatibus contendebant."

She translates, "There were in that legion two very brave men, centurions who were approaching the first rank, Titus Pullo and Lucius Vorenus. These two always had... disputes? Disputes among themselves... And..." She tails off.

Elizabeth smiles as she steps in. "Over which should be preferred." She waves a hand delicately, then sits back in her chair. "Should I continue? Every year they quarrelled over which should be... promoted... with great animosity." She smiles at Strelley. "Was this section picked carefully, Master Strelley?"

Strelley returns a wry smile. "What does the lady mean?" Elizabeth does not pursue her line of questioning out loud, though, simply shaking her head slightly at Strelley and returning to the lesson.

As the translation comes to an end, Jane Grey pulls out another book from somewhere within her clothes. It is a tiny duodecimo, recently printed by the look of it. The title is 'Institutio Christianiae Religionis', and the name of the author, barely discernible in its gilt on the spine, is Calvinus.

"I wonder if we might discuss this work of Calvin's?" she says. "I understand that the Lady Elizabeth is capable of deep discourse on such a subject and I would know her thoughts...?"

Elizabeth angles her head as she looks at Jane. "Calvin, you say? Another one of these reformers, isn't he?"

Strelley and Grindal look at each other. Grindal gives a flicker of a half-smile, indicating his consent that the discussion should go ahead. Jane has a hurt look, Elizabeth's casual dismissal of her choice of text rankling her. Strelley still has his sardonic smile, watching with interest as Elizabeth attempts to assert herself over her rival, though over what exactly they are rivals remains unclear.

"He is not merely some polemic voice of reform, My Lady," Jane returns. "His is the definitive statement of the position."

Elizabeth raises her eyebrows. "What do you take *the position* to be?"

"That man is not justified by his works on Earth, nor by his participation in the sacraments, but by faith and faith alone." Jane's voice is firm, her pride evident in every word. Grindal takes it in without comment. Strelley risks a look at Elizabeth that says 'go on then, answer that!'

"And this satisfies you?" Elizabeth asks with something of a sneer, mainly directed at Strelley rather than Jane. "Do you not think it odd that God should allow us our freedom to choose our path, to make our life's work whatever we wish, give us His church, and then whatever decision he makes about who goes to heaven is already made?"

"God knows each of us thoroughly, and he knows what choices we shall make before we make them." Jane frowns, discomposed by Elizabeth's badinage.

"Then," Elizabeth says, her tone lightening to breeziness, "we might as well say that all of our fates are decided before we even began. So the whole point and purpose of life is diminished to nothing..." She inspects her fingernails carefully, leaving her point hanging for Jane to bite back. But the younger girl masters herself.

"If God exists outside time, then whilst he may know our decisions before we make them, time still has to pass for those decisions to happen. Our life is our path to heaven, or to hell. I know which choices I shall be making." Jane puts the book away, chastened by the experience.

"And what would you have had to say to my dear father, I wonder?" Elizabeth leans forward, in false earnest. "Would you have contradicted him as you do with me? How confident would you have been in the presence of the great King Henry, not mollycoddled by these-" she gestures from Strelley, who is now suppressing a grin, to Grindal, whose eyes have rolled upwards - "*tutors* who allow us such leeway with our own thoughts?" Jane does not reply.

Strelley takes advantage of the momentary silence to speak. "Madam, might I remind you that we give you your head so that we might refine your thought, not so that you can think and speak whatever your wilder convictions lead you to conceive?"

Elizabeth eyeballs him. "Do you commit, Master Strelley, to your own position? I have not heard you say anything definite for months, and yet you sit in judgement of my opinions daily!" Her tone has risen once again from delicate to bantering. "Would you care to present your thoughts on the justification?"

Strelley ignores Grindal's rising hand, and sets off. "I do not think God would have such prejudices, Madam. He sees all that transpires within a man's heart and his mind. He knows what faith a man truly has, and what his works are done for, and if a man does good only for a reward, or he has faith only to open the gates of St Peter, then God will not be fooled."

"Bah!" Elizabeth says, equally ignoring Grindal's half-hearted attempt to silence this exchange. "Yet more avoiding the question! You can't possibly assert that Calvin and Luther are wrong, and that the Pope is just as wrong!"

Jane Grey smiles, briefly and with little ostentation, at Strelley. He notices, but keeps his face straight and his eyes locked to Elizabeth's.

"I can, and I just have. God is no man's – or woman's – fool, Madam, and He knows what lies beneath. Works done for the reward of heaven, or faith held for fear of damnation are neither of them enough to confound Him."

"So what do you do?" Elizabeth asks him, genuinely quite astonished at Strelley's bluntness. "Do you do all out of a disinterested desire to do, and to be, good?"

"No. I have made my peace, Madam, and I do as I wish."

Grindal cannot hold in a burst of laughter at Strelley's statement. Jane looks from Elizabeth to Grindal, to Strelley, but does not break into frown or smile. Elizabeth stands, and nods the tiniest of courtesies to Jane.

"Good day, Madam," Elizabeth says sharply. "If there is more of this... *lesson*, it shall be my pleasure to hear it from you tomorrow." Strelley watches her go, amusement playing across his face.

Grindal stares at Strelley. "And what was that for?"

"To show the lady that she is not the only one who can strike at another's opinion." He turns his eyes, finally, to Jane. "You must not allow her to intimidate you. She is clever, but from what I have heard, so are you."

Jane Grey is again a picture of equanimity. She holds Strelley's gaze for a little longer than she ought to, then returns to the discussion with enthusiasm.

"Do you truly have no faith, Master Strelley?" she asks. Her voice betrays a little of her shock at the directness of Strelley's statements.

"My faith, Madam, is my own affair. I shall say, though, that whatever Pope Paul, and all those Swiss and Germans arguing about wine and blood, God would have us be *good*. And autos-da-fe are not men being *good*."

Grindal sits stony-faced, listening to this apostasy. His head shakes slightly as Strelley finishes speaking. "Master Strelley," he says, quietly but firmly, "I must remind you of your status in this household."

Strelley smiles wryly. "Ah... My position. Yes... I should not give My Lord Sudeley the reason to terminate my employ, you think." Grindal frowns, but Strelley does not stop. "The baron has enough reason to dismiss me should he so wish. I think rather he keeps me here to punish me."

Jane's expression shows that she does not understand his comment. Grindal rolls his eyes. "Enough!" he sighs. "On with the lesson."

48: Longshawe

The estate at Longshawe looks out north-west, its pale under the heights of Carl Wark and Higger Tor. These bleak landmarks, in the time of our story, are covered with a dense forest. The hall is an impressive half-timbered building, much like the Bishops' House that we saw many months ago as our story began. It nestles in the shelter of the lees, protected from the fierce weather that blows in all the way from the North Sea. From the hilltop above it, one might see Sheffield to the north-east, its furnaces and foundries spewing out black smoke. In the distance, it is even possible to see Doncaster.

Now, looking out northwards, we can see two mounted figures cresting the hill, riding southwards. One is slight, young perhaps. The other has the build of a warrior. The reader will no doubt have recognised our old friends James Longshawe, and his lackey Guy Fletcher. They wear riding cloaks against the late autumn wind, and though each has the baggage of the long-distance traveller, neither carries the campaign weaponry that we have seen them with only a few weeks ago. Longshawe has his sword hanging at his thigh as a gentleman might, but he wears no armour, nor does he carry the halberd of the household guard. Guy Fletcher wears a smart riding cloak bearing the coat of arms of the Talbots, a gift from the heir to the Earldom of Shrewsbury, perhaps.

"You haven't seen your father since we before we fought at Ancrum?" Guy Fletcher says.

"No." Longshawe replies, chewing his lip. "I haven't. He and I... Well, you know already."

"So why now?"

"Because..." He thinks for a moment. "Because, when I realised I might have died, I wanted to see him. I mean, when I woke up, I thought about him. Before I thought about anyone else." Longshawe's lips curl into an ironic smile that Fletcher doesn't notice. His head turns out eastwards, looking in the direction of Sheffield and its northerly outlying villages.

"Do you want him to apologise?" Fletcher asks. "For the way he was with you when you were young?"

"It's not that. I don't think he was a bad father." Longshawe turns his head back to look at Guy.

"Were you a bad son, then?"

"Probably. I thought I knew everything. It's not that I think *he* does. But I wanted to tell him that I understand some of the things he said now. That I didn't before."

"What do you mean?"

"Well... I always thought he was selfish. He told me that what I wanted – to go to war – was senseless. And I thought he was selfish because he wanted me to stay at home with him. But that wasn't it. He wanted *me*. Not to constantly worry about me because I was away on some foreign field dodging bullets and blades."

"So he was frightened of you dying in battle?"

"Yes, of course. *I* was frightened of dying in battle. Not nearly enough, but I *was* frightened. He was frightened of losing his son."

"Aren't all of our parents scared of us dying?"

"Probably. But I was a little more enthusiastic about trying to die..."

"And that's all over now, is it?"

"I shan't be standing across a field from twenty thousand feral hairy Scotsmen again."

"No desire for glory?" Guy Fletcher smiles as he asks.

"No. I don't think glory attaches itself to the common soldiery."

"Nor very often to the nobility."

"I don't know. I think Henry would have told us that Flodden was glorious."

"And was it?"

"Not for the men who died there, no."

A few minutes later, Longshawe and his young lackey arrive at the wicket gate and allow themselves into the grounds of the estate. There is little activity in the late autumn sun, but as they become visible to the house, a retainer makes his way out from the front door.

"May I ask whom I welcome to the house of Longshawe?" The retainer is an old man, white-haired and wrinkled. He is slightly stooped with age, but his eyes still crackle with energy. Longshawe gives him a moment for recognition to dawn.

"Ah!" the domestic exclaims. "Young Master Longshawe! We had not thought to see you again. The Master will be overjoyed!"

Longshawe nods to Guy Fletcher, then tilts his head at the

servant. "This," he says to Guy, "Is my father's majordomo, Ralph." He turns back to Ralph. "We shall be staying a while. Can you have the horses stabled and my rooms made ready?"

"I shall, young Master, but I must tell you that your father is at Sheffield. He has business with the Earl of Shrewsbury and the Baron of Sheffield."

"Has he indeed? It is a little late for us to set off to follow him, and we wish to rest. Please do not announce my return to my father, Ralph. I should like to do so myself on his return."

"As you wish, young Master." Ralph bows deeply to Longshawe, which hides his smile. He has straightened his face when he returns to his almost-upright posture. Longshawe bounds into the house, leading Guy Fletcher inside. Ralph turns and follows slowly, mustering his dignity.

Longshawe shows Guy Fletcher around the house, and they find a pleasantly warm sitting room, fire burning against the autumn chill. Longshawe hall is rustic, without the ornamentation we have been used to seeing in the great houses of the royal family or the nobility. As well as its homely aspect, it is high up in the hills at the northern extent of the Derbyshire Dales, and has to be well-girt against the cold wind. It has a few ancient weapons adorning the walls, antique firearms and huge broadswords that might have been borne by some ancestral Longshawe. There are two portraits, one showing a young man who bears a striking resemblance to our Longshawe, James, and another that shows an older, wizened man in the armour of a medieval knight.

Longshawe stands in front of the fire looking at the portraits. He points to the one that looks like him. "That's my father. About thirty years ago, a long time before I was born. Everyone says I look like him, but he always insists that I look like my mother."

"It could be your portrait, Master Longshawe," Guy says, taking in the portrait himself.

"I'm 'Master Longshawe', am I? I haven't been that for a long time."

"It's what your servant calls you."

"He's my father's servant, not mine."

"Am I your servant?" Guy asks, followed by a little laugh.

"Not any more. If you ever were. More of a helper than a

137

servant."

"What about a surgeon?"

"Indeed. I had briefly forgotten that." He touches his shoulder, still bandaged underneath his riding gear. "I might not be here at all without you."

"I will tell your father that you said that," Guy says, smiling up at Longshawe. Longshawe joshes him gently. Then Guy says, "perhaps he will reward me..." and they both laugh, but the sound of activity outside the house shuts them both up quickly. Shortly afterwards, they see the dancing light from the windows indicative of the movement of bodies.

"He is here," Longshawe says, quietly, bouncing up and down on the balls of his feet. He fixes his eyes on the door, listening as the servants bustle around, organising his father's return. There is the sound of clicking footsteps on the stone floor of the corridor, and the door opens. The man who enters is clearly Longshawe's father. Their jawlines, eyebrows and cheekbones are identical, separated only by the thirty years of age that the father has over the son. The older man's face shows a little surprise mixed with the genuine delight of the relieved parent.

"James!" he exclaims, coming over to his son. He stops a couple of feet away, straightens himself and looks his son over. "I am glad to see you." His tone has flattened almost immediately after the burst of emotion he showed a moment ago, conscious of the outward display of emotion. His face settles into an expectant expression.

"I am glad to have returned, father."

"We did not part as I would have wished. For that, I am sorry." The old man's voice quavers slightly but noticeably. "I have missed your presence much. Since your mother-"

Longshawe puts his hand on his father's shoulder. The son moves a half-step closer to the father, and the father's head falls forward.

"I know," James says. "I understand a little more now."

"For that I am grateful. But I should never have let you go without my blessing."

"It was my choice to leave without it. And for that, I am sorry." A quarter minute passes, in which neither father nor son says anything. Guy Fletcher watches without blinking, taking in this exchange of

138

sentiment that signifies so much to his master, and to his master's father.

"Father," James says, "this is Guy Fletcher, my associate and saviour."

"Your saviour?" his father asks. "Then truly I owe you a debt of extraordinary gratitude. In what manner do you deserve such a title?" The old man looks solicitously at Guy Fletcher, whom the young man encourages with a raising of his eyebrows. Fletcher looks down at his feet, unwilling to allow himself to become the centre of attention.

"Master Longshawe – your son, Sir – was wounded at Pinkie. He took a ball in the side. I just helped him with his recovery."

"Nonsense!" James shouts in a bantering tone, "without Guy I would be rotting in a damp corner of that God-forsaken field. Take your credit, young man, for without you my father would be childless." He puts his arm around Guy's shoulders. His father looks from one to the other, eyes lifting and lowering to their markedly different heights.

"I feared to lose you. To be alone in the world is a great burden, son," he says. "Your sister married and gone away, then when we lost your mother – do not stop me, I would speak for once – when we lost your mother, all I felt was fear. Fear of losing you, and I could not see that every thing I said, each opportunity to go out into the world that I denied you pushed you further away. I thank God that you have returned, because it gives me the chance to tell you: I am proud of you, James. Whatever you are, whatever you have done, you have made your choices in spite of me. Your return is my salvation."

James Longshawe looks out of the window, blinking rapidly. He doesn't quite manage to stop the tears leaking from his eyes.

Later that afternoon, James Longshawe steps out of the hall, heading up the hill that looks down in one direction over the Hope valley, and in the other out towards Sheffield and the villages around it. He is clad against the cold in a hooded cloak, with fur around his face that wafts on the blustery wind. He finds a dry outcrop of rock and sits on it, facing north-east, staring out. He looks at Sheffield Castle, nestled in the confluence of rivers and their valleys that mark out the centre of the town, then follows the line a little further to a small group of houses above it. The reader may remember it as the little village of Byron Greave.

An hour or two passes, and Longshawe's shadow lengthens and rotates around him. He doesn't move, sitting in silent contemplation, watched for the last fifteen minutes by Guy Fletcher, who stands down the hill from his friend and master, watching him, with the sun at his back. As the sun begins to dip down below the horizon, Fletcher goes over to Longshawe, who evidently notices the new presence as he shifts his shoulders and shuffles across the rock.

"Sit down, Guy," Longshawe says, "and enjoy this view."

"We don't get so much of this at Doncaster."

"No. You barely notice it until it's gone. It's taken me nearly three years of war, intrigue and getting shot at to realise it." Longshawe's eyes are narrow against the wind, focused on the distant far side of Sheffield. "One can hardly see to the next street in London."

"And the smell..." Fletcher says.

"And the smell," Longshawe repeats. "Do you know what, Guy? I almost found myself missing it – the smell, I mean – when we were out on campaign."

"Do you want to go back?" There is a plea in Guy's question, which seems to surprise even him.

"To London?" Longshawe replies. "Yes. I made a promise to the old king that I intend to keep. I can't look after that boy from Scotland. Or from here. So yes, soon enough, we shall return to London."

Fletcher stands, his fresh and relatively warm limbs moving quickly and easily, and holds out his hand to Longshawe, hauling him up from his seating position by leaning back against the weight. There is a broad smile on his face.

"Shall we go inside, Master Longshawe?" he says.

49: How Strelley receives the admonition of his betters, then provokes the rage of his Lord.

Edward Strelley sits in the window of his garret room, reading. The book he has open is very old, hand-written in some seemingly indecipherable ancient language. He has out in front of him a set of papers in his own neat hand, and every now and again scratches the pen across the work as he construes a new sentence, or arrives at a better translation than was already recorded. The autumn sun is strong and the weather is warm and pleasant. Elizabeth sits outside with her stepmother, Dowager Queen Catherine, and they are playing some card game as they take a drink. They play together happily, enjoying the last of the good weather.

Strelley watches them for a minute or two. He reads on their faces something of a thawing in the relationship between them. The queen occasionally puts her hand on Elizabeth's, or smiles warmly at her. For her part, Elizabeth is less stern and frosty, showing more enjoyment of the queen's company, indeed perhaps a little affection as well.

Strelley returns to his work, glancing up occasionally as this domestic scene continues. His attention is caught by the arrival of Thomas Seymour, who strolls up to the two women with some swagger. Seymour twirls his moustaches, smoothes his doublet and leans demonstratively over the card game. Strelley cannot hear at this distance what is said, but he watches as Elizabeth laughs at whatever joke has been told. Catherine smiles, but is not so enraptured as her stepdaughter. Seymour calls over a servant, who fetches him a chair, and he sits with them, getting involved in their game.

Strelley watches for a minute or two, before trying to concentrate on his translation. He is unable to focus, though, and finds himself frequently looking up to see what is happening. Frustration colours his face, and he scribbles angrily at a poorly-constructed sentence. Then he looks out of the window again, seemingly giving up on the work. After a short while, the Baron takes Elizabeth's wrist in his hand. She looks at him in surprise and confusion. He smiles back at her, utters some mollifying words, and she softens. Catherine forces a smile of encouragement, but when Seymour looks away, her face betrays her own misgivings.

Strelley pushes his work aside, and watches more intently. Baron Sudeley continues to smile broadly, kissing Catherine vigorously, pushing her close to Elizabeth as he does so. Strelley strains his eyes to see, but he is sure that Sudeley looks at Elizabeth whilst kissing her stepmother. The girl looks away, finding some distant bird or animal to attend. She maintains this stern removal of her attention from Catherine and Seymour for a half-minute after this momentary crude display of affection. Catherine looks briefly to Seymour, upbraiding him perhaps. He doesn't seem to notice.

The card game restarts, with Seymour as a part. He is effusive, his every movement and gesture exaggerated. Elizabeth seems restrained, awkward by comparison. It is clear that Catherine is doing her best to mediate between the two, trying to involve Elizabeth in the baron's exuberance, and to tame his excesses to make her less uncomfortable. The queen plays this part with dignity, and Elizabeth gradually seems to relax, forgetting the baron's earlier strange behaviour.

Strelley rolls his eyes, and focuses his attention again on the paper before him. The effort involved in not watching the drama playing itself out in the gardens is palpable, and he frequently shakes his head, crosses out and wrinkles his nose in disgust at his own poor construal. He does not notice that Seymour more than once looks up to his garret room, seeing him framed in the glass. He manages for perhaps fifteen minutes before casting his eyes out of the window once more.

What he sees is extraordinary. The Baron Sudeley has in his hands a pair of scissors of the sort that might belong to a tailor or seamstress, and he is cutting away at Lady Elizabeth's skirts. Elizabeth herself is pinned in her seat by Queen Catherine, who has her arms wrapped around Elizabeth's shoulders, tipping her backwards so her legs are off the ground. Elizabeth's face is hidden, but her feet kick about as though in protest. Catherine is smiling, occasionally nodding her head almost automatically. Sudeley pursues his work with considerable enthusiasm, tearing to pieces Elizabeth's dress such that after only a few minutes, she is left in little more than a bodice and her petticoats. Sudeley sits back to admire his handiwork, and Elizabeth is released from Catherine's pinioning.

The young woman stands, red-faced. It is not clear if she has been crying or not, but after a few breaths, each accompanied by the pronounced rising and falling of her chest and shoulders, she walks quickly away into the house. Strelley continues to watch for a minute or two more as Catherine rises, slaps Seymour firmly in the face, and follows Elizabeth into the house. Despite the blow, to which Seymour responds by rubbing his chin gently, his face is creased into a malevolent and victorious smile. Strelley glowers at him, but when he sees Seymour lift his head up to look in the direction of the house, he returns to his papers in front of him. Once again he does not realise that Seymour is looking at him.

Strelley does his best to be quiet as he descends from the attic down into the main house. He twists around a passing uniformed servant, and threads his way towards Elizabeth's rooms. When nearby, he opens a door hidden in the wall, and slips through, pulling it to behind him.

The door opens into a narrow, unplastered corridor that leads into the midst of Elizabeth's quarters. He creeps along, careful not to indicate his presence by the slightest sound. His discretion is hardly needed, as Elizabeth's furious voice can quite clearly be heard from his listening post.

"Bastard!" she yells. "How dare he!"

The voice that replies is that of Elizabeth's governess, Kat Astley. "I am sure he didn't mean anything by it, My Lady." Astley's voice is shot through with concern. "What on earth were you all doing?"

"Playing cards. He said that we should gamble, as he does with his friends when they play. I didn't fully understand his implication."

"Did the queen not intervene?" Astley asks, surprised. "I mean, did she not say anything to stop him?"

"She helped him!" Elizabeth howls. "She held me while he did it."

"Truly? Queen Catherine did this with him?" Astley looks out from underneath knitted brows, quite skeptical of her young charge's story.

"I am frightened of him, Mistress Astley. If he behaves in this way, I do not feel safe in this house."

"Well, I shall tell the queen, then." Astley speaks with a sort of firm finality that shakes Elizabeth's confidence.

"Please, Kat, do not! I would not wish it that he should think to have intimidated me."

"But you *are* frightened, Elizabeth. And Catherine has enough power with him to stop it."

"If you think it right..."

Strelley sneaks back along his passage. He waits for a minute at the door, listening carefully. When he is sure no one is in the corridor, he opens the door as gently as he can. As he does so, he swears loudly as he notices Kat Astley watching him.

She shakes her head. "No, not the saviour himself, just a governess." She narrows her eyes. "What did you hear?"

"What?" Strelley says, arranging himself, trying desperately to look innocent, and failing miserably.

"I mean what did you hear the lady say to me just now?" Astley purses her lips. "Come, now, Master Strelley, I am no fool, nor are you. You were in that wall, listening. I had an idea it might be you, actually."

"What?" Strelley says again, this time without dissimulation.

"You have Elizabeth's best interest at heart – most of the time – unlike a lot of the other people in this God-forsaken house. And a cunning mind. And not a lot of shame."

Strelley frowns. "I heard nothing that I had not already seen with my own eyes," he says, waving his hand vaguely in the direction of the gardens.

"If Seymour persists in this madness," Astley whispers, "we shall all hang, whether it be for treason against Edward, or for refusing whatever Baron Sudeley wants out of this."

"I shall not hang for nothing," Strelley says.

"Make no mistake, my boy, that man will have us all strung up if we stand in his way."

"No. I mean that if I shall hang, it may as well be for something."

"What do you mean? Do not challenge him. He already has his evil eye on you. I have heard him say so myself."

"Then it would be a shame to disappoint him." Strelley looks past her along the corridor, at nothing in particular.

"Master Strelley!" Astley hisses, trying to get his attention. "I can forgive you your anger. Christ only knows, I am angry myself. But if you place Elizabeth in danger I shall call down every one of Heaven's avenging angels on you! Control yourself, for all of our sakes!"

Strelley lowers his head. "I cannot stand to see Sudeley abuse the lady thus. I shall make it my business to bring it to an end, but I shall employ every caution. If any danger results, it shall be mine alone."

"I hope you are as clever as you think you are, young man. These people could end your life in a moment, in nothing more than a fit of rage at being gainsaid or frustrated. You have already roused his anger with your trick at that ball! Oh yes," she says, noticing the confused look on Strelley's face, "we all know everything about it, Sir! It is not your *place* to chaperone the lady, nor to act as moral compass for the nobility." She accompanies this with a jab of a pointed finger.

Strelley pushes out his bottom lip, and swallows hard. "What would you have me do?"

"For the best? Nothing. Accept that life will always be thus. Some people get what they want, and others must do as they are told."

Strelley breathes out slowly. "I understand. Shall you tell the queen of Elizabeth's feelings?"

Astley shakes her head. "Just as it isn't your place to govern the baron, it is not your place to govern me! Now go before I lose my patience altogether." She dismisses him with a gesture, and he turns and leaves. As soon as he is out of hearing, she lets out a long, exasperated sigh.

Strelley sits in his garret, reading from a weathered leather-bound book. There is a knock at his door, and he carefully puts the book down, wedging another piece of paper in it so that the paper protrudes from between the leaves. He frowns a little as he rises to go to the door. It is Grindal, whose face is flushed red from the exertion of the climb to the top of the house.

"Edward," Grindal says, flatly, barely raising his eyebrows in acknowledgement. "May I come in?" He doesn't wait for an answer, instead pushing in to the room as Strelley backs out of his way. He sits in Strelley's chair, looks at the book, then puts it down.

"I do not approve," Grindal continues, "of your continued poor behaviour regarding Lady Elizabeth. Firstly, you persist in challenging her every thought. I do not think it is right for her to be thus frustrated, least of all by her tutors." Strelley starts to make a response, but Grindal silences him by continuing more forcefully. "Then there is the matter of what we shall call your interventions with the baron. I can understand your attitude to him, but I must counsel you against any more meddling."

"Have you spoken to Kat Astley?" Strelley asks, his voice hard.

"Of course I have. Both she and I like you, Edward, and we have great respect for your learning and your unfathomable ability to keep the good graces of the lady despite your desire to argue with her at every turn. Does it surprise you that we discuss you?"

"I suppose it does."

"You do not go unnoticed. Elizabeth speaks very highly of you in your absence. Does that surprise you?"

"Umm..." Strelley tries to think of a suitable answer.

"It should. She is a but young girl next to you, Master Strelley, and whatever the intention in your reproaches, it is rather by good fortune than any stratagem of yours that she stands for your belligerence." Grindal wipes his brow. "Forgive me," he says in a much quieter voice. "I do not feel well."

"Do you wish me to fetch some curative from Gilbert?"

"Perhaps. Have you listened to what I have told you? Will you restrain yourself?"

"I apologise for my rashness. I am conscious of the danger to myself, but I do not wish to bring harm to you or Mistress Astley, nor any other member of the household."

"You would do well to remember that. And try not to be discovered reading such material. It does not sit well in these times." Grindal stands, and leaves. After the door is closed, Strelley bangs his fist down on his writing-desk in frustration.

Later on, in the gloom of the autumn evening, Strelley sits alone in the servants' refectory, eating absently from a wooden bowl as he reads the same volume as he was reading earlier. There is a sound of approaching footsteps. At first, Strelley doesn't seem to notice, but the footsteps stop close by. The silence is intense enough to draw his attention, and he looks up. Standing across from him is Baron Sudeley, who is sneering down at him. Sudeley is conspicuously armed with sword and poniard at either hip. He twirls his finely-honed moustaches.

"Good evening," Sudeley intones, rather unctuously. Strelley, after a considered pause, stands in recognition of his superior. "So," the baron continues, "you *do* recognise me as your master...?" Sudeley leaves the words hanging for some moments, then pulls away Strelley's chair, pointedly sitting on it, pushing it backwards on to its back legs, bracing his feet against the table-leg.

"Sir?" Strelley says. "As Master of the House-" Sudeley waves his hand to shut Strelley up.

"Don't be disingenuous. You understand that Lady Elizabeth is *mine,* don't you?"

"She is your ward, Sir, as you are husband to the Queen Dowager Catherine."

"Ah, Master Strelley, this pretended naivety is rather touching. She is *mine* to do with as I wish." Sudeley looks up at him and sniffs, revelling in the awkwardness of the situation.

"I do not follow you," Strelley says, eyes narrow, buying himself time to think. He looks about the room, fixing briefly on the door that leads out. Sudeley has positioned himself so as to interpose, facing Strelley. There is no route to escape, not without getting too close to the baron.

"Oh, but I think you do," Sudeley says. "Whatever power you think you might have over her, or the queen, or over me, it is naught but ashes and dust."

Strelley takes a half step back. "I do not follow," he says again, firmly this time. "I do not hold any power over Elizabeth." His eyes flick to the door again.

"Indeed not." Sudeley laughs, loudly and for a little too long. "Elizabeth is mine. Catherine is mine. You are nothing but a *servant,* boy!"

Strelley frowns. "I know that." He scowls at Sudeley, weight back on his heels.

"And yet it seems that Elizabeth does not."

"I confess myself baffled, My Lord." Strelley shuffles backwards again.

"Elizabeth's childish infatuation with you is-" Sudeley stops speaking as Strelley begins to laugh, and leaps to his feet, covering the distance between them in no time at all. He leans in, flecking Strelley

147

with spit as he bellows. "You are an insolent blackguard! I shall have you dismissed! How dare you presume..." Sudeley runs out of words.

Strelley arranges his countenance in the most serious manner he can muster. "I do not hope for, encourage or seek the affection of the Lady Elizabeth." He fights to restrain the thousand things that he might say.

"And yet!" Sudeley spits. He notices that Strelley's eyes have fixed themselves on the exit, wrinkles his nose, then turns to look. Standing behind him, watching with eyebrows raised, is Elizabeth herself. "What!?" he shouts. "How long-?" He doesn't finish his question, instead spinning on his heel and striding towards Elizabeth. "Out!" he screams. "Out!" And he pushes Elizabeth out of the refectory. Strelley sits down, shoulders rising and falling.

It is night. Grindal and Strelley sit opposite each other in Grindal's room. There is a heavy silence between them which neither seems able to break. Eventually, Grindal says, quietly, "Perhaps you should leave the house for a few days? Could you go to London? Stay with your friend?"

"I should not have to leave for his wounded pride," Strelley says, shaking his head.

"But his pride *is* wounded, and you, your presence here, it is like salt rubbing into that wound. Leave, whilst you are able. Before any ill should befall you. I shall smooth the path of your return if I can."

"That is admitting defeat."

"Indeed it is. You are beaten, though. You must see that."

"I could appeal to-" Strelley begins. He sees Grindal's face darken. "That would only make matters worse."

"It would. Whatever value the lady, or the queen, place in you, an appeal to them is only likely to rouse the baron's anger yet further. You must retreat, Master Strelley, to fight another day. Surely you learned that in your experiences of war? You counsel Elizabeth every day to bend before the wind, such that she might live."

"*Live*? You can't think that Sudeley would go as far as that?" Strelley's eyes have widened at the very real danger he has created for himself.

"Neither of us know, do we?" Grindal replies, with a resigned sigh. "But we both see that he is enraged, and his next move will be made in that anger."

"I shall go to London. Perhaps I can find employ in Mary's household with de Winter."

"You mistake my suggestion, Edward. You cannot be visible."

"What about seeking the king's own protection?"

"Sudeley is the king's uncle. He has his ear. You have but a little chance of the king remembering you and even less of him standing as your protector."

"I see. I shall go to Gilbert, first of all."

"That is a more appropriate suggestion. You must hide yourself, Edward, away from this raging beast that you have unleashed."

It is early in the morning when Edward Strelley departs Chelsea Manor, riding a horse that he has chosen specifically as it will not be missed from the stables. His saddlebags bulge with his books, giving them the oddly blocky look that is characteristic of the scholar's satchel. His sword and poniard are in his belt, his hands gloved against the cold, and the hood of his riding cloak is raised and tightened to hide his face. The hoofbeats echo around the Manor's courtyard, and he is soon gone from sight and hearing as he presses his mount to a canter. Looking back at the house, it is possible to see that there are two windows with faces in them watching him disappear. One is Grindal, whose developing illness has left him grey-skinned and miserable. The other is Elizabeth, whose expression as she sits framed in the embrasure is inscrutable.

During the morning, Thomas Seymour can be heard more than once berating one or another unlucky servant who has failed to impress in some minor fashion. His anger shows in his flushed appearance, and those who meet him cannot fail to notice the rancid stink of yesterday's liquor on his breath. The domestics that are the victims of his random outbursts all pull faces as they catch the smell, but he is not put off his course.

Some time after breakfast, Sudeley is sitting in one of the parlour-rooms staring out of the window. His dress is disarranged, but not in the studied, almost elegant manner that we have seen him adopt previously, rather showing a real lack of care for his morning toilet. A door creaks open, and Grindal emerges into the light. The brightness of it accentuates his pallor, and as he notices the baron sitting his eyes close in frustration. He makes to withdraw, but Sudeley has noticed him and it is too late.

"Grindal!" Sudeley growls. "Get over here." The unceremonious language is accompanied with a wagging finger. Grindal sighs out his despair, and pads across to the other side of Sudeley, standing in the light of one of the tall windows to hide his expression as much as possible.

"My Lord," Grindal says, acknowledging the baron with a bow of his head. "What might I do-" His question is interrupted by a derisive snort.

"That boy you keep. Strelley. He must go. He is disgrace to this house." Grindal listens to the baron's words without comment and without a change in his expression. "Do you understand me? I want him gone. By the afternoon."

"My Lord already has his wish. Edward Strelley left Chelsea this morning." Grindal again bows his head, showing supplication but hiding the faintest hint of a smile.

"My wish, tutor, is that his black heart had never darkened my home, my ward and my wife. We are well rid of him. If you are to take on another secretary, I forbid you to choose one with so little regard for his betters."

"As you wish, My Lord." Grindal takes a step forward, making to leave Baron Sudeley's presence. Sudeley raises a hand, palm outwards, to stop him.

"Your continued employment depends on it. You are thought of rather highly by some, considering your lack of judgement. Should you wish to take up this same position with any other young person of standing, you have much work to do to repair your reputation."

Grindal finds there is nothing to say, so says nothing.

Sudeley stares at him, the knot of anger in his stomach forcing itself out a little more. "I would not keep you, Sir, were it my choice." There is a jeering edge to his voice. "Soon enough I shall have what I want."

Grindal bows his head a third time, and takes another step forward. Finding his way unbarred, he makes his exit as quickly as his faltering legs will allow, and shuts the door behind himself before blowing out his breath through pursed lips, with eyes screwed shut.

"Gone?" Elizabeth says. She sits in her withdrawing room, attended by Kat Astley and Grindal, whose colour has risen a little so that he looks more like a living, breathing human being.

"Yes, Madam," Grindal replies, "gone this morning. I am given to think that Madam understands the reasons for his departure." Astley lays a gentle hand on Elizabeth's shoulder. The girl puts her own on top of it, looks up to her governess, then back at Grindal.

"Gone?" She repeats, stressing the word into several syllables. "I had not foreseen it."

Astley adopts a soft voice, almost a whisper. "It is for the best,

Madam. He and the baron could not adapt themselves to each other."

"You mean that Strelley cared for me and meant to keep that bastard away from me?" Elizabeth spits. "You mean that Sudeley saw in him a protector who had only my interests and not his own in mind?"

Grindal shakes his head at her. "You must be careful, My Lady. Above all do not anger the baron further."

"He is the architect of all of this. It was he that confronted Strelley. It was he that conceived the ludicrous notion that Strelley had some sort of inappropriate interest in me. It was jealousy that led him to it. Why must I suffer for his arrogance?" The governess and the tutor listen to this impassioned speech of their ward, and look at each other.

"I repeat my warning," Grindal says, "that the baron's anger is not a trifle to be played with. He is a powerful man and he has few scruples as we have already seen."

Astley waits for him to finish, then adds her own thoughts. "Baron Sudeley may have been right that you should never have had a young man like him in your lessons. He was too free with you."

Elizabeth glares at her aslant. "I encouraged him to be thus. Mistress Astley, *you* encouraged him to be thus. He was free with me because I would have it so."

"But," Astley says, sternly, "that freedom may be acceptable in a counsellor or a friend. Not in a servant."

"You are a servant," Elizabeth shoots back, "and you practise great freedom with me."

"I am a woman, Madam." Astley's reply is curt.

"He was my friend. Not some ridiculous romantic lover!"

"I should think not," Astley says, looking to Grindal for some support. He makes a face of great sadness, composing his reply.

"Baron Sudeley only knew that you held him in great regard. Sudeley also knew that Edward Strelley influenced you, and Sudeley knew that Edward Strelley does not like him."

"So he was a threat," Elizabeth says. "I should rather have had him for my influence than you two. Neither of you has it in you to stand up to him."

"With respect, Madam," Grindal says, patiently trying to bring her out of her anger, "Neither of us has pricked the baron so. Whatever your thoughts, keep them to yourself when Sudeley is about or you risk yourself and your friend, if you insist on thinking of him as such." He nods to Astley, bows to Elizabeth, and turns about. Over his shoulder, he adds, "we will continue our lessons this afternoon. We must not be felt to be lamenting his absence."

As Grindal suggests, Elizabeth's lessons carry on that day, although there is a sombre quality to their exchanges which reflects their mood. Elizabeth herself is distracted, barely focusing on the words in front of her. In the absence of the crib which would have been prepared by Strelley, progress is slow and frustration is quick to surface. Grindal's own difficulties concentrating are partly due to worry at Strelley's absence but mainly due to his own poor health, which manifests itself in heavy, laboured breathing and sallow skin.

"My Lady," Gilbert is saying, "you must learn to recognise this subjunctive mood of the verb. As we have discussed, it indicates doubt rather than certainty, possibility rather than necessity."

"How apposite, Master Grindal, when doubt and possibility are all we have?" Her voice has an edge of irritability to it that Grindal is quite aware of but chooses not to notice.

"Madam must also learn that change is inevitable and that there will be times in her life when she must cope with that change or be swallowed up by it." Grindal manages to summon some patience with Elizabeth, and he speaks soothingly to her. "Madam, whatever our thoughts or regrets, if we are to do the best by both ourselves and our departed friend, we must not bemoan our situation, but rather bend ourselves to turning it to our advantage."

"I have not got the energy for such machinations today, Sir," Elizabeth says quietly. "I am not altogether well."

"You are quite well, Madam, as we both know. Do not make excuses." She seems about to interrupt, but he continues, the force of his greater age, wisdom or perhaps just determination allowing him the victory. "If you reckon me harsh or unsympathetic, it is a misapprehension. I have more care for you than almost anyone else in the world does, Madam, and it is not out of spite or a lack of pity that I continue to counsel you as I do."

She shakes her head at him, narrow-eyed and angry, but says nothing. Grindal looks at her with his watery eyes, and thinks about how to carry on. Eventually he settles on his decision.

"Madam, I too regret Strelley's having gone. But we both must hide it as best we can. Else the baron will be further angered and may act out of spite."

Again, the teenager says nothing, but this time she doesn't look at Grindal either. His features are all compassion, but Elizabeth does not see, whether deliberately or otherwise. It is after only the briefest time spent in this uncommunicative situation when the door opens and Baron Sudeley steps into the room. His doublet is unfastened, his beard untrimmed. The red circles under his eyes have, if anything, grown since the morning.

Grindal manages to control his expression, remaining neutral enough for Sudeley not to remark it. Elizabeth, on the other hand, wrinkles her nose and scowls at him. The baron does not fail to notice her combative mien, and immediately there is a sense of tension between them.

"Your scribe has not returned?" Sudeley asks Grindal. "It is for the best. He has failed to endear himself to several members of this household, myself included." His eyes flick to Elizabeth, to check her reaction to what he says. She has not changed, still frowning at him. He decides to continue with his brazen calumny. "I must ask you before your pupil that you more carefully consider your next choice of assistant."

Grindal nods resignedly. "As you have already suggested, My Lord." Elizabeth watches him as he speaks, her face going from anger to disbelief.

"You aren't going to let him get away with that?" she says to Grindal. "Master Strelley only failed to endear himself to you, My Lord Sudeley, because he challenged you when you did wrong to me." Grindal sighs and rolls his eyes, recognising that whatever advice he has given Elizabeth in the past day has gone unheeded. Sudeley pulls a wry, menacing smile.

"Well, Madam," the baron says, "he is gone whether it be to your liking or not. I will take my leave, Master Grindal, until you can impress upon your pupil the need for her to have respect for the master of her house." He sniffs pointedly, and flounces out of the room with a hint of a smile on his face. Grindal shakes his head in a mixture of disappointment and censure, but says nothing further.

A few days later, Baron Sudeley leaves Chelsea Manor without great fanfare, only accompanied by a single footman, although both Sudeley and the footman are armed with swords, poniards and pistols. They take the road east towards Westminster, and ultimately follow it through towards St Paul's. Their final destination is the warehouse of the merchant Gilbert. Sudeley enters alone, his retainer standing watch outside the door in a manner calculated to be inconspicuous, but all the more obvious for it.

Sudeley stands before Gilbert, who is writing on some papers at his desk. It takes him a full half-minute to satisfy himself that all is in order, and he stands the papers up on end, tapping them against the desktop to line them up, as he takes in the nobleman in front of him. Both are familiar to the other. Sudeley has a malicious glint in his eye. Gilbert, by contrast, has a wary, circumspect look.

"My Lord Sudeley," Gilbert says, remaining seated and not inviting the baron to sit himself, "to what do we owe this most agreeable surprise?"

Sudeley, who obviously knows Gilbert and his irreverent manner, ignores the flattery. "Gilbert, I need you to do something for me."

"Ah," Gilbert replies, eyebrows raised. "If it is me you have sought, it is a matter of delicacy, perhaps?"

"One might say so. Or, one might say, it is a matter of the greatest indelicacy. I need you to help me be rid of someone."

"We are an honourable house of dealers, importers and exporters of fine goods, Sir." Gilbert teases him with his playful tone. "We are not in the business of, as you so aptly put it, matters of indelicacy."

Sudeley thinks about threatening Gilbert for just a moment, but masters himself. He is dressed, unlike when we saw him earlier, as befits a nobleman, finely cut clothes and impressive adornments. "Come, Master Gilbert, we both know that you are a well-connected man. I do not ask you personally to conduct the work I require."

"And you expect me to arrange matters? Why?"

"Because," Sudeley says, producing a large cloth bag of evidently considerable weight, "I will pay your black heart in the way you most desire. Half now, half when the job is done."

Gilbert looks at the bag. "For a person of your station, Sir, that is a tenth-"

"Your target is not a person of my station." Gilbert accepts the baron's interruption without comment, but draws breath audibly, contemplating.

"Name your victim, then," Gilbert says, eyes still on the bag.

"His name is Edward Strelley, formerly a servant in my household." Gilbert shows no sign of recognition of this familiar name. "There is one additional difficulty," Sudeley continues, "that I do not know where he is. He fled my house yesterday."

"That is of little consequence. Anyone can be found." He pouts his bottom lip. "But that does require a touch more effort on the part of my associates. That," he points to the bag, "is a quarter of the total I expect. But you may bring the rest on completion of the job."

"So it is arranged?"

"You have engaged my services, Baron Sudeley. But a name alone is rather more of a challenge than either of us would wish."

"Very well. He was the servant of William Grindal, who is tutor to Lady Elizabeth in my household. He is about my height, with dark hair which he doesn't trouble himself to cut short. I do not think he could grow a beard even if he wished it. Speaks with a northern accent. Sly, with a ready wit which he turns to mischief whenever he can."

"Grindal has sent him here to make purchases. I know him. Consider it done, My Lord Sudeley," Gilbert says with a sort of finality that the baron picks up on immediately.

"Then, I take my leave of you. I wish to see him, Gilbert. Dead."

"You have seen the last of him." Sudeley turns and leaves, the brief flash of light from outside illuminating Gilbert's office for a moment. Gilbert sits back in his chair, touching the tips of his fingers together. His smile is unfathomable, but it lights up his whole face.

51: Caroline de Winter provides a glimmer of hope in the darkness

James Longshawe sets out with Guy Fletcher for Sheffield, some ten miles distant, tucked away behind the hills of Fulwood. Their destination is the castle, property as we have seen of the Earl of Shrewsbury. Their invitation has arrived, prompted by a letter from the earl's son, that they might visit the earl again and join him for a feast in celebration of the victories in Scotland. Longshawe has shaved himself clean, ridding himself of the dirty blond beard that he has worn for the time we have known him. His hair has been cut back, taking away some of the look of the soldier that he has previously been, and returning some of the look of the gentleman that he has chosen to become. He sits high in the saddle, but the shoulder above his wound hangs a little, betraying the stiffness and pain it still gives him. Guy Fletcher rides a six-year-old from the stables at Longshawe House, needing for the first time a fully grown mount rather than the smaller one he has previously ridden. The first wisps of his own beard are visible around his chin, evidence of his ascent into manhood.

They ride in the bright early winter light as a fine mist fills the valleys before them. The scene, as they ride side-by-side at a walking pace, is one of calm, so unlike the war of which they have recently been a part. Fletcher looks happy, almost without care. Longshawe, despite all these changes, has an apprehensive countenance.

"Shall we meet the baron?" Fletcher asks. "That's George's father, isn't it?"

"Yes, I imagine we will," Longshawe answers. His frown grows more intense.

"Do you not wish to see him?"

"It is not that. The baron is an old fool. I doubt if he would even recognise me."

"Well... What, then?" Fletcher speaks confidently, less the lackey and more the companion.

"There may be other people there."

"You are speaking in riddles."

"People whom I have not seen since... Well, since before I met you."

"That will be most of them. You haven't been back, have you?"

"Not since after Ancrum Moor. Do you know why we were sent

157

to war in the first place?"

"You and George de Winter were caught fighting. I know that."

"Do you know why, though?"

"Umm... No, I never asked."

"And we never spoke about it. I don't think George ever truly forgave me."

Fletcher sighs. Then he asks, pointedly, "for what?"

"I spoke... inappropriately... to his sister. The baron's daughter."

"Ah! So you fear she will remember the insult."

"I don't know. Perhaps I want her to remember. Remember *me*."

Guy allows himself a half-smile, then coughs to disguise it. "You are apprehensive?" He raises his eyebrows at Longshawe, who returns him a look that says Guy has the right idea.

"When I think about all that has happened in the past couple of years, it hardly seems to matter. But when I think of *her*..."

Fletcher has the sense to say nothing. Longshawe loses himself in reflection for a long period, during which Guy glances over to him occasionally, without getting a response. Neither of them seems to want to break the silence, but Guy is animated, looking at the sights that he vaguely remembers from two years previously.

"So," Guy says, after a quarter hour of silence, "this lady..." He doesn't go so far as to ask a direct question.

"This lady..." Longshawe repeats, mechanically. "She is rather pretty, Guy, and very clever. Like Edward. Clever. Not pretty. Edward is not pretty. She is probably married to some lord or other by now."

"She is a baron's daughter. That is her curse to bear."

"Indeed. Though I imagine she will make some old man very happy, if only for a short while."

"You mean she is a shrew?"

"No. She is intolerant of fools. I do not think a future as a mother of noble babies appeals to her. I don't think marriage and family is her goal."

"So she may have closeted herself in some nunnery by now?"

"Perhaps. Not so many of them around any more, though. Not for them..."

"The Catholics, you mean?" Guy asks.

"Yes. I wonder how the baron carries on. He probably does as he's told by Shrewsbury. I don't think George got his strength of mind

158

from his father."

"Do you really think that Edward and his Evangelism have taken hold? Up here?"

"What?" Longshawe asks, nonplussed.

"I mean that all of our contact is with people who are close to the king. The Protector, his men... All of them courtiers or attached to them. What about the *people*?"

"Surely the king's word..." Longshawe doesn't complete his thought.

"I mean, does some yeoman farmer actually understand what the priest says to him at church? What about the husbandmen? What about their wives?"

"Why this sudden concern for the people?" Longshawe angles his head skeptically.

"Because, Master Longshawe," Guy returns with a pointed look, "I am one of them, even if you are not."

"You can read," Longshawe says bluntly. "Edward has taught you that."

"I can read. I can follow the Mass now, actually."

"Truly?"

"I know what it says. I know the meaning of most of it. But, were I ever to make it to church, Master Longshawe, and the priest were to tell me how *I* should worship God, I do not know how I would react."

"What do you mean, 'were I ever to make it'? We attend a service when we can."

"I have counted and recorded it, Master. Since I have been in your service, I have attended thirty-two services. In over two years. You have been present at thirteen of those."

"Do you worry for your soul?" Longshawe asks, laughing loudly. "Or mine?"

"I do not think God counts our attendance, but our devotion."

"And you think me un-Christian, do you?" The laughter has subsided, but Longshawe's smile is still broad.

"No..." Guy's voice falters. Longshawe shakes his head.

Two hours later, they arrive at Sheffield Castle. The earl's household is there, liveried footmen in their scores indicating the presence of the earl himself. There are others, wearing insignias of the Baron of Sheffield, and one or two can be seen wearing the Strelley family crest. Longshawe points these out to Guy. They notice that their arrival seems to have sparked extra activity, as some of the servants respond to them by turning and disappearing into the interior of the castle.

It is only a few minutes before they have their answer. The earl arrives at the head of a large company and welcomes them warmly. Longshawe is only the son of a gentleman, but the earl treats him as if he were a lord. Guy Fletcher follows them, paying close attention to the conversation but finding that it consists of little but pleasantries. Shrewsbury thanks Longshawe again for his continued interest in his son George, and commiserates with him over his wound.

"George told me," Shrewsbury says, gesturing vaguely in the direction of Guy, "that this lackey of yours was your saviour!"

Longshawe turns to Guy, and they stop their progress through the castle. "Yes," he says quietly. "I confess that I did not know much about it. Master Fletcher here is a master surgeon."

Guy smiles at the memory, but says nothing. Shrewsbury picks up, "a good lackey on the battlefield is a precious commodity. Fletcher, is it?" Guy nods. "Well, if Longshawe ever releases you, my son would have you for his own." Fletcher colours to his ears.

Longshawe pats him on the shoulder. "He's too good at saving my skin for that."

Shrewsbury personally leads them into a large hall, where final preparations are being made for the feast. Baron de Winter sits across the hall, his face displaying the characteristic ruddiness of the habitual drunk. His daughter Caroline stands on seeing the earl and his companions, and walks directly over to them.

"My Lord Shrewsbury," she says, making a slight courtesy. "May I speak with these gentlemen?" Shrewsbury pouts his bottom lip. Caroline de Winter frowns at him. "Alone, if I may?"

Shrewsbury raises his eyebrows, but after a moment's consideration, he shuffles off in the direction of the Baron de Winter, and seats himself next to him.

"Longshawe," Caroline says without further introductions, "I have received a letter. From my brother. The news it brings... Well, it concerns you and your footman. Please sit down." She directs him to a table nearby, where Longshawe settles, his nerves showing clearly on his face. He says nothing, waiting for Caroline to continue.

She inhales deeply, takes a letter from inside her sleeve, and begins to read.

"Dearest Sister,

"I write with sad news. My friend and yours, Master Edward Strelley, has disappeared. He has not been seen at Chelsea Manor for a fortnight, and Master Grindal knows nothing of his whereabouts beyond that he left precipitately those few nights ago. Grindal says that Strelley crossed words with the Baron Sudeley, and that he left immediately afterwards. He has not seen him since. I have not been able to see Sudeley myself, as he does not receive.

"I have taken the trouble to visit the mortuaries around London and Westminster, and as far as Kingston and Dartford I have not found his body. It may not signify, but it gives me the faintest hope. Pray for him. I shall write again soon, and I hope it shall be with happier tidings. Yours ever in affection..." She breaks off.

Longshawe strokes his chin, one eye narrow. He struggles to find a word to say. Guy Fletcher rests a comforting hand on his shoulder, and Longshawe puts his own over it.

"I am sure..." Caroline begins, but cannot continue.

Longshawe looks up at her. Her eyes shine, but the tears do not fall. He fights his own urge to weep. "I thank you for informing me," he says, rising. "I had rather wished that we might share some pleasant words today." He laughs, just briefly, then lifts his head, blinking repeatedly. Caroline takes his hand.

"Do not grieve. George would have found him if..." Again, she cannot finish her thought.

Longshawe looks down at his hand in hers, and forces a smile. He brings it up to his mouth, and kisses it gently. "I have wanted and waited to do that for a long time."

Caroline shakes her head. Her dark hair, gathered into a simple but elegant cap, comes a little loose, framing her face. She too forces a smile. "My brother has forgiven you for your presumption. My father-" She glances over her shoulder at the baron, who is guffawing loudly at some remark of the earl's, "-My father put it down to youthful high spirits."

"I was in earnest," Longshawe says, flatly, quietly, and without looking into Caroline de Winter's eyes.

"Then you do presume." She folds her hands over her bodice. "We shall speak again in happier circumstances, Master Longshawe." As she turns, Longshawe's eyes screw up closed. He does not see the smile that passes over Caroline's face as she returns to her father on the other side of the hall.

Half an hour later, Sir Nicholas Strelley is announced. Several heads turn to the door, including Longshawe's, Caroline de Winter's and the Baron de Winter's. Longshawe moves to rise to greet his friend's family, and to pass on his news if they have not yet heard it. However, he falls back into his seat when he realises that Strelley's mother and sister are wearing mourning-black. Their eyes are shot red with weeping. Sir Nicholas has a grim, stony expression on his face, but makes the customary obeisances to the earl and then to the baron. The women are proper in their etiquette, but without enthusiasm.

Longshawe turns to Guy Fletcher. "I must speak with them," he says, steeling himself for the task by long, slow breaths. He stands, walks slowly over and nods his acknowledgement to Sir Nicholas, before trying his best to smile at Elizabeth Strelley and her mother. Neither is able to reciprocate.

Shrewsbury is leaning in, listening to Sir Nicholas' words.

"The letter says that Baron Sudeley was shown the body earlier in the week. Dragged out of the Thames, he was told, by a merchant at St Paul's. Drowned." Nicholas Strelley's voice matches his countenance. "I had high hopes for that boy, Your Grace. He showed such promise when he was young."At this, Longshawe angles his head in thought.

Shrewsbury raises an eyebrow. "He was tutor to a royal daughter, Sir. Hardly a failure."

"He was sent down from the University for his non-conformity. I have heard from him only twice since he left on your war."

Shrewsbury, though he is by now in his late forties, shifts his weight around with the ease of a much younger man. He straightens himself, smoothes his beard.

"His part in the war in Scotland was not the reason for your lack of accord."

Strelley sighs. "It was not. Nor is it now much comfort that he was so dearly beloved of his sister and her mother." He speaks of the women as if they are not present. "My only relief is that he did not go the stake apostate as I imagined he might."

Shrewsbury wrinkles his nose at this comment, and moves away without ceremony. Longshawe steps forward and takes the hand of Strelley's mother, kisses it, then holds it between his own.

"I share your grief, Madam. And yours, Mistress." He addresses this last to Elizabeth, now grown into a striking young woman. She has her brother's dark hair, and a rare fineness of features even as an adolescent. They nod their heads at Longshawe's words, but say nothing. Sir Nicholas eyeballs Longshawe, daring him to say anything further. Longshawe wisely withdraws, and goes back to his table to sit with Guy Fletcher. Fletcher watches him, not knowing what to say. Longshawe thinks for some minutes before he speaks again.

"Did you ever see Edward swim, Guy?"

"Not that I remember."

"No. When we were boys we used to go up to the Don, or the Ponds. He used to beat me by miles."

"Why are you thinking about swimming?"

"The Strelleys said that Edward's body was found in the Thames. That he drowned."

"And...?"

"Well, he wouldn't have drowned if he was... Unless he was already dead when he went in."

"You think he was murdered?"

"Well, I don't know. But there's more to this, somehow. He hated that Seymour, didn't he? The one that married the queen? Perhaps he said something to him, did something to rouse his anger."

Guy Fletcher closes his eyes and lets himself think through what he has heard. After a half-minute, he says, speaking quietly, quickly, "Do you remember that George said in his letter that he hadn't found the body? Why wouldn't he have seen it if it had been found? Especially so close. St Paul's is hardly out of the way. It's downstream of where Strelley lived with Sudeley."

"George might not have been to the right places."

"He might not, but once a merchant had pulled a body out of the water, he wouldn't go to the trouble of burying it himself."

"So?"

"So if Edward's body came out of the Thames at St Paul's, George should have seen it."

"But Sudeley himself wrote to the Strelleys about the body!" Longshawe's voice has an edge to it, as though he is tired of this game of Guy's.

"You said yourself that Edward hated Sudeley. George's letter said they crossed words before he left."

"So what? Sudeley did what? Hid Edward's body so George couldn't find it? Lied about Edward being dead?"

"To lie about it wouldn't have satisfied Sudeley. He must have been convinced."

"Guy... my friend..." He gives up. "Edward is dead. We both have to accept that."

Guy gets up and goes to the Strelleys. He bows, paying particular attention to the depth and correctness of his bow to Elizabeth Strelley. She is unmoved, but Sir Nicholas is immediately impatient.

"You do not have an introduction, young man," he snaps.

"I am your son's former servant, Sir." Guy returns. "Am I wrong to presume that is introduction enough?" He retains his composure, even though Nicholas Strelley frowns markedly. Elizabeth Strelley and her mother both sit forward a little, intrigued if not yet convinced. Fletcher, sensing their enthusiasm, directs his next words to Strelley's mother. "Madam... Do you have Baron Sudeley's letter? Edward was my mentor, and my friend. I should like to read it with my own eyes."

"You may address me as Lady Margaret, young man. What is your name?"

"Why," Guy answers, a little stung, "I am Guy Fletcher. Has Edward not written of me?"

Elizabeth Strelley's face softens a little. "He mentioned you in his letters to me. I am not sure that father has heard your name before now." She darts a caustic glance at her father. "I have the letter myself."

Both of Elizabeth Strelley's parents turn to her with a mixture of anger and surprise, but neither stops her handing over a piece of expensive-looking paper to Guy Fletcher.

"May I," Guy asks, "take this over to Longshawe for a moment?"

Nicholas Strelley is about stop him, but Margaret Strelley stops him with a gesture. "You may," she says, "but please return it to us."

164

Fletcher bows deeply, turning himself so that he gets a little closer to Elizabeth. "I shall," he says, then stands, turns flamboyantly and goes back to Longshawe.

"I have Sudeley's letter," he says, flatly, and sits down. Longshawe stares ahead, barely moving in response to Fletcher, eyes fixed on nothing in particular across the room. Guy reads the letter in silence, before fixing on a portion of it, which he rereads several times.

"Listen to this," he says to Longshawe, who moves around in his chair, but doesn't turn his head. "It says here that Strelley was found under the wharves just downstream from the Fleet."

"Guy, my patience for this is thin."

"The merchant that he used... Gilbert. You went there yourself. That was St Paul's. Did George ever go there?"

"Not that I know of. There are hundreds of warehouses there."

"Hmm. How would you describe Gilbert?"

"Guy!" Longshawe closes his eyes firmly, screwing them up so that his face creases and wrinkles.

"Please, James." Longshawe bites his bottom lip, perhaps in response to the use of his Christian name.

"Well, then... He was canny. Knew things."

"The kind of man to have spies in every tavern and on every corner?"

"Yes. That kind of man. Why, for heaven's sake?"

"Because Gilbert would know if a body was pulled out of the Thames, wouldn't he? And Gilbert knew Edward, and he knew whom he worked for."

"So...?" Longshawe

"Perhaps it was Gilbert who found him."

"I still do not follow your reasoning, Guy."

"I'm not sure I do either, Master Longshawe. But can I borrow a horse? And have ten days' leave?"

"Will you let Edward rest in peace? I need you to let him be dead, if dead he is. If Gilbert says so..."

"I will, Master Longshawe. But if not...?"

"Away, Guy." Longshawe breathes in and out slowly, trying to master the combination of anger, sadness and confusion in his mind. He takes a long draught of beer.

Across the room, Guy bows extravagantly once again, as he

returns the letter from Baron Sudeley into the hand of Elizabeth Strelley. His smile as he leaves her is impenetrable, of hope for a friend lost, or of something else altogether?

Guy Fletcher rides out from Sheffield Castle within twenty minutes of his conversation with Longshawe. He is properly armed, his sword hanging at his hip. He checks a pair of pistols that the armoury at the castle has been provided and smiles to see that they have been loaded. The horse that he rides is one of the earl's, loaned on the strength of Longshawe's exasperated recommendation, with tack of fine-but-understated quality. The animal itself is tall, sleek and fast. Fletcher strokes its muzzle, already regretting that it will be exchanged too soon at some country inn for a lesser beast. Nevertheless, it is speed now that he needs, and he will not regret its loss if it serves his greater purpose.

He spurs the horse and flies south, taking the most direct if not the safest roads. He trusts to Providence, and that a lone rider, well-armed but without any possessions other than those arms, is a poor target for a bandit. It is gathering dark when he arrives at the village of Alfreton, and he heads straight to the least conspicuous of the inns. A five-minute stop is all it takes for him to exchange his horse, and he sells the earl's fine saddle to the proprietor, taking instead the cheapest on his new mount, keeping the coins in different places about his person. He makes no attempt to conceal his arms, but does not show them off to the other patrons, judging that either course might identify him as a target for pursuit. He is soon on the road again, and he rides just as hard over the next two hours to Nottingham. His face betrays his struggle as he resigns himself to having to stop for the night there, rather than press on. Even his bravery and strategy do not equip him to ride through the night across country.

Instead, he rises at first light after six hours sleep, and is off again at an even more frenetic pace, stopping every fifteen miles for a change of mount. He makes good progress, and it is late in the evening when he passes Tyburn on his way to Westminster. Fletcher does his best not to show his nerves in the city, peopled as it is already by the denizens of the night. He is much more comfortable in the open, where the knowledge he gained in his youth gives him the advantage. Here, after the relative calm of the open country, he is surrounded on all sides even as the light fades to night. The people who inhabit this strange city of the night are indifferent to him, ignoring him or occasionally taunting him over the relative size of horse and rider.

Trying to give no thought to any matter other than the one that presses, Guy Fletcher makes a series of turns through the narrow streets, in an attempt not to give away the fact that he does not know precisely where the object of his search is, but also to take in the shape of the place, giving him some reference points that he can use to build his map. He passes up and down the old city walls just west of St Paul's, which gives him a good marker to navigate by. The tower and spire reach to such a height that they are visible from almost any angle.

It is after about an hour and a half of searching that he spots the sign of Gilbert's warehouse. He approaches the building cautiously, well aware that customers would not be expected at this time of night. It is with some relief that he sees the building is occupied, lights flickering at some ground-floor windows. He approaches, and for want of a more subtle stratagem, he bangs his fist against the door.

It is Gilbert himself who answers. "Christ Almighty!" Gilbert shouts. "I do not recognise *you*. By what authority are you here?"

"By none but my own, Sir." Gilbert's eyes widen, his demeanour and movements now thoroughly alert. Fletcher picks up his own words. "I seek a man called Gilbert."

"And my name being displayed on my premises, here, you fixed on me as your target. I am not your father, boy, so be on your way." Gilbert smiles at his own joke. But as he does so he scrutinises Guy carefully, and there is something in the look of the youngster that catches his attention. There is a moment during which Guy expects Gilbert to close the door in his face, and it does not happen. Guy uses the opportunity to keep speaking.

"Sir," Fletcher, aware of Gilbert's close scrutiny, and somewhat put out by it, continues, "I understand that you know my friend. My mentor, indeed. Master Strelley?"

"Inside," Gilbert says, quietly, leaving the door open as he turns and disappears into the offices. Guy follows him. Two paces through the door, Gilbert turns and holds a pistol to Guy's forehead, stopping the boy instantly. Guy turns pale, and his shoulders rise in tension.

Gilbert speaks slowly and carefully. "Your next words will determine your fate." With his free hand, he gestures for Guy to explain himself. Guy Fletcher summons all of his bravery and intelligence in weighing his words, taking his time,

"I am Guy Fletcher, sometime valet to Edward Strelley. Yesterday I was at Sheffield Castle with James Longshawe, who has also been your customer. We were told by the de Winters that Edward had disappeared. And we were told by the Strelleys that Edward's body had been pulled out of the river at St Paul's." Gilbert listens to this with a frown. He signs that Guy should continue. "I knew that Edward had been here many times. If someone had found him, you would have recognised him."

"I did indeed. Drowned in the river." Gilbert tries to sound offhand, but Guy has unsettled him. Even Gilbert's habitual irreverence can't hide the tension.

"But James Longshawe said that Strelley was a strong swimmer." Guy's tone is pleading, but he allows himself a hint of a smile at this counter-argument. "He would not have drowned, even in the Thames."

"Listen, lad, I don't know how or why you've come all this way, and it's very touching that you did. But I saw your friend dead on that quay out there. So did fifty other people. So has Baron Sudeley. If he was such a strong swimmer, perhaps he wasn't awake when he went in the river. People are *bad* around here," he says, pointedly looking at his gun, "and bad people do bad things. Do you understand?" He lowers the gun slightly. "I was very fond of Edward Strelley. He made me laugh. But that doesn't bring him back from the dead, does it?"

Fletcher shakes his head. Some of the colour has returned to the skin. For all of Gilbert's efforts spent in appraisal of him, Guy has made his own judgements, and he recognises that his mention of Strelley's name is what set off this odd event. Furthermore, if Gilbert had wanted to kill him, he had had the chance and not taken it.

This reflection lasts only a moment, before Gilbert fills the quiet again. "Where are you staying? You might find it hard to get a room at this hour, 'specially with your young face and your long sword." He looks at it, recognising it as one that he may have sold. "How about I take you to an inn I know, and I'll put you up there for the night. As a gesture of... good will?"

Guy, outmanoeuvred for now but not totally beaten, recognises this compromise as a good one, and accepts it with a nod. Gilbert leads him out on to the streets, where he takes his horse in hand and leads it, following the turns as Gilbert makes them. After three minutes, but out of sight of the warehouse, they come to an inn. Gilbert ushers Fletcher inside, and a stable-boy takes the horse through an alley. Gilbert approaches the innkeeper, engages him in conversation for a minute or two, and then comes back to show Fletcher to his room. As they mount the stairs together, Gilbert asks, "where's your stuff? You can't have ridden here from Sheffield with no pack."

"I did, Sir. In the clothes I stand in and with nothing else."

"For Strelley?"

"For Strelley."

"He had some good friends. Shame." At the bottom of the stairs, a rough-looking man stations himself on a pallet-bed, his legs across the step in such a way that no one could descend without waking him. The stable boy sits under Fletcher's window, a shiny coin in his hand. Gilbert leaves, unmolested, indeed the inhabitants of the inn seem to show him a respect that hints at prior acquaintance. Fletcher takes note of these precautions, subtly arranged as they seem to be. Gilbert does not want him to leave, at least not without him knowing. But, crucially, he doesn't seem to mind him being aware of this fact. Fletcher sits on his pallet-bed, trying desperately to make sense of the events, but the journey and the shock have left him unable to, stuck in the kind of loop of thought that prevents enlightenment. He wavers between an attempt to escape and awaiting Gilbert's next move. Intransigent disgust at his being a captive threatens to overcome him, but Guy is a strategist. He realises that whilst Gilbert is a wily thinker, he too knows that he has shown Guy that he has touched on something. Unwilling to force things by an all-too-likely-to-fail effort at flight, he sees that he has to leave Gilbert to show his hand. All the same, he sleeps with his sword at his side and his pistols close to hand. He doesn't anticipate using them, as if he were to find himself in a situation to use them, he would not have been left with them.

Fletcher rises with the dawn again. He fusses about his room, trying to fathom his next move. As he looks out of the window, he notices that there is another stable-boy watching his window. He opens the door to his room a little, and sees that the man at the bottom of the stairs is still there. Guy shuts the door again, and paces around the room for a few minutes. Eventually, he stops, and then, mustering his resolve, he opens the door and walks confidently down the stairs. The man at the bottom stirs, but does not move. Fletcher steps over him, glances around the room and sets off for the outer door. No one stops him, but there is a general movement of bodies about the inn. Fletcher opens the door and steps outside. He looks up and down the street, considering, then walks around the back of the inn to the stables. He unties his horse, and leads it away. As he walks, he turns his head left and right, doing his best to see if there is anyone following him. He doesn't notice a boy detach himself from a conversation and begin to track him, hidden among the already growing crowds in the streets.

Fletcher heads out west, and is soon on the road to Chelsea. He continues to look behind himself frequently, but his shadow is rather too subtle to be caught so easily, mixing himself in with the traffic and remaining far enough behind to be inconspicuous. Some time later, Guy arrives at Chelsea manor, where he is met by a liveried retainer. The servant recognises him as Strelley's former lackey, and shows him inside. Fletcher sits in a hallway as the retainer disappears into the house, trying to find a more senior servant who can deal with this unexpected visitor.

Eventually, the majordomo arrives. He looks down his nose at Guy, dishevelled and dirty from the journey of the previous day. "Young master Fletcher," he sneers, inspecting the back of his gloves as he speaks, "I trust you have worthwhile news to deliver."

Fletcher stands. "I would speak with Grindal."

"Master Grindal is at study with Lady Elizabeth. He cannot receive you."

"Please allow him to judge that for himself. Announce me, and if he refuses to see me, I shall leave."

"I shall do you the honour of repeating myself. Master Fletcher, Grindal will not receive you." The majordomo stares at Guy, and flicks his hand to the other servant, who scurries away down the corridor. A moment later, an armed guard appears with him.

Fletcher narrows his eyes. "I am not a peasant to be dismissed without an audience, Sir!" Guy raises his voice, consciously trying to be noticed by someone whom he can persuade. "I am here regarding the fate of the lady's former tutor!" The guard steps forward. He is a head taller than Guy, and much broader. "Edward Strelley!" Guy shouts. A door opens slightly further down the corridor. Grindal, looking old, grey and worn, puts his head out. He recognises Guy immediately, shuffles towards them, watched by four pairs of eyes, none of whom seems to be able to conjure the correct reaction. The majordomo is bristling with rage, the guard and the other servant seem wryly amused. Guy smiles, but along with the other three, does nothing for the quarter-minute it takes Grindal to walk half of even such a short distance.

"I do hope you have welcomed Master Fletcher to this house," Grindal mumbles. The majordomo sighs, but does not say anything further, his face contorted into something like disgust at being over-ruled. Before Grindal has finished making his way to the knot of men, he turns and struts away, dismissing the guard and the other servant with pointed gestures. That leaves Grindal and Fletcher alone in the corridor. Grindal comes to a halt a few yards away. "Guy... It is good to see you. Though I wish the circumstances were different." Guy rushes over to Grindal, who is out of breath even after these few steps. He takes his hands, and holds them for a moment.

"I have been to Gilbert's," Fletcher says. "He said they pulled Strelley out of the river."

"Yes..." Grindal answers, his voice creaking. "I have my suspicions. Come inside."

Elizabeth is at her study, eyes fixed on a piece of parchment that she occasionally writes on. She looks up at Fletcher as he enters with Grindal, nods her head slightly in response to his deep bow, and returns to her studies. She looks tired, and there is no trace of her usual flickering smile.

Grindal shows Guy to a seat across the room from his pupil, far enough away so that Elizabeth will not hear their whispered conversation. Guy settles himself, and leans in to Grindal.

"What do you suspect?" Guy asks urgently.

"Master Strelley disappeared after an exchange with the master of this house. Do you know him? No, well, Baron Sudeley is a proud man who does not take well to being challenged. Something Edward said to him, or perhaps didn't say to him, set him to anger."

"So Sudeley...?"

"Baron Sudeley is not so unsubtle as to take arms himself. But he may have engaged others to do so."

"Gilbert did not say whether Strelley had been wounded. Would he not have said so if he had been?"

"They could have knocked him out and thrown him in the river." Grindal accompanies his description with a feeble blow of his right hand into his left. "Or drugged him senseless. Or he may have chosen to ignore a wound he did see. So it doesn't signify."

"But you think Sudeley had Strelley murdered?"

"Yes. Sudeley has taken an interest in Elizabeth." Grindal glances over at her. She notices but pretends not to. "For whatever reason, Sudeley has marked Strelley as... well, a rival..." Grindal considers. "If not for her affection, then at least for her respect, her good opinion."

"But why this? Rather drastic, isn't it?" For the first time since his arrival, Fletcher's face displays the merest hint of a smile. "Murder?"

"As I say, Sudeley is not a man to be trifled with."

"There was another letter. From George de Winter."

"Strelley's friend? The one who is in Lady Mary's household?" Grindal asks, getting a nod of confirmation from Guy Fletcher. "And?"

"George said that he went to every mortuary in London and that he didn't see the body."

"So? Sudeley was shown it himself. He played quite the concerned master."

"Shown it by...?"

"Gilbert. What do you mean?"

Guy scratches his chin. "Whose friend is Gilbert?" he asks, giving a knowing rhetorical flourish of his hand.

"Mine. We have known each other for a long time. And I understand he had some affection for Edward."

"He said so himself, in fact. When I went to him, he threatened me."

"What do you mean?"

"I mean he pulled a pistol out and aimed it at my head."

"Why?" Grindal asks, suddenly animated.

"Gilbert was very wary of me. Asking about Strelley. He had me watched overnight. I shouldn't be surprised if someone followed me all the way here. I have been suffered to enter by his spy, which must mean something. Why?"

"Well... Sudeley himself is not here at Chelsea. So he has nothing to fear from you. But what if Gilbert himself, or one of his men, killed Edward? They may be waiting to see your next move. You have shown it to them." Grindal speaks in a hissing, rattling whisper, only partly as a result of his failing breath.

"Would Gilbert have any truck with Sudeley?" Guy asks, changing the focus.

Grindal frowns at him. "Are you suggesting that Gilbert lied to Sudeley? Somehow deceived him into thinking he'd seen Strelley's dead body?"

"Why else would he react so strangely?"

"Perhaps because he put Strelley in the river himself." Grindal's voice has a sharp edge. "You are just like Edward. Everything is an intrigue."

"If Strelley had been killed, why did George not see the body?"

"Because Gilbert found it."

"And did what with it? He's not in the business of burying folk himself, is he?"

"Master Fletcher, you are upsetting me. I appreciate your affection for Edward, but you must accept that he is gone."

Fletcher rises. Elizabeth's head lifts at the noise. He smiles at her, as Grindal wearily lifts himself out of his seat. Fletcher seizes the moment, strides across to Elizabeth and leans over her work.

"My Lady," he says, quickly and in low whisper, "Do not grieve for Edward just yet."

She looks up at him, sees his earnestness and reacts simply by putting down her pen. "Master Fletcher," she says, drily, "you are distracting me from my work. Please leave now." Fletcher looks back at her, eyes aslant. She shuffles her papers around on the desk. One, deeply buried in the pile, is unmistakeably in Strelley's handwriting.

Guy rushes out, before Grindal is even able to make his way over to Elizabeth's desk. Grindal, huffing and blowing, sits heavily in the chair next to her.

"I am sorry, Madam," he says. "Master Fletcher has rather excited himself over nothing."

Elizabeth's fingers tap at her pile of papers, her eyes drop twice to them, then fix on Grindal. "Indeed," she replies.

53: Benedic' Domine, nos et dona tua

The reader will no doubt by now be eager to learn the truth about the fate of our friend Edward Strelley. All in its time. It is a story which must begin three weeks ago as Mary Tudor kneels before the altar in the otherwise deserted chapel at Hunsdon, praying earnestly. Snatches of words here and there come through audible in the babble of her constant stream. A 'Pater Noster,' a 'Sancta Maria, mater Dei', the repetition of the common prayers. After a while, the words become less familiar, less easy to recognise as parts of these formulaic collects. She intones prayers that range from the quiet plea of the supplicant through to the confident statements of the wronged.

After many minutes, she begins to rise. "Guide me," she says in English, "Lord, for I know not what to do." She stands facing the altar, not moving.

The cowled figure of a Benedictine monk emerges from behind the rood screen, silhouetted against the light from the far end of the church. His hands are hidden by his sleeves, his head is bowed slightly. He does not speak for a moment, but Mary turns away from the altar to him. Her eyes narrow.

"I did not know there were any ecclesiastics left," she says, almost to herself. "Welcome to my chapel, brother monk."

"Thank you, My Lady. Not all of my brethren have left behind their vows, even if they have been forced from their monasteries."

"I am glad to see that the habit has survived my father's reign."

"Does God speak to you?" the monk asks, nodding his head at the apse to which Mary has been praying. The reader will no doubt have recognised him as de Winter's hireling. "Does he respond to your prayers?"

"No. I find myself lost." She takes two steps towards him, focusing her eyes. His black habit is immaculate, almost as though it has not been worn before today. There is a moment during which she considers this intrusion, her thoughts visible on her face that the Benedictine may be an assassin, sent by her brother or the Lord Protector. It passes, and she relaxes visibly. If there had been a threat, it could have been enacted by now. "Why are you here?" she asks, sharply.

"God speaks to me. And through me, he speaks to you."

Benedict plays the part well, injecting his voice with mystery and authority. "I have a vision."

"You have a vision?" Mary returns. There is something of weariness in her tone, but her eyes light up just enough for Benedict to notice, and he finds an even greater level of emotion.

"I have seen the future. You shall be queen of this land." He speaks almost dreamily, as though his vision is appearing to him even now.

"What do you mean?"

"I mean that I see you, crown and sceptre in hand, ruling this nation of England." Benedict leans in towards Mary. She looks up at him, scrutinising.

"And this vision of yours, why does God send it to you but not to me?"

There is a moment's pause. "Because I am able to quiet my mind, and to hear God's word. He sends me to comfort you in your need."

"And my brother?"

"He has rejected God, and does not hear Him. Edward shall not produce an heir that England will accept, and it shall be your glory to return this people to God's Holy Church of Rome."

"I do not wish to gain the throne by violence. Least of all against my brother."

The monk's confidence in his story begins to grow. "You shall be Queen of England, My Lady, through no sin of your own. There are those who believe you to be the rightful ruler, and they shall act in your interests."

"My brother is but a child. I will not allow it."

"No harm will come to your brother through your devotees. But the people of England, the good Catholic people of England, they await your accession. They have faith that you will rescue them from this ungodliness."

"There is still time to save my brother's soul...?" Mary asks. Benedict smiles underneath his cowl. Her solicitousness for her brother has made his task even easier.

"Yes. I shall pray for him, as should you."

"Oh, I do, brother monk. Every day. I would not wish the fate he has chosen for himself on anyone. I ask God to forgive him for his sins."

"They are not *his* sins, Madam. He is led by his advisers, and God will see that."

"I am comforted by your words, Sir, but I cannot take pleasure in the overthrow of my brother."

"It is not for your pleasure that God has chosen you, Madam." Benedict pauses before applying the coup de grâce. "It is for His glory, and His Church's glory."

"I am chosen..." Mary says. "Then I must await with forbearance as I have through my life. God's tests are exacting indeed."

"Perhaps his tests are to show you your own strength."

"I do not feel strong sometimes."

"God is with you. Take your strength from that."

Mary looks at the Benedictine again. A frown passes across her face. "Who-" she considers the question, begins it again, and then stops. "Will you remain? Here at Beaulieu?"

"If My Lady wishes it."

"I do." She strides out of the chapel, and heads off through the palace in search of her lady, Susan Clarencieux.

De Winter has strategically arranged for it to be himself waiting on Susan Clarencieux at this moment. She sits with her needlework, embroidering a pair of gloves for Lady Mary. De Winter stands at the door of the room, solicitously offering drinks or food as often as he dares, giving away a little of his nervousness in trying to be useful. His eyes widen visibly when he hears the footsteps of his mistress. Clarencieux, with no foreknowledge of the encounter, rises and turns to make her courtesy to the lady.

"Susan," Mary says abruptly, "I have need of your counsel."

"My Lady...?" Clarencieux says, expectant. De Winter's eyes flick between the two, gauging whether his strategy has worked.

"At prayer, I have had an encounter. With a religious. A visionary."

"What did he tell you, My Lady?"

"That I shall be queen."

"You shall be queen!" Clarencieux exclaims. She does not know whether to be delighted or despondent, congratulating or commiserating. She desperately tries to arrange her face so as to be

177

neutral, following Mary's lead. Her mistress, though, is inscrutable.

"That I shall be Queen of England. He told me that I am chosen by God. To bring about the return of His church to this country."

"Is this news not what you wished to hear?" Clarencieux asks, calmer but still searching for the response Mary wants.

"I do not know. I have prayed every day that my brother's folly – his heresy – would be arrested and reversed, but I have never wished harm upon him. The monk said that Edward would come to no misfortune. But I cannot see that I could be queen with him still alive. Even if my mother is recognised and I retain my place in the succession, even restored to legitimacy, how could I sit peacefully upon the throne with my brother alive?"

"Do you believe his prophecy?"

"I... I don't know. I cannot fathom that God would speak to me in this way, but I also know that I have so rarely felt the presence of His Spirit, He might choose another channel to communicate. Besides, what could an ascetic ecclesiastic gain from dissimulation? He would risk his own soul, were it a fabrication."

De Winter, standing away from the dialogue of the two women, cannot suppress the merest hint of a smile at this. It goes unnoticed.

Clarencieux, given as she is to occasional moments of emotion in relation to the Lady Mary's situation, takes her hands and sheds a tear as she speaks.

"It is My Lady's destiny to lead this country. God speaks to us all in His way, and this must be the way He has chosen to speak to you."

"I wish that I could believe it. I want it to be true, but that I want it is not enough."

"You do not have faith in this monk, then?"

"I have faith in God, but not in men. My father put that out of me. I still wonder what God's plan was for him. He discarded my mother for that whore, then Edward's mother died, then there was that awful Howard girl. How could God suffer his rule – his misrule – for nearly forty years? And then put my heretic brother on the throne?"

"Surely it is God's way of testing his faithful?"

"That was the monk's reasoning. Does it not shake your faith, Susan?"

"My faith is strong. If you need proof, then surely this prophet is the beginnings of it. His bell tolls for you, Madam, even should you need to wait."

"Of course, you are right. God needs *me* to show my faith, rather than Him lay it all out before me." Mary purses her lips. "I curse my weakness. But I bless your strength, Susan."

"I believe in you, My Lady."

The following day, de Winter rides out alone from Hunsdon south towards London, at a furious gallop. His horse is sweating and blowing, but he keeps up the pace. He even changes horses at a coaching inn near Epping, desperate to maintain his speed. He pays no mind to the potential robbers and bandits on the way, either through preoccupation or conviction that he will outrun any pursuer. Within an hour-and-a-half, he is approaching the Fleet prison. He exchanges words with the jailer, and is admitted without delay.

Gardiner sits crooked on his pallet-bed, thinking. He looks up as de Winter enters, but shows little sign of pleasure at the visit. "You," he says drily. "I should hope that you have good news."

De Winter's nose turns just a fraction at the former bishop's lack of enthusiasm. "I do, as it happens."

"Well, what then?"

De Winter takes the opportunity to shake his head, ostentatiously removing a pair of fine leather gloves a finger at a time. He puts the gloves down on a bedside table that is already buried under books and manuscript sheets, all covered with dense writing, and stands over Gardiner.

"I have arranged matters as you wished, My Lord Bishop. It seems that Lady Mary has rather a fancy for these notions of her future regency."

"Do not joke with me, boy," Gardiner spits. "I will have you whipped when I am free."

"But Sir, I doubt you shall remember my name then."

Gardiner smiles. "I shall make a note of it."

"Put it in your ledger in the column that says 'saviour of English Roman Catholicism'." De Winter laughs out loud. "I have the greatest of respect for My Lord's theology, and his conviction. But you are a prisoner here, and it is those of us that are left free that are fighting the Lord's fight. You are the safest of us all, despite your confinement."

"How dare you speak to me thus? I am here as a prisoner of conscience!" Gardiner colours as he speaks, but does not rise from his seated position on his bed.

De Winter shakes his head at him. "You are here as a prisoner of your own pride." He accompanies this accusation with a pointed finger.

"What would you have done, then, in my position? Resist arrest? Flee to the continent?"

"No. I would have used my name and my power to press the Catholic church's case. But it is rather late for that, wouldn't you say?"

"I have never been so insulted by a commoner before."

"Rather you should say that a commoner has never spoken such truth to power before."

Gardiner finally rises from his bed. He is a head shorter than de Winter, and he looks up into the young man's finely-cut, darkly handsome face with eyes that sparkle with passion. He considers, briefly, then with a waved gesture says, "speak your mind, then. I would hear it before I dismiss you."

"Very well, My Lord. You are the figure-head of our religion in this country. Our cause, which I take it we agree is a return to the Papal fold, is not helped by your imprisonment. It is not in my power, nor in Mary's, to secure your release. Do you agree with these statements?"

"I do. But they do not reveal anything previously unknown."

"Well, I shall continue: Mary is frightened and alone. Her handmaid does what she can to mollify her, but we suffer for two reasons. Susan Clarencieux is no man, and she is not of the cloth. Your guidance at her side – your presence – would be more valuable to our future queen than any prophet."

"And? How do you propose to engineer this situation?"

"You must find it within yourself to bow to Cranmer."

It is Gardiner's turn to laugh. "You understand nothing, do you? Cranmer is a fool, an ideologue who has latched on to the wrong end of an argument. I will not bow to him."

"Then you remain as you are, a prisoner who plays no role in this game of thrones."

"I do not fear my insignificance."

"Nor do I. What I fear, if such is the right word, is your impotence. Your influence with Mary is great, and you do not wield it usefully from here. For strategy, then, My Lord, make your apologies, and get yourself released to where you can fight the good fight."

De Winter turns, making to leave. Gardiner struggles with himself, but, before de Winter has reached the door, says, "You will not take such a tone with me again."

"I hope I shall not need to," de Winter replies, before disappearing through the prison door.

An hour later, de Winter enters the Dutchman Van Der Delft's office once more, and leaves again no more than three minutes after that, a smile of victory playing about his features. As he exits the Imperial ambassador's house, though, he sees a man being led through the streets by another man, in a way which suggests coercion. They are moving away from him, but he takes advantage of the slow pace of the two to get ahead, and gasps when he realises that it is Edward Strelley who is the one being led. He stands aggressively upright before them, blocking their path.

The man who is forcing Strelley along is big, powerful-looking and has a facial expression that suggests physical violence is familiar to him. De Winter assesses him quickly, rating him as a thug with a strong arm but likely no great wit, and relaxes as he decides that if it came to a fight, it would not end in defeat. He cocks his head to one side, flush with his already-accumulating earlier victories.

"You seem to have my friend here in a compromising position," he says, trying to see if the big man is armed, particularly if he is pressing a knife to Strelley's back. "But you obviously don't just want to kill him. If it were the case, he could be dead many times over already."

Strelley looks at him, but remains silent. He has not yet seen de Winter's strategy, but he recognises that there is a play afoot. De Winter continues, in the same bantering tone, "so you must be taking him somewhere. If you were just trying to kill him, you would have knocked him out and dragged him away. Or found him in the dark."

Strelley's assailant pushes him forward, towards de Winter. "Get out of my way, you greasy twat!" he grunts. De Winter snorts a laugh, derisive of the threat.

"You'll look even more like a pig when I cut off your nose!" De Winter's hand flies to the handle of his sword.

Strelley finally speaks. "George, no!" he says, freeing his arm to wave frantically. "You,", he says, bending himself to address his captor, "where are you taking me? Your answer might save your life."

"I told you once. Someone wants to see you."

Strelley closes his eyes, and says slowly, "if you do not answer me, my friend will kill you, whatever happens to me. Are you taking me to Gilbert?" At the name, the burly man tightens his grip on Strelley. He chews his lip, frowning all the while he thinks about his next move. He looks around him. No one has stopped to intervene in this altercation, despite the street being packed with people.

Strelley takes advantage of the pause to speak again. "You are taking me to Gilbert. Let my friend accompany us, and I give you my word I will not try to escape." The man looks at de Winter, pointedly. Strelley responds in a soothing tone. "And my friend will keep his sword where it is." De Winter raises his eyebrows, but falls in with them.

As they walk, Strelley whispers to de Winter. "I have, shall we say, left the service of the Lady Elizabeth. In circumstances that were not of my choosing."

De Winter returns a puzzled look. "And what leads to this?"

"My guess? That this man was hired by my erstwhile employer, Baron Sudeley. Via Gilbert. I owe my continued survival to Gilbert's decision to spare me. Any other assassin and I would be at the bottom of the Thames by now."

The man notices this conversation and puts an end to it with a threatening look. It is only five minutes later that they arrive at the familiar warehouse of Thos. Gilbert.

Strelley leads them inside, with de Winter following behind the other. Gilbert is seated at his desk. He lifts his eyes from whatever document he is scrutinising, and is about to begin some raillery when he notices de Winter.

"Who is the spare?" he asks his man.

Strelley answers, "George de Winter, Sir, a friend of mine, and for now, my protector."

Gilbert laughs. "As I am sure you are aware by now, Edward, I am your protector. Your friend, however he comes to be here, would not have saved you should I have so wished it." He gestures to his hired muscle, who leaves the office by the front door, back out to the street. "Sit!" Gilbert calls, and a second man rushes to put chairs behind de

Winter and Strelley.

He looks from one to the other. "You," he says, bending the word around so it takes longer than it should, and addressing it to Strelley, "have made yourself some rather powerful enemies, it seems. Powerful enemies who pay well to have men *removed from circulation*. I am not a violent man myself, but I know a few. He-" he gestures to the door, after the one who has left, "is not the most subtle or the most cruel of my acquaintances. But he has the singular virtue of doing as he is told. By me."

"Sudeley?" Strelley asks.

"You must know that I never betray the confidences of a client. How many men who can afford an assassin have you angered?" Strelley half-smiles in response to this gibe, but says nothing. Gilbert picks up, "nevertheless, I understood immediately that you were the target, before my client even mentioned your name. In any case, I have a great affection for your Master Grindal, and I rather feel that you might have something to offer me."

De Winter looks at Strelley, eyebrows raised, but keeps silent.

"So," Gilbert continues, "I thought rather than waste your life, I might take it for my own."

"For which I am thankful," Strelley says.

"You say that now, young Master..." Gilbert throws his best enigmatic look at the two young men. "Well, we have some arrangements to make. Your friend cannot divulge our arrangement or we are all dead men. Can I trust him?"

Strelley looks to de Winter. "James?" he says. Gilbert frowns.

"I have gone out of my way to preserve your life, Master Strelley. I do not expect half of London to be in on that particular secret. 'James' is the large fry you brought here?" There is a hint of exasperation in his voice. "No. He will have to remain ignorant. If I come to regret my decision, Strelley, I will be taking your head to show Baron Sudeley myself. And yours." He angles his head at de Winter.

De Winter narrows his eyes in response. "What will you do with him?"

"There are a number of ways to occupy a young man of his talents. But that I shall not be divulging. You, de Winter, may leave now." Gilbert gestures at the door. "I am sorry to say that if you return to this place, you will die. Whilst the Baron Sudeley lives, Strelley is dead. Do you understand?"

De Winter rises and looks down at Strelley, who nods at him to acquiesce. "Adieu, then, Edward. I shall remember you in my prayers." He briefly takes Strelley's hand, then turns and walks away. Gilbert, once the door has closed, snaps his fingers, and a cloaked figure emerges from within the warehouse.

"Follow him. Make sure that he does not go to Sudeley. If he does, you come back immediately." Strelley swallows loudly. Such a message would mean his own death, and possibly de Winter's. "You don't trust your friend? I do. He seems *subtle*, somehow. Anyway, we must both hope it does not signify. You can lie low with me for a little while, we shall test the waters, and then decide on your future. Meanwhile, I have some papers for you to peruse." He reaches into his desk, and pulls out a thin bundle of papers. They are written in a foreign language, dense and impenetrable.

"Well?" Gilbert asks.

"Give me a couple of hours. I don't recognise some of the words, but it shouldn't take long to work it out." Strelley breathes in and out, slowly, trying to master himself and regain his composure. Gilbert looks at him, for slightly too long. "I am grateful, Sir," Strelley murmurs, still fixing his eyes on the papers. "I truly am."

"Do not get comfortable just yet. I shall need your clothes," Gilbert says, eyebrow raised.

The sun rises, late as it does in the winter, over Chelsea Manor. The outside air is crisply cool, the sun providing no warmth to heat it. Inside, William Grindal sits up in his sick-bed, coughing. His room has been blocked to the light, and there is a fierce fire burning, keeping it swelteringly warm. The sweat is visible on his brow. A dark-robed physician sits by the door, reading from an old but beautifully illuminated Galen. There is a knock, and Grindal weakly calls to enter.

Elizabeth opens the door, and sighs as the heat hits her. She frowns at the doctor, and makes her way over to the window, throwing off the curtain and letting the light into the room. She opens the casement and the cool air rushes in. Grindal's face loses its vivid redness, and he breathes a little more easily. The physician looks at her, disapproval evident on his sullen features.

"You are killing him," Elizabeth says. "He will sweat out his soul if you do not cool him."

"My Lady." The doctor shakes his head as he acknowledges her. "You should not be here."

"And yet here I am. Do wish to summon my illustrious mother? She would be interested to know that you had allowed me admittance."

"The queen is not your mother..." He stops himself and focuses. "Please allow me to conduct my duties. I must treat Master Grindal's fever." He waves a book in Elizabeth's face rather aggressively.

"Galen?" she says, snatching it out of his hands. "Do you still practise what he recommends?"

"Mistress Elizabeth, please," he says, exasperated by her taking the book.

"Master Owen," she replies, echoing his patronising tone, "Galen is fifteen-hundred years past. Have you not read Avicenna? Al-Nafis? They show how Galen is wrong in both his particulars and his philosophy."

"Madam," Owen says, forcing a smile, "let us forget the fact that you are fourteen years old, and that you refer to heathen medics who don't even believe in God as we do. Let us ignore that your instruction is in its infancy, and that even at its peak it will not include disease and its treatment. Let us remember that, notwithstanding your helpful advice, I have read a great deal more of the latest in physick than you. Even so, I have my instructions from the king. They do not allow me to seek advice on matters concerning the health of your tutor from you." As he speaks, he reaches into a pocket in his cloak, and draws out a piece of paper, conspicuously bearing the privy seal.

Elizabeth holds out Owen's copy of Galen, pretending acquiescence. As he takes it, she grabs his letter and looks over it. "This is Sudeley's signature!" she snaps. "You told me you had instructions from the king."

"Sudeley writes that it is on the king's orders that I am here. Madam, our discussion is distressing Master Grindal." He points over to the patient, whose appearance has improved drastically in the minutes since Elizabeth came in. Elizabeth follows his gesture.

"He at least looks like he might last another day of your tender ministrations!" she snarls, and struts over to the supine body of Grindal. "My prayers are with you, Master Grindal. I hope you do not need them." Grindal grips her hand, but does not speak. A moment passes, and he lets go. Elizabeth turns and leaves, pointing to the open window as she does so.

Owen goes to Grindal. "You understand, don't you? Her prayers cannot save you now."

Grindal blinks his eyes.

"I thought so. I will do what I can to ease your passing."

Later that day, Elizabeth watches as the doctor leaves, wrapping his cloak around himself against the winter chill. His breath billows visibly as he mounts his horse and rides away. She takes the chance to enter Grindal's room.

Grindal is awake, eyes open but glazed over. The window has remained unshut, perhaps a simple concession to the young woman's desires, perhaps because it truly has improved Grindal's pain, if not effected a cure for his condition. Some alertness returns to his face as he notices the door open. His eyes flicker into life, darting around the room, settling on the young woman. She goes to him, kneeling by his side and taking his hand. He summons himself for the effort of this conversation.

"Elizabeth..." he croaks. She strokes the back of his hand.

"Master Grindal. I must speak with you. It is a matter of some significance."

"Please, then, go on..." His voice trails off indefinitely.

"You are dying." She says it with some conviction, almost as though she needs to say it to herself to really believe it. "I am sorry."

"Not why you came..." He flexes his hand a little.

"No. Not why I came." Grindal coughs and hacks. Elizabeth waits for his fit to subside before continuing. "I came to pass on some news. Our friend, whom we thought lost, yet lives." Grindal says nothing, but nods his head once, very gently. She continues, "I thought you would want to know. Before..." Grindal nods again.

She stands up, and walks over to the window, letting the cool air rush against her face. She stands looking out across the grounds of the manor, following a footman with her gaze as he goes about his duties. It is five minutes before she turns back to Grindal. Her face is streaked with tear lines, her mouth is twisted.

"How can you both leave me like this?" she wails, taking two steps towards Grindal, before stopping and drawing herself up. "You were my rocks. My mentors..." She lowers her head and says nothing. "When Strelley left, you guided me in my grief. But then he sent me hope, he came back. Like our Lord Jesus himself, he rose from the grave. Now I lose you as well."

Grindal is unable to speak. His breath rattles as he takes it in, and again as he lets it out. He watches her, passive, as she continues her speech.

"He thinks of you. He knew... even before he left, he knew that you were sickening. He must have known that what ails you would be fatal. He left something."

She takes out a scrap of paper, written in Strelley's hand. It displays the signs of being rushed, blotted ink and scratched pen marks almost obscuring the words. She reads, in Latin. Her words are those of Catullus's elegy to his brother. "Atque in perpetuum, frater, ave atque vale."

As she reaches the end, Grindal weeps without sobbing. He closes his eyes for a moment, then he gathers himself, and says, quietly but clearly, "adieu, my brother."

Elizabeth folds the paper. "It is yours," she says. "But I cannot give it to you." Grindal's eyes show that he understands, though he does not have the energy to reply. Elizabeth stands still, looking at him. After a quarter minute in thought, she speaks again. "I cannot communicate with him. Even should I wish it. A condition of his exile." She closes her eyes against the tears. "I shall return to you later, Master Grindal. Now I must go." She does as she says, rushing her exit in a flustered attempt to hide her grief.

The sun sets early, the twilight evanesces into a dark, moonless night. Chelsea Manor is dimly lit, signifying the absence its master, the Baron Sudeley, and now also his wife Catherine. Two cloaked riders approach the gatehouse. One of them approaches the keeper, and after the exchange of a few words and the flash of a letter, they are admitted without further delay. As they approach the house, the rider who spoke with the gatekeeper advances to the fore. The footman at the door challenges him. The reader will have guessed that our riders are already known to us. It is de Winter who speaks.

"I am sent to the good Doctor Grindal via a friend of his, Master Gilbert. I have my credentials." He holds the sheet of paper out for the guard to see.

"I am sorry, sir. I cannot admit you."

"You haven't read the letter," de Winter states bluntly. His companion, still veiled by a thick riding-hood and cloak, coughs pointedly. De Winter smiles. "Ah. You can't read the letter. Allow me."

He shakes out the letter, then smooths it with the back of his hand, sitting deliberately tall in the saddle. "Sir, the man who presents this letter to you is Master George de Winter of my household. I understand that my dear sister's tutor is desperately ill, and I have sent my servant to bring him this preparation against the pain." At this point, de Winter extracts and waves a clay pot for emphasis. "Whenever he should arrive, please admit him immediately. I would not countenance a delay in the delivery of this medicine." De Winter eyeballs the guard, one brow raised. "Need I read the signature? I shall, for I trust not to your perspicacity: yours, Mary Tudor."

The poor footman is quite flustered, knowing not what to do. He half-turns, opening the door behind him. "I shall fetch the majordomo," he says, as much to himself as to the two riders. "Wait here."

De Winter turns in the saddle to face his companion. From under the hood, we might just recognise the face of Edward Strelley, despite his best efforts to remain hidden.

"We are undone if I am recognised," Strelley says. "All bloody

188

hell..."

"Then you must not be recognised. Do not underestimate the capacity of people to ignore the evidence of their eyes."

"How good is the signature?"

"I could not tell it apart from the genuine one. Your friend Gilbert certainly knows some useful people."

"Perhaps we could pay him to have Sudeley assassinated...?"

"Now that, my friend, is political." De Winter laughs. "I don't think Gilbert would expose himself to such risk."

"As risky as letting me live?"

"Remember, Edward, you are dead. Everyone thinks you were dragged out of the river a month ago."

"So when I turn up alive...?"

"You won't. After today, you're gone."

"I know. I shall miss this place, you know."

"The manor? Or its occupants?"

"I have lived with that girl for a long time, now. One grows accustomed to her... idiosyncrasies. And Grindal's. Though he cannot be long for the world."

They turn to the door. Strelley, just in time to avoid being exposed to the majordomo, drops his head and disappears into his hood.

"Master de Winter, is it?" The majordomo is immaculately presented, despite the late hour. "I should like to see this supposed letter."

De Winter leaps down from his horse and approaches, swaggering to show off his height and physique. The majordomo snatches the letter from him, looks out at him from underneath his eyebrows, then settles to reading in the flickering light from inside. There is an audible exclamation of surprise as he reaches the word 'sister', and another as he reads the signature.

"Very well," he says, and waves his hand several times at the footman. This seems to be the signal for him to act as the guests' guide, as the majordomo disappears into the house without waiting for further questions to be asked. There is a brief pause as the footman shouts down the corridor to a colleague to replace him at the door, then beckons them with a finger.

He leads them to Grindal's room and opens the door. De Winter asks him to stand outside, and he does so, pushing the door closed behind them as they enter. Strelley takes several paces into the room before removing his hood, although it is nearly dark in Grindal's chamber, then stands for several minutes contemplating the ruined, dying body of his great friend. De Winter stands behind him, taking in the scene without becoming part of it, watching Strelley as his face changes from grief to resolve and back again.

Strelley goes to Grindal, leaning over him and taking his hands in his own. "Master..." he says quietly. Grindal's eyes show some flicker of recognition, but he does not say anything. "I know I should not have come. I know indeed that you would have forbidden it should you have learned of my intention. But I am here. I would not let your spirit leave this world without bidding you adieu, and to show you that I have not been beaten by Sudeley just yet."

Grindal holds his eyes open for a few moments. With a supreme effort, he speaks, his words barely distinct in the rattle of his breath. "Do not waste this chance that God has given you, Edward. Use your life for some good. Protect Elizabeth. And her brother... from those that would... do them harm... Find God, Edward. He will guide you."

Strelley smoothes his hand over Grindal's brow. "You do not have long. Owen has extended your days but only by a little. We have brought something to ease the pain." De Winter steps forward and hands him the little clay pot. Strelley dips his fingers into the unguent, and rubs it into Grindal's gums. "You may only need one or two more applications."

Grindal waits until the preparation is administered, then with his eyes closed and even quieter than before, he speaks again. "You are gifted with intelligence, Edward. Now you must find wisdom. Listen to God. He will speak to you if you listen. Now go. Owen will return. He must not see you. Go!"

Strelley leans over and kisses Grindal's forehead. As he does so, Grindal whispers to him. "Guy Fletcher was here. He has worked out your secret." Strelley places the pot on a table beside the bed, and turns to leave. De Winter follows a moment later, with a shrewd expression about his face.

As they leave Chelsea, de Winter asks Strelley, "Did he he say that Guy Fletcher had been there?"

"Yes. That Guy had worked it out."

"I shall make sure I see him when I can. Put the doubt from his

190

mind." De Winter rubs his hands together. "This is starting to get dangerous!"

55: Between the truth and fiction, the truth seems the less likely of the two

Dumbarton Castle nestles in the cleft of two mighty pinnacles on the north bank of the Clyde. As a stronghold, it is nearly impregnable, a retreat for those crises when the very existence of Scotland has been at issue. The reader will no doubt wish to learn why, then, the train of Mary of Guise, the Queen Mother, and her daughter, Mary, Queen of Scots, is approaching. All will become clear.

Mary of Guise is by this time in her mid-thirties, twice a widow despite her relative youth, charming without ever having been truly beautiful. Her eyes have the characteristic quickness of a sharp, penetrative mind, constantly shifting from one focus to another as she rides the last of the journey to Dumbarton. Her daughter, a vigorous and energetic child of about six years, sits on a pony beside her mother. They are flanked on either side, and before and behind, by a guard of household cavalry in gleaming armour. All the trappings of a royal procession are in evidence, but the destination gives us a clue as to the purpose.

The gate in the sheer, imposing stone wall opens before the queen, her mother, and their retinue. Guards raise their halberds to allow their passage, and they are ushered in to the courtyard, where they are met, still mounted, by the Earl of Glencairn, Alexander Cunningham. He is between thirty and thirty-five years old, a huge bear of a man with wild russet hair and beard. Glencairn offers his hand to Mary of Guise to help her dismount, which she accepts. Guise herself takes the queen from her pony, and stands her by her side.

"My Lord Glencairn," Guise says, her French accent rather pronounced, "we welcome your hospitality. With the English back again, we cannot take any risks with our daughter's safety."

Glencairn bows in acknowledgement. "Whilst Protector Somerset still wishes to unite the crowns of England and Scotland, Your Majesty, we shall defend Your Majesties, and our sovereignty, with whatever lies at our disposal."

"Your loyalty is most welcome, Sir." Guise offers her hand for him to kiss, which he does, bending to one knee to lower himself. She continues, "my daughter and I are weary from our journey. Please show us to our rooms, that we might rest a while."

The earl summons a number of his retainers, who hustle off with the queen's baggage. His chief servant directs mother and daughter into the keep of the castle. The soldiers surrounding the queen disperse, leading their horses to the stables. Glencairn watches them as they disappear, then turns to one of his own armed guardsmen.

"And what of our prisoner? Has he spoken?"

"He maintains his claim, My Lord."

"I shall see him again myself, then."

The earl, preceded by the castle gaoler, descends into the dungeon beneath the keep. Carved out of the rocks on which the castle is built, it is cold and dark, but the cell which he visits is not cruel in its dimensions or its furnishings. Indeed, for a prison, it is tolerable, with straw-stuffed sacks for a bed, and a wooden chair on which the prisoner sits. Lit from the outside by torches through the iron-barred wall, every move the prisoner might make is visible to his captors. The gaoler fetches a second chair, positions it facing into the cell and steps away. Glencairn removes the furred cloak from his shoulders, hands it to the gaoler, and sits.

All the while the prisoner has been following this activity with his eyes, but has not otherwise moved an inch. His face is thoroughly covered in matted, unkempt beard and moustache, such that only his grimed forehead shows. His hair is long, unwashed in months or even years, and though his bared arms and legs show the signs of cuts and bruises, he is fit and healthy underneath the filthy exterior. His clothes, what at least is left of them, are so dirty as to prevent their original colour being identified.

Glencairn strokes his own beard, observing his prisoner's. His eyebrow rises a touch. "We are not so different in appearance, you and I," he says, with a little laugh. The prisoner looks at him, his penetrative stare almost unnerving the earl. It is a quarter-minute, during which the prisoner does not lower his gaze, before the earl speaks again. "My servants tell me that you are an Englishman, by your voice. The English are not welcome here in Scotland, as you will know."

At this, the prisoner relaxes his eyes and looks down at his feet. But he does not reply.

Glencairn picks up, "as I say, an Englishman loose on the Scottish moors is a suspicious character indeed. What might you offer me to allay my suspicions?" He sits forward in the chair, expectant. It creaks under his considerable weight.

The prisoner lifts his head again. "Little," he says, quietly. "But I am no spy."

"A pilgrim, perhaps?" Glencairn laughs again, this time heartily. "There are no holy relics on the moors above Dumbarton."

"Were I a spy, I would have avoided capture." There is a little sparkle in the prisoner's eyes as he says this. "You were closer suggesting I am a pilgrim."

"You have no trappings of the religious hermit about you."

"I sought God, nevertheless."

"In the Scottish moors? What brings an Englishman north to a foreign land with which his own nation is at war?" Perhaps the reader will have guessed the answer by now, but let us continue to follow this conversation, fascinating as it is to the Earl of Glencairn.

"War itself," the prisoner says. His accent is rustic, Yorkshire or Derbyshire, but it is half-hidden by his quietness.

"War? The last English army left many of my countrymen dead, but few of its own behind. Besides, you are not wounded."

"Not in the body, perhaps."

"Your cryptic replies do you no credit, Sir!" Glencairn spits. "I see no reason why I shouldn't hang you from the castle walls."

"It would be an odd way for my life to end," the prisoner replies, still calm. He summons himself and continues, "I am William Pike, and I served with Somerset's army at Pinkie. I deserted the service because of my conscience, after I killed a man who was fighting for the Scots with whom I had once served. I have wandered your moors this autumn and winter, finding what sustenance and shelter I can, that I might speak to and hear God, and receive absolution for my sin."

"Not a spy?" Glencairn smiles. "As good a cover as I have heard, though."

"The man I killed was an Italian named Lorenzo. He and I fought, with several of my friends, at the defeat at Ancrum. But he fought with the Scots at Pinkie."

"Whose man are you? What house? What colours?" Glencairn struggles for the right question.

"I served the Baron of Sheffield, then the Earl of Shrewsbury, then King Henry. I am a gamekeeper, Sir. Soldiery was forced upon me."

"A gamekeeper? I am impressed by your persistence, Englishman." He signals the gaoler. "Gently, to begin with," he says to him. "I do not want him damaged if we can avoid it." Then, he returns to addressing the prisoner. "We shall test this story of yours. I shall return, in the morning." And he stands, takes his cloak back and fixes it around his shoulders, then disappears up the stairs. The turnkey looks down at Pike with something approaching pity.

"If you confess to being a spy, we can dispense with all..." He gestures around himself. "This..."

Pike inhales deeply. "I am telling you the truth."

Later that night, the queen and her mother descend from their apartments for their meal. The earl has requested that they do him the honour of dining with him, and so Queen Mary and Queen Mother arrive in the hall dressed in what finery they can muster. The child wears an elaborate ruff and pearl headdress, together with an elegant red dress. The mother wears black, her red hair gathered under a black cloth cap that accentuates her graceful paleness. The three of them sit to dine at a rustic oak table set with silverware that has seen better days, but has been polished to a shine in anticipation of the royal visit. Their conversation is of little interest to us, until partway through the meal when a dreadful scream, distant but clear, rings out.

The queen and her mother stop eating and look up at Glencairn. Guise narrows her eyes. "A prisoner?" she says. "You did not mention any other inmates." There is a hint of banter in her tone.

Glencairn chews thoughtfully. "A wild man. We picked him up a few miles away on the moors when we were out hunting. He was asleep under a rock. Didn't take well to being chained."

"You do not think a wild man on the moors about Dumbarton is of significance? The English are-"

"Yes, Madam," Glencairn interrupts. "You will have observed the uncomfortable nature of my other guest's reception." He returns the raillery. "If he is a spy, he is ineffective enough here."

"I do not-" Guise begins, but Glencairn silences her a second time.

"If Madam is unsure of my judgement, perhaps she should like to interrogate the prisoner herself?" He smiles, mockingly. "I am experienced in matters of war and policy, and in the ways in which one might learn what one wishes from a prisoner."

Guise tilts her head. "I accept."

"What?" Glencairn asks, uncomprehending.

"I accept your offer. I will speak with the prisoner myself."

"We are at table. Afterwards, perhaps," Glencairn backtracks.

"No, My Lord. Now. I should not be able to rest easy, nor to enjoy this fine repast to its fullest, unless I settle my qualms."

He rises, slowly, pointedly. As Guise stands, so does the young girl.

"Her too?" Glencairn shakes his head as he speaks.

"Her too." Mary of Guise smoothes her skirts, and they set off.

Glencairn does his best to hide his frustration at being made to leave his table for this excursion, but is little given to dissimulation, and he is soon harrumphing audibly. Queen Mary trots up beside him, taking three steps to his one, and pulls a little at his jacket.

"Master Glencairn," she says, with the peculiar over-pronunciation of a child still learning her accent, "I wish to thank you personally for guarding us here. I can't imagine any army taking this castle."

"Well, young Madam," he replies, his voice a little kinder and warmer than during his exchange with her mother, "We shall defend you here as best we can. But one should never trust alone to rocks and stone walls. You're here rather because you can put to sea at a moment's notice than because we can hold out for eighteen months in the keep."

"Oh," she replies, a little put out by the earl's doom-mongering.

"This castle has been taken more than once," Glencairn says, looking down at the top of her head. "The English cannon would batter down the walls in a few days if they held the river. There isn't much to be gained from hiding behind this stone, not any more. If they come, you're going, not staying."

Mary of Guise listens to this conversation without comment. The little girl looks up at Glencairn. "Will you come with us?" she says.

"I have my people here, Madam. I am needed. To fight the English!" This last he enlivens by drawing his sword and holding it in front of him, which elicits first a giggle and then a cheer from the queen. Glencairn, revelling in this minor victory, eyeballs her mother, who meets his gaze with a frown.

"My Lord Glencairn," Guise snaps, observing the formalities earlier ignored by her daughter, "we have rather lost sight of our aim. I wish to see this prisoner, of whom we were only informed by his own screams, rather than your report. Your report which, I remind you, you should have made immediately on our arrival."

Glencairn smiles, showing a set of teeth remarkable for their erratic directions and sizes. "As you wish, Madam." He leads them deeper into the castle keep, wakes the turnkey who is sleeping outside the dungeon and points to the cells. The gaoler is about to question the presence of the woman and most especially the girl-child, but a look from his master silences him. He leads them through the main gate into the cells, then to Pike's particular chamber, then retires, allowing Glencairn to point out the prisoner to his guests.

Pike, lying with his head propped against the back wall of his cell, looks at the mother and daughter from under the mess of his hair. His face, what is visible of it at least, is impassive. As he shifts himself, his left hand can briefly be seen missing the nails from its third and little finger. They are curled under the others, in a vain attempt to hide the raw flesh from view. He draws breath, and sits upright, gingerly keeping his injured hand away from anything that might touch it.

"Your Majesties will excuse me if I do not stand," he says, summoning a little smile underneath his beard. He indicates his cell with a gesture of his good hand. "It would not be my choice of accommodation." The young queen giggles at this small piece of humour from the prisoner. Pike sees that he has made an impact, and instantly follows up. "I do not much rate the food, either, Madam."

Glencairn smiles at this banter from his prisoner. Mary of Guise stares at him, trying to weigh him up.

Guise speaks next. "My host says that you are an English spy. Are you?"

Pike looks past them at Glencairn, who is half-hidden in a dark recess. "I do not believe he truly thinks I am a spy."

Queen Mary breathes in sharply. "Oh! That is just what a spy would say!" She beams in triumph at her mother, who ruffles her hair.

Pike sighs. "And that is why I am doomed. Like a witch: if I float, I am condemned, if I sink, I am absolved, but little good it will do me."

Queen Mary laughs again. "You are not a witch. A witch would not allow himself to be so imprisoned."

"Nor, Madam, am I a spy, by the same logic," Pike adds quickly.

"Mother," the queen says, "I do not think he is a spy."

Guise looks down at Pike, one eye closed in contemplation. "What would you do if you were released?" Glencairn's ears prick at this question and he watches the exchange, focused.

"I do not know. Return to Sheffield, perhaps, and try to regain my old job as gamekeeper to Baron de Winter."

"Why did you desert?" Guise asks.

"I killed a man I knew. At Pinkie. The English won that battle, as you know. My friend fought on the other side, and I shot him. After that, I couldn't be a soldier any longer."

"But you went into the wilds," Guise says, unimpressed. "Not back home."

"I sought God, Madam. I did not think I would find him if I surrounded myself with the comforts of home. Nor would I burden my friends with my guilt."

Guise shakes her head. "I do not agree with my daughter." She grabs the little queen's shoulders and starts pushing her away, back out of the dungeon. Glencairn follows, after a moment's significant look at Pike.

James Longshawe rides out from his father's house in the direction of Sheffield, alone, in the crisp early spring sun. As he rides, his breath is visible in the cool morning air, his horse maintaining a steady trot, covering the distance down the hill into the town in an hour. He heads for the castle, and presents himself at the gate. He is admitted instantly, and dismounts within the castle grounds. His horse is led away by a retainer of the Baron de Winter, and he is shown into the keep by another.

The Earl of Shrewsbury sits on a carved wood chair opposite the Baron, himself occupying a slightly lower, less ornate seat, in a warm, fire-lit room. Longshawe is announced as he enters. Both the earl and the baron look up at him with an air of sympathy.

"Master Longshawe," the earl begins, "I have heard the sad news. It is terrible to lose a friend. You have my condolences. If there is anything I can do, please tell me." Longshawe bows, his eyes shining a little. The baron says nothing, looking from Longshawe to the earl. After a pause, during which each seems to be waiting for the others to speak, the earl picks up, "I understand you are to travel to London to act as fencing-master to the king. That is some good news, at least."

Longshawe smiles weakly. "I am glad to be out of the service for now. Pinkie was too close, even if we won the battle."

"It seems your former commanders are still pursuing that same campaign even now. George has written to me from Haddington... The Scots are still vigorous in their defence, in spite of your victory last September. The queen still eludes capture."

Baron de Winter stirs, saying, seemingly to himself, "Seymour still wants her for the king."

There is another pause, but this time it is Longshawe who breaks the silence. "I wondered if I might present my respects to Lady Caroline, My Lord." Shrewsbury's mouth turns up at this, and there is a little glint in his eye. The baron's face is indifferent, but grunts his assent.

"She is here somewhere." Baron de Winter points vaguely elsewhere in the castle. Longshawe does not wait further, turning on his heels and leaving the two men to each other's company. There is no serving-man waiting outside the door, so Longshawe sets off through the castle, looking for a sign of the lady for whom he searches. He passes along a corridor, finding himself out in the open again, and heads off for a set of buildings within the castle walls that serve as living quarters to most of the Baron's household.

Within, he is immediately attended by a young serving-girl, who approaches him head-bowed and deferential. "Sir," she says, nervously, "what might we do for you?"

"I wish to see the Lady Caroline." Longshawe looks down at the girl, who continues to lower her eyes. After a pause, she seems to sense his stare and looks up at him, holding his gaze for just a moment longer than she ought. She drops her head again, but Longshawe can see the poorly-hidden smile on her face.

"Yes, Sir, I will show you to her." The girl is desperate to hide her interest, but cannot manage it. Her face betrays the fact that her mistress is expecting – anticipating, perhaps – this visit. Longshawe follows her through a series of doors, leading through to a large and comfortable sitting room. Lady Caroline is seated next to another young lady, whom Longshawe does not immediately recognise.

Longshawe bows, respectfully but not ostentatiously. The servant girl speaks his name with a snap of her heels, then steps out of the room. The other lady, seated next to Caroline, looks up at him, then at Caroline, who nods without taking her eyes off her sewing, which looks like a fine linen shirt of a size to fit her brother.

"Please excuse Miss Furnival, Master Longshawe," Caroline de Winter says. "Whatever you have to say to me, you can say before her."

Longshawe repeats his bow to Miss Furnival, a look of some slight recognition on his features. "I believe we have met before, Miss. At one of the baron's dinners."

Miss Furnival, a fair-complexioned young girl of perhaps eighteen years, looks up at Longshawe. "I remember you well, Sir, but it is a long time since you have resided at Longshawe."

"That is true," Longshawe replies, then turns to Caroline. "In that time, Madam, I have had much to reflect on. As a younger man I was perhaps boorish and unsubtle. I regret that now. But what has happened since then has made me consider." He leaves the sentence hanging, more from not knowing what to say next than from any clever conversational tactic.

"And where did these reflections lead you?" Caroline asks after a moment's pause.

"I wanted to go away to war and win glory on the battlefield. It is clear to me now that war is not where I shall find glory."

"So you seek your fulfilment somehow otherwise?" Caroline smiles at him, warmly. Miss Furnival watches the conversation with deep interest but does her best not to appear so.

"I do not think my fulfilment will come from killing other men, or winning battles for my king."

Caroline glances briefly at her friend, before looking back at Longshawe. He has his eyes lowered, and waits for her reply, which comes after a few seconds that seem an age.

"As women, our fulfilment cannot come from dying or ending lives on a battlefield. We must make what we can of life, mustn't we, Lucy?"

Lucy Furnival nods her head in reply, before adding, "Being dead rather dampens one's fire..."

Caroline de Winter laughs a little. "Master Longshawe, I understand, came rather closer to dying than he anticipated." As she speaks, her face straightens and her tone melts into sympathy. "But he is here, now. Well, Master Longshawe, you are not here simply to tell two young women that you are withdrawing yourself from a life of soldiery. So, what is it?" She leans forward, and her hands twitch as though she wishes to take Longshawe's in her own.

Longshawe clicks his heels together and stands up straight. "I leave for London within the week. The last time I spoke to you of my feelings, it did not go as I had planned. I went to war immediately afterwards. And in the time that has passed, my thoughts have often returned to that day."

"My brother challenged you for your impertinence," Caroline says. "I did not ask him to."

Longshawe bows his head again. "I have been trying to say... What came across as impertinent was in fact in earnest."

Lucy Furnival jumps into the gap, saying, "perhaps your approach *was* a little too daring, Sir."

Longshawe sighs a little. "Romantic...?"

The two young women smile at each other, which does not escaped Longshawe's notice. Lucy Furnival stands. "I will leave you for a while. Caroline, I shall be in the green long-room." She leaves, throwing Caroline de Winter a suggestive glance as she passes through the door.

Longshawe relaxes a little, steps closer to Caroline's chair and bends lower. "My Lady... Caroline... I'm sorry. I should have been plain. Losing Edward has made me brave in a way I had not considered before, so I shall say: Caroline, I hold you in the highest regard. I wish to make my affection for you clear before I leave. You may do as you please with what I say."

Caroline, eyes glistening a little, replies, "doubt thou the stars are fire, doubt that the sun doth move, doubt truth to be a liar, but never doubt I love."

Longshawe stares at her. "I will doubt no more. Are those your words?"

"Yes." She opens a little pocket-book and shows him the manuscript lines. "I told you, a woman's life cannot be lived through the sword. Why not the pen?"

Longshawe bows. "You are truly magnificent." He kneels before her and takes her hand. "May I?" She nods, and her presses a gentle kiss on her right hand. Then, he stands and steps back a little. "I will write to you. As soon as I can."

"I will await your letter with great expectation." She holds her right hand in her left. "My brother asks that you visit him when your duties allow." Her mouth turns upwards, just a hint.

"I shall. I do not forget his friendship."

"He does not forget yours. I will see you soon, one way or another."

Longshawe turns and walks to the door. There is a sound of scuffling feet as he approaches, and he tactfully waits a moment or two before turning the handle and opening it. He uses the moment to turn back to Caroline de Winter and give her his most charming smile. Once he is out of the door, he clenches his fist in a gesture of victory. He turns a corner and sees Lucy Furnival coming the other way. She does her best to seem surprised to see him.

"Master Longshawe... I was just returning to offer you and Caroline some of this wonderful mead." She produces a glass bottle of yellow liquid, holding it out in front of herself to show him.

He bows his head at her. "Please, Miss Furnival. Speak well of me to Caroline. I love her."

She tries to keep a straight face, but the smile breaks through. "I shall, Sir."

Longshawe goes outside. We shall follow Lucy Furnival back to Miss de Winter, and see what passes there. Lucy enters to see Caroline still caressing her right hand in her left. She rushes over to her friend and kneels beside her.

"Well?" Lucy asks, rather breathless.

"He expressed his affection."

"He told me to speak well of him to you. Said that he loved you."

"When?"

"I saw him leaving just now. Looking a little love-struck."

"I wish he did not have to go."

"Caro... If you use your brother's connection, you could be at court yourself in a matter of months."

"My brother serves the king's sister, not the king himself. I do not think, from what he has told me, the king and Mary are close."

"She is still heir to the throne."

"Don't be morbid. The king is a little boy with many years ahead of him. Though if he has his father's troubles, not so many sons!" They giggle at this innuendo.

"But a position with the Princess Mary would get you close."

"Hunsdon is hardly the centre of the universe."

"It is much closer than Sheffield. *I* would serve her."

"You would not make much of a lady-in-waiting. You do not have the patience."

"You do not have the temperament either, dear. Too much independence of spirit." Lucy Furnival smiles conspiratorially. "Besides, the ladies-in-waiting are all *unmarried*!"

De Winter shakes her head. "We have not quite got to that stage yet, Lucy. I shall not *marry* him after just a moment of tenderness."

"No... You shall make him work for your hand."

"I don't mean that. Just that it is too much to speak of marriage just now."

"Well, you may not be able to live in Hathersage..." Lucy says, and waits for Caroline to deliver the punchline.

"But we can always live in Hope!"

Let us now return to Longshawe, who is re-entering the room in which he left Shrewsbury and Baron de Winter. Shrewsbury looks up as he enters, and raises his eyebrows in inquiry. Longshawe returns him a confirmatory smile. De Winter does not seem to pick up on the silent exchange, but after a second or two he too turns to Longshawe, who bows, and speaks.

"My Lords, I am leaving for London tomorrow. I thank you both for all your consideration. I shall remember you always."

Shrewsbury claps a hand over his shoulder. "Master Longshawe, you are a colossus. If you ever find yourself without a master, apply to me. Or to my son, if I am gone. Edward's personal gain is his army's great loss."

Longshawe tilts his head. "I could not face battle again." He touches his side. "Some good must come of all this."

Shrewsbury lowers his hand. "Your friend Strelley did not die in battle. Despite your wound, you did not die in battle. Your grief is understandable, young man, but you should not let it stop you living."

""I have not," Longshawe replies. He looks pointedly at Baron de Winter, but does not need to elaborate in words.

Shrewsbury's face breaks into a grin. "Then whatever you choose, in this at least you have my blessing."

"Will you...?" Longshawe begins. He does not finish. Baron de Winter watches the exchange but does not seem interested.

"I will say what needs to be said. Trust me, Master Longshawe. Now, go." He gestures to the door. Longshawe does as he is told, closing the door behind him.

57: He lives!

Greenwich dock is crowded with merchantmen, some smaller, most likely conducting their business with the Low Countries, some larger, intended perhaps to sail across the North Sea or into the Mediterranean. Edward Strelley, whom the reader will recognise despite his changed clothes, dirty, bearded appearance and slouchy demeanour, stands waiting to board one of the larger vessels. To the casual observer, he is the weathered sailor of the routes south around Spain and through the Pillars of Hercules. To the more trained eye, observant of the minute details, he might appear a little green and naïve. His tan is mostly composed of smeared dirt, and his hands in particular have none of the hallmarks of time spent serving on a ship.§ Strelley is, as we know by now, a master of the art of observation, and as he feigns a sluggard nature and the devil of a hangover he manages to cover some of his lack of experience. His ship, rather grandiosely named 'Argo', is a caravel of perhaps 150 tons and 3 masts, sleeker by far than the channel-boats that it rides next to. It is being loaded with wooden crates by a kind of crane, that swings over the deck and lowers the heavy boxes down into the hold.

A man, shabbily dressed but wearing three large gold rings, approaches Strelley. He nods his greeting without smiling. Strelley, unused to such laconic company, frowns to stop himself from speaking and revealing his ignorance. The man comes closer. He looks Strelley up and down.

"Not much use as a fighter. No sailing before. Woman's hands. What use are you, boy?" His voice is gruff, his accent indistinctly of the west country.

"I read. I write." Strelley copies the man's curt speech. "I reckon."

"Hmm." His interlocutor smiles ironically. "Not much need of that aboard ship. Can you work? Haul?"

"I can." Strelley allows himself a smile, much like that of his new acquaintance. "I have served in the army as well."

"Interesting. You'll meet one or two who will try their hand agin you if you let on. Keep your wits – such as they are – about you. Gilbert wants y'out of England, but he kept mum on the subject of your condition *after* your voyage. Don't give them an excuse, because I won't step in for you. Understand?" Strelley nods. "Name's Thatch. Captain Thatch." He does not hold out his hand for Strelley to shake.

They go aboard. Strelley follows Thatch up the gangplank, concentrating on not making a false step. He looks around at his new station in life, and wrinkles his nose.

Thatch shakes his head. "You'll learn to love it. Or, if you don't, you'll pitch yourself overboard and rid us all of your trouble."

Strelley ignores the gibe. "Where are we headed?"

"Not sure you need to know that." Thatch's voice suggests Bristol or Somerset. "Perhaps I'll tell you when we're underway."

"I might be able to speak the language." Strelley tries to sound casual, but ends up sounding earnest. He notices his own mis-step, and doesn't follow up the comment during the quarter minute or so that Thatch seems to have ignored him.

"Master Strelley..." Thatch says, after this over-long pause. "I do not *need* you to speak for me. I shouldn't think you'd be much use negotiatin'".

Strelley looks out from under his brow at Thatch. The seaman is old, perhaps in his late forties, weathered to a leathery-brown, wrinkled finish. His exterior does not disguise his rapidity of eye and the strength of his movements. Strelley takes him in, contemplating.

"What do you have need of?" he asks. "Since I am such a burden, what would you have me be instead?"

Thatch laughs, this time genuinely. "My crew is full. I do not need an extra body. Gilbert has paid rather well to get you on this ship, Master Strelley. You can do most good by doing no harm."

Strelley stands alone on the deck as Thatch goes about his preparations for launch. He turns back in the direction of the palace, and stares at it for a long time without moving.

Some hours later, the ship is on its way down the Thames towards the North Sea. Thatch watches Strelley, who is reading. He takes a couple of steps closer, trying not to let Strelley see that he is interested. Strelley is sensitive to it, though, and closes his volume demonstratively.

Thatch weighs up his options. After a moment's hesitation, he decides to sacrifice his earlier aloofness and asks, "What is that?"

Strelley, alert to the situation, answers, "Not sure you need to know that." There is the tiniest hint in his voice that he is copying Thatch's accent.

"Perhaps," Thatch says, as nonchalant as he can manage, "you got the wrong impression of me. Sailor I may be, but I like a good read."

Strelley stifles a snigger. "This is Ovid. The Tristia. Actually, the Ex Ponto." He leans back and awaits the effect of his statement. His face slackens as Thatch takes him up.

"*laeta fere laetus cecini, cano tristia tristis.*"

"You know it?" Strelley asks, incredulous.

"I do, young man. Now... I don't need you adding your efforts to those of my crew. They are capable of doing what they do. But not a one of them has a poetic bone in his body. Read to me once in a while and I'll look out for you."

Strelley nods, bottom lip pouted out. "No one else has acknowledged me, yet."

"We're not used to passengers. Normally run spices and oil back from the Med. Take all sorts out, sometimes wool, sometimes more specialist cargo. This run is a mix, tin, wool, trade goods."

"Where are we going? You wouldn't tell me before."

"We're heading to Rome, Cyprus, the Levant eventually. We'll be away months."

"More than that, I suppose."

"I don't know why Gilbert's put you on this ship, Strelley. But he wants you... disappeared."

"If you're going to toss me overboard, or sink a knife-"

"No, Master Strelley. He doesn't want you to come back with us. This is a one-way trip for you."

"I see."

"Well, I'm not sure you do. What do you propose to do when we drop you?"

"I told you. I can speak French, Italian. A bit of Arabic."

"Speak, perhaps. But how will you live? It would be a shame to set you down half a world away only for you to get killed."

"I have escaped death once already."

"Hmm. Be that as it may, I will do my best to ready you. You're not a worldly man... Are you?"

Strelley does his best not to appear sour in response. "Perhaps

207

not."

"You can go anywhere once we're done with you."

"I shall, Cap'n Thatch. I shall."

At around the same time as Strelley's departure, Longshawe is getting ready to leave his family home to travel to court. As he scans over his belongings laid out on a table, he hears the sound of a halloo from outside. A retainer rushes inside.

"Master Longshawe! A rider approaches."

Longshawe turns quickly, and barges his way outside. The rider, although distant, is recognisable. It is Guy Fletcher.

Longshawe sets off at a jog out to meet his friend and former servant. Fletcher, seeing this, puts his horse to the gallop, and closes the gap between them in just a couple of minutes.

Longshawe starts to shout when they are still a hundred yards apart. "Guy Fletcher! I had thought you lost!"

Fletcher makes no reply until he is close, when he executes a perfect dismount and embraces Longshawe. He whispers in Longshawe's ear. "He lives."

Longshawe pushes him back, holding his shoulders, shaking them a little. "Guy!" he admonishes.

"James," Guy says, stern, "he lives. De Winter told me. We do not share this, or he dies."

Longshawe's face goes from disbelief to delight, via bewilderment. "He lives, you say."

"He lives."

11314941R00123

Printed in Great Britain
by Amazon.co.uk, Ltd.,
Marston Gate.